BOOK ONE IN THE ***PROSPERINE*** SERIES

THE ALIEN CORPS

PJ MCDERMOTT

All characters and events in this publication, other than those clearly in the public domain, are fictitious, and any resemblance to actual persons, living or dead, is purely coincidental.

Copyright © 2024 PJ McDermott
All rights reserved.
ISBN: 9781096033158

For Joe

Contents

Chapter		Page
one	Aquarius IV 2176	1
two	The Alien Corps	6
three	Heirloom	18
four	Mission	24
five	Arrival	34
six	Dominion Island	49
seven	Ezekan	72
eight	Eyewitnesses	95
nine	Imprisonment	109
ten	Murder	123
eleven	Dark Suns	136
twelve	Pharlaxians	150
thirteen	Conspiracy	161
fourteen	Teacher	169
fifteen	Pursuit	178
sixteen	Escape	202
seventeen	Ultimatum	212
eighteen	Charakai	228
nineteen	Alone	243
twenty	Return to Ezekan	257
Twenty-one	Rescue	268
twenty-two	War	287
twenty-three	Retribution	307
twenty-four	Return to Earth	314
appendix	Cast of Characters	323
illustrations	Prosperine	34
	Ezekan	94
	Western Avanaux	177

Acknowledgments

Special thanks to my daughter, Gillian, for sharing my journey. David Patrick was invaluable as my Beta reader and provided many constructive suggestions. The very talented Lauren MacGregor created the maps in this edition.

By this sign, you shall know that the world's end is at hand. The Lord of Light will be revealed to all the people of the universe, man and not man alike. He will lead his followers to Earth, where they will join the dead and the living in the final battle, and they shall prevail over the evil one.

Extract from a manuscript discovered near Hierapolis, Turkey, in 2095 AD

Aquarius IV 2176CE

Hickory leaned on one knee and examined the tracks left by her quarry. Thanks to her empathic skills, she could sense faint traces of their passing, but the snatchers were still two hours ahead.

She resumed the pursuit, cursing her stupidity. She had deactivated her comms channel during the breakup with Jacob. The last thing Hickory wanted was to air her dirty laundry in public. But, by the time she'd reconnected to the network, the religious fanatics had already made their move.

Hickory's heart sank at the thought of failure. She and Jacob were finished, but their brief liaison might yet result in a permanent scar. She glanced at her ex-lover, running parallel twenty meters to her left, and gritted her teeth. *Two-timing jerk.*

Sweat trickled down Hickory's face, and tiny flies swarmed before her eyes whenever she paused to take a breather. Their teeth were needle-sharp, and the mites carried many exotic diseases endemic to

P J McDermott

Aquarius IV. Frantically, she batted at them, but they persisted, nipping at her exposed skin. She'd been jabbed for every disease known to man before she arrived, but it didn't prevent the insects from leaving a tiny, itchy swelling with every bite.

The space pilot Jess Parker loped over to her. "Any sign of them?" she asked, her eyes flicking across the terrain ahead.

"They've hardly moved in the last half hour—they could have stopped for the night. About ten miles north of us." She panted as she spoke. *Too much Tequila.*

Hickory had spent a wild month with Jacob, visiting every bar and tavern in the planet's spaceport. Besotted though she was with the liquor and the man, she hadn't entirely lost sight of her responsibilities in the investigation of the alien mystic, Crxtor Aliaq.

She'd deduced at their first meeting that he wasn't the one they were looking for. Aliaq was a miracle worker, all right, but of the sorcerer kind—party tricks and stage magic—there was no spiritual side to him, just fakery.

Another failure for the Alien Corps to add to their growing list. Is there any point in continuing this stupid search? Hickory swore under her breath, but she couldn't dispute the facts. Every new release of COLIN* over the last twenty years had certified Philip's manuscript as genuine. The bio-computer was as close to infallible as it was possible to get. It achieved this state of God-like omniscience by harnessing the unique skills of brilliant individuals to multiply its own artificial intelligence. Over the years, this collaborative intelligence had solved many seemingly impossible problems leading to miraculous discoveries such as an immunization that protected against all major Earthly diseases, the "immortality" pill, and the secret to interstellar travel.

COLIN had concluded that "Philip's manuscript" was written by a contemporary of Jesus of Nazareth. Analysis of the manuscript provided new insights into the biblical events presaging the end of days.

The document contained a prophecy from Jesus that the "Lord of Light" would gather a vast armada from worlds throughout the universe to join in the final battle against the forces of evil on Earth.

The inference, of course, was that alien beings were just as much children of God as Earthlings. Not surprisingly, this polarized world opinion.

Controversy raged as the authenticity of the manuscript was called into question. Some orthodox and new-age religions took a belligerent stand. These included the popular but xenophobic People's Crusade. They declared the manuscript a forgery, a magic trick staged by the Vatican to bolster the waning influence of the Catholic Church.

When the Vatican finally released the scroll for

public scrutiny, the fuse to World War Three was lit.**

Another take on the four horsemen of the Apocalypse, thought Hickory. *Even scarier because it was written at a time when the existence of extraterrestrial beings couldn't possibly have been imagined.*

The Vatican formed the Alien Corps to search for signs of the prophecy on inhabited planets. It argued that finding the "Lord of Light" could provide direct access to the creator, which seemed the only hope of preventing Armageddon. Hickory marveled at the vision and arrogance of the cardinals who could conceive of such a thing.

Since its inception, the Corps had discovered many would-be messiahs, but all had proven to be false. Crxtor Aliaq of Aquarius IV was the latest.

Jess broke into Hickory's thoughts. "Let's hope the snatchers stop there for a while. My legs will fall off if we don't catch up with them soon. I don't suppose it'll matter because there won't be much left of me by the time these midges get done."

Jess complained, but Hickory could sense no lessening of effort from her, and she wasn't surprised. She'd known Jess since they'd studied together at Rome University and been friends ever since. Hickory managed a grin despite her mood and forced her legs to move faster.

Two hours later, their mission ended abruptly. They found Crxtor Aliaq stripped naked, his arms and legs staked to the ground, and his eyes milky-white in death.

Jacob knelt to examine the body and shook his head. "How are we going to explain this? We're looking at the end of our careers right here."

Hickory bent over, hands on knees, and retched.

* Collaborative Intelligence Advanced Reasoning Organism

** As told in *Born of Fire*, the prequel to the Prosperine Series.

Alien Corps 2179 CE

Hickory's hollo-channel signaled a new message just as she'd finished her class for the day. She placed her thumb on the ID panel to authorize the transmission. Prefect Cortherien's pixigraph materialized in front of her. The message was direct and to the point. "Meet me in my office at seven. There's an important matter we need to discuss." Her eyebrows rose. She hadn't spoken to the prefect in months.

Hickory arrived a few minutes early and sat in reception, alternately cracking her knuckles and glancing at the wall clock. At seven precisely, the security door buzzed, and she strode through.

The prefect lowered the shield on his console and rose from his nineteenth-century walnut writing desk. He reached for Hickory's hands and held her at arm's length. "My dear, how good to see you again. You look well. Teaching must agree with you."

"You would say so, Pierre. You're the one who recommended me for the job." She smiled pleasantly

He frowned at her familiarity, then turned his scowl into a smile to match her own. "I terminated your employment with the Alien Corps for your own good—I was concerned for your welfare, child." He patted her hand.

Hickory emitted a brief snort. After finding the lifeless body of Crxtor Aliaq, she'd spent weeks trudging through the flea-infested swamps and jungles of Aquarius IV, fruitlessly chasing up clues to his murder. When Hickory returned to Earth, physically and emotionally exhausted, Cortherien had sacked her. She shook her head. "My welfare? I needed your support, Pierre, not your concern."

His smile faded, and he let her hands drop. He crossed to his desk and shuffled some papers. "Your father dropped by the other day. He asked me to pass on his good wishes and says he hopes to be able to spend some time with you on his next visit."

Hickory swallowed. She opened the French windows to the balcony and stepped into the fresh air. Leaning over the parapet, she breathed deeply and gazed at the vista of New Rome. After the war, the United World Government rebuilt the city as a shining example of the new order, declaring it Earth's capital and the epicenter of world government.

Ancient monuments like the Coliseum and the Pantheon, which were obliterated during the war, were reconstructed from original drawings. They now took pride of place in the city's central parklands. The parklands themselves were a kaleidoscope of color designed to showcase the beauty of nature. Hundreds of artists, gardeners, and sculptors from Japan, Austria, Singapore, and the USA were chosen to create a vision of paradise.

From Hickory's viewpoint on the balcony, spiraling towers and shimmering domes stretched as far as the eye could see. Constructed from glass and plasteelskin, they changed color and shape depending on the weather and time of day. Public transport capsules and automated cabs traveled on multi-layered highways that looped around buildings and other floating roads like tangled spaghetti. Heavy vehicles were prohibited from using these highways; instead, they used a matrix of underground subways that circumvented the city's central precinct.

"That's nice," she said finally. "What did the admiral come to see you about?" Hickory kept her back to the prefect. When her mother died giving birth to Michael, her younger brother, her father had offloaded both his offspring to his sister, Maddie. For fifteen years, the only communication she'd received was an occasional birthday card with his name printed on it. In the last five years, there'd been nothing. George Lace held the rank of flag officer in the navy. He rarely made it back to Earth and never so much as called her when he did.

The Alien Corps

Cortherien came to her side and spoke in a soft voice. "Your father does care for you, you know. As the head of the Intragalactic Agency, he carries enormous responsibility for the security of the Alliance. Over forty known planets are at a stage of development comparable to Earth. I don't want to preach at you, Hickory, but not all of these are friendly, and your father is responsible for neutralizing potential threats. He can't just drop everything and come home, much as he might want to." He patted her on the shoulder.

How much of his precious time would it take to say hello? I bet he caught up with Michael. She turned away from the railing and sighed. "I'm amazed he knows I teach here." She paused, struck by the truth of her own words. No way would her father have known. Something else must be going on. She sought the prefect's gaze, but he averted his eyes. *Cortherien is hiding something from me.*

Hickory was a neoteric, an empath—one of a small percentage of the population born in the aftermath of World War Three with a mutated supramarginal gyrus in their cerebral cortex. As Hickory grew, so did the mutation and her empathic power. By the time Hickory turned fifteen, her spontaneous piggybacking onto other people's feelings had reached the point where she had trouble distinguishing which thoughts were her own.

Her doctor arranged for her to be hooked up to COLIN, which allowed eminent surgeons from New York, London, Moscow, and Tel Aviv to work on her mind. Under the guidance of the bio-computer, they applied patches and created new gateways in her brain to reduce the intensity of her empathic responses.

Ever since then, Hickory could generally tell if someone was lying or avoiding the truth by sensing minute changes in their body language. But Cortherien was aware of her talents and skilled at masking his feelings.

"That's probably enough about your family issues, Hickory. We have more important things to concern ourselves with than whether your father loves you."

She smiled, knowing the barb was aimed at deflecting her from the truth.

Cortherien lit a Sobranie Black Russian and inhaled deeply. "Disgusting habit, I know." He exhaled a long stream of smoke. "But it calms my nerves."

Hickory's nose wrinkled at the pungent aroma.

The prefect continued, "Admiral Lace brought some exciting news from the far side of the Eridanus constellation, about sixteen light-years from Earth. They've discovered an inhabited planet. It's called Prosperine and has an oxygen-based atmosphere and a dominant life form similar in body plan to humans."

The Alien Corps

He switched on a holographic image. "As you can see, the species is bipedal. They call themselves Avanauri, after their homeland in the northern continent."

Hickory stared. The alien wore a three-quarter-length cloak draped over its shoulders. It appeared tall and thin, with long stick-like legs and arms. Its skin was predominantly white, with dark pigmentation on its neck and around the eyes. The oval-shaped head was devoid of hair except for a thin strip running along the top of the skull like a Mohawk. *Created in God's image.* The irreverent thought flitted through her mind. "How intelligent are they?" she asked.

Cortherien stubbed out his cigarette and lit another. "I'm told the Avanauri race is more ancient than humankind, but their brains have developed more slowly. According to the admiral, their society is medieval. Scientists have studied their genetic makeup and say they are approaching a critical point in the evolution of their species.

"It seems their intellect will rapidly increase over the next century. It's estimated the Avanauri will be on a par with humanity within a few hundred years."

Hickory felt a flutter of anticipation in her belly. Why was the prefect telling her this? She said nothing, waiting.

The prefect cleared his throat. "How long has it

been since you were on assignment, Hickory?"

She could have told him to the day, even the hour when she returned from her last mission. *Three years, two months, and ten days.* "Three years," she said.

He smiled at her and nodded. "And no doubt you miss being in the field. The good news is Admiral Lace has asked that you be released from your academic duties to work with the Intragalactic Agency in the Avanaux capital, Ezekan."

Hickory's heartbeat raced, and she felt her cheeks glow. She averted her eyes so Cortherien wouldn't see the excitement shining through. The prefect walked to the wall dispenser and said, "Coffee, black with two." He raised his eyebrows at Hickory, who shook her head. He took a sip from the steaming brew, then lit his third cigarette. "Reports have been coming in over the last few months that religious fanaticism is on the rise. There have also been claims of miracles by a local mystic who goes by the name of Kar-sèr-Sephiryth. Loosely translated, it means 'Kar, beloved son.' His followers call him 'Teacher.'" He strolled over to the window.

Hickory felt strangely lightheaded. She forced herself to focus on the prefect's words. "You think this Teacher might be the one?"

The prefect hesitated. "How long have the Corps been looking?" He glanced down at the plaza below before continuing. "It's been eighty years since the

The Alien Corps

discovery of Philip's manuscript, and in that time, we've investigated fourteen potential messiahs." He turned and blew a stream of smoke in her direction. "Including the one unfortunately killed during your last mission. I suppose it's possible this 'beloved son' is the one we've been searching for. At the least, we need to explore the possibility. But there is a problem.

"Agency spies on the planet say the Teacher is a thorn in the side of the government, which, I guess, is what one might expect. He also seems to be the target of a disgruntled cleric. Apparently, this cleric considers anyone who strays from past traditions to be a heretic. I'm told he would like nothing better than to return the planet to the dark ages."

"So, the chances are the Teacher will be dead by the time I arrive?" *Or just after.* Hickory felt her stomach churn.

Cortherien grimaced and exhaled a cloud of smoke before continuing. "Hickory, do you believe in our mission?"

It was a fair question. One she'd struggled with, especially since her return from Aquarius IV. "Honestly? I don't know whether I do, but I believe we can't stop searching."

"Agreed, although I would put it a little more positively. Someday, Hickory, we will find another Christ on some remote, insignificant little planet. What happens then will be pivotal in determining whether the human race, indeed all life in the universe, continues to exist."

"I doubt either of us will be alive to see it."

"What an experience that would be, though. To meet the Son of God in the flesh, perhaps to speak with the Almighty through Him. Think about it!" His eyes gleamed.

"I wish I could share your vision, Pierre." Such a possibility was inconceivable to Hickory. She brought the subject back to Prosperine. "What I don't understand is why the Alliance is so interested in a medieval planet."

The prefect's fingers flicked at his cigarette, dislodging ash onto the floor as he paced back and forth. The fervor left his eyes, and he turned to face Hickory. "Politics—what else? There's been an upsurge in violence and rumors of revolution in the capital. The civil government has asked the Galactic Alliance for help."

Hickory shook her head, bemused. "The Alliance doesn't get involved in local squabbles."

"Which is why they've requested the Corps to join their investigation. We have a vital interest in this Teacher, and…" Hickory waited. "And," Cortherien began again, taking a deep breath, "the admiral has been negotiating sole buyer status for Avanaux's crynidium—"

The Alien Corps

"Crynidium? They have crynidium?" Hickory's eyes widened. The liquid metal, a catalyst essential for faster-than-light travel, had so far been discovered on only a handful of planets. Calling it rare did not do it justice. No wonder the Alliance was involved.

"Yes, and Admiral Lace was quite explicit. He's personally running point on this mission, and he's never dealt with a species so different. Given the sensitivity and importance of the relationship, he wants the Alien Corps on the team—he believes your rather unique talents could come in useful."

Hickory sensed a whiff of duplicity. Perhaps the admiral thought her skills might be helpful, but the prefect had other ideas. She dropped her eyes. She was desperate for another chance to prove herself in the field, but after the debacle on Aquarius IV, she didn't know if she still had what it took. And why would Cortherien approve her secondment to a vital operation against his better judgment? Did he want her to fail again? "As I recall, you were the one who said I was no longer up to the rigors of the Corps."

A bead of sweat glistened on Cortherien's forehead and trickled slowly toward his eyebrow. "Your father insisted—and I agree with him—that this mission will benefit from someone with your training and skill set. Guile will be more helpful than athleticism, and besides, you have four months to get into shape."

That still didn't answer the question: why her?

Either Cortherien didn't know, or he wasn't prepared to say. She probed, but all she could feel was an intense pressure to deny her. She thought the request for her transfer must have been persuasive, but who had the authority to demand compliance from the Vatican? She let the question lie unanswered. *Time for that later*.

They negotiated terms. Hickory would be assigned the rank of commander and could hand-pick her crew. She and her team would be given access to the Agency's elite fitness program and any classified intelligence on Prosperine and its people. Once she arrived on the planet, Hickory would have sole discretion, reporting only to the admiral but keeping Cortherien updated on her progress whenever possible.

"One more thing," said Cortherien, "The Alliance's presence on Prosperine is subject to their non-interference directive. Modern weapons and technology will not be available, and you and your team will of course be incognito. The Agency will brief you further and provide you with the equipment and training you'll need."

That evening, Hickory began working out at the university gym, stretching, boxing, and cycling. Her first session lasted two hours, and she walked home tired and aching. She stared at the unopened bottle of ten-year-old Barbaresco, then poured a glass of cold water and took it to bed with her.

Early the following day, she jogged around the lake in the gardens of Villa Borghese. The autumn sunlight shimmered through the leaves of Chestnuts and Oaks, casting dappled light along her path. After the first ten minutes, she was too puffed to appreciate its beauty and was forced to stop to ease the stitch in her side.

Into the second week, Hickory began to see improvement in her muscle tone and aerobic capacity and purchased a road bike. On Saturday, she called her grandmother to say she was coming over for some pasta.

Heirloom

Maria Lucerne looked up at her critically. "You are much too thin, my little one." She spun round on her heels, gesturing for Hickory to follow. "Come, play for me while I make lunch."

Her reflection notwithstanding, Maria, at five-foot-five, was dwarfed by the much taller Hickory. Her olive complexion and dark hair contrasted starkly with Hickory's pale face and burnished red hair. But the two had been a comfort to each other after the tragic death of Hickory's mother, Angela, and were still great friends.

Hickory laughed as she made her way into the expansive lounge. "Don't make too much for me. I'm in training."

Maria popped her head around the doorway, her eyes wide. "You're back in service?"

"That's what I wanted to talk to you about. Whether I should accept or not," said Hickory.

Her grandmother nodded at the grand piano in the

center of the room. "Play something for me, gattina. I will fix some puntarella, and we can talk over lunch."

Hickory was taught classical piano as a child, and it was still a favorite way for her to relax. She settled onto the stool, centered herself, and let her fingers fall lightly on the keys to stroke the first notes of Claire de Lune.

When lunch was ready, they took their plates and glasses onto the balcony and sat at a small table. Hickory glimpsed the spire of the Basilica of Santa Maria Maggiore, peeking above the rooftops. It was hard to believe the fifth-century church had survived the war. So many historical buildings were gone. "It's beautiful here. You're lucky to have this place, Nonna, and the salad smells delicious." She smiled and forked some chicory sprouts into her mouth.

"It sounds like you've had some luck too. Don't keep me in suspense; tell me all about it."

Hickory outlined Cortherien's proposal. "But I don't know whether to accept. I'd have to work pretty closely with the admiral."

Maria looked over her sunglasses. "Surely, that's no reason to reject this opportunity? You're mature enough not to let a poor relationship stop you, and you never know, this might be a good chance for the two of you to—well, to get to know each other better."

"Nonna, I'm sure he's not interested in knowing me better." Hickory smiled wryly. "You understand more than most how self-centered he is. But you're right—I could work with him professionally. I know it's just an excuse. I'm not sure I'm capable of working in the field anymore. After my last mission, Cortherien was adamant that I didn't have what it took. He only agreed to this because the admiral insisted." She put her fork down.

Maria tilted her head to one side and smiled affectionately at her granddaughter. "Gattina, you love the Corps. It's what you were born to do." She patted Hickory on the knee and reached for the salad bowl. "You have it in your blood to be an inspiring leader. You know your great-grandmother was among the first women to join the Corps. Talya was a courageous woman. Would you like me to tell you about her?"

"My great-grandmother? Talya?" Hickory frowned. "I know the name. Have you told me about her before?" She searched her memory, but it eluded her.

"Yes, but not this part of her life. It all began just before the war broke out. Talya fled to the planet Sumer. She met my father, one thing led to another, and they were married. He worked on the land, a farmer." Maria paused, thinking. "I can't remember much about papà except him bouncing me on his knee. He died of Spinaker disease when I was only four. The grief, plus the harsh climate and having to

The Alien Corps

work the farm by herself, aged Mamma quickly, but I don't remember ever hearing her complain.

"At night, we would watch the stars and roast potatoes on an open fire, and she would tell me about her life on Earth. She often talked about the priest she worked for, the one who discovered the gospel of Philip. They were both supposed to take the manuscript to Sumer for safekeeping, but a mob of Crusaders killed the priest before they could escape."

Hickory's eyes widened. "Nonna! Why haven't you told me this before now?"

Lines appeared on Maria's forehead. "For some reason, I never thought to. Talya passed away before you were born, and then when your mamma died, you went to live with your father's people. Only in recent years have you and I come to know each other so well. My memory isn't as sharp as it used to be." Her shoulders slumped, then her eyes brightened and she rose from her seat. "Wait here. I have something for you."

She went inside the apartment and returned a few moments later, carrying a tiny jewelry box. "This was a gift from Cardinal Rousseau to my mother after she retired from the Corps." She opened the box and gently took out a pendant necklace.

The elegant chain supported a stylish golden crucifix encrusted with tiny green emeralds. Hickory felt her skin tingle. "It's beautiful."

Maria arranged the chain around Hickory's neck. "It's yours," she said.

"No, no. I can't accept this. Talya gave it to you."

Maria smiled. "Yes, she gave it to me on my thirtieth birthday, but it would come to you eventually. You're only twenty-two, but I want you to have it now. It has quite a history. Peter III of Russia presented it as a wedding gift to Catherine the Great. After her husband died, the Empress donated it to the Church. Perhaps it will bring you luck."

Hickory nodded. Tears threatened to fill her eyes. She'd missed out on a lot since her mother died. "Tell me more about Talya," she urged.

The story of Talya's journey to Sumer was new to her. It was a valuable piece of the jigsaw connecting the discovery of Philip's gospel in Turkey to its current home in the People's Museum in New Rome. She gazed at the remarkable heirloom, and her heart filled with pride. *You don't receive an award like this unless you've achieved something out of the ordinary.*

Her grandmother continued, "After the war, when Earth started to recover, Rousseau asked Talya to help him rebuild the Alien Corps. The new Corps was born two years later, and Mamma became its first field officer."

Hickory blinked away some moisture and looked at the pendant again. "She must have been quite a lady."

"She was, gattina, and so are you."

Later that night, Hickory called Cortherien to accept the assignment.

Mission

Hickory hadn't felt this hyped since she was thirteen and won her second gymnastics silver medal at the New Rome Olympics.

She was ready for anything.

Admittedly, the level of competition this morning hadn't quite been up to that standard, but boy, did she feel fit.

Three months ago, she would have been in bed fast asleep this early in the morning. But after she'd accepted the mission, Cortherien arranged for intensive one-on-one training to rapidly increase her strength and aerobic fitness. That proved tricky enough before taking on the plyometric exercises that boosted her flexibility and reaction times. It was worth the pain, though, to be able to channel her energy into the powerful and explosive athleticism she'd unleashed this morning on the cycle track.

As an Olympian, her delight at being among the best athletes in the world didn't last long. In the following two years, she'd grown twelve inches and become uncompetitive at the elite level. The Academy had seen something special in her, though, and offered her a scholarship. When she graduated, aged nineteen, she'd signed up with the Corps for the first time. Now she was back.

Hickory made herself a coffee and waited for Jess and Gareth to arrive. She replayed the vid she'd retrieved from the library archives for the third time. Along with eyewitness accounts by Battista and Talya covering the finding of St. Philip's tomb, the appendices added a lot of detail about the initial assessment of the manuscript.

She paused the vid on a closeup of her great-grandmother, taken at her award ceremony. Long black hair in a braid, blue smiling eyes, and a generous mouth seemed to look out at her mischievously. Talya's hand reached towards the golden pendant hanging around her neck. *How strong and confident she looks.*

Hickory fast-forwarded to the critical passage. *By this sign, you will know that the world's end is at hand. The Lord of Light will be revealed to all the people of the universe, man and not man alike. He will lead his followers to Earth, where they will join the dead and the living in the final battle, and He shall prevail over the evil one.*

Jess Parker's full-sized image flickered to life in the chair opposite Hickory.

"Hi, Jess. Great to see you. How are the twins?"

asked Hickory, closing down the vid.

Jess's husband had died two years after they married, leaving her to raise twin girls on her own. Andrea and Erica were in their final year, studying alien biology at the University of Melbourne, Australia.

"Same as usual. They're both too smart and too slippery for their own good. They send their love and a reminder that they are available if you need them." The twins often helped Hickory prepare assignments for her students.

"Isn't it about time you introduced me to these two geniuses?" Gareth Blanquette materialized at the end of the table and grinned at the two women. "They sound just my type."

Jess tutted and shook her head. "Not on my watch, boyo. I don't want to be the one having to pick up what's left after the girls are done with you."

Hickory's eyes crinkled at his mock-crestfallen look. Gareth was a bright-eyed twenty-year-old who'd graduated maxima cum laude two years earlier. Hickory had met him after Gareth joined the Alien Corps to continue his research. He was a brilliant engineer specializing in propulsion systems, including the latest Lightwave "surfing" technology. Despite many offers, he didn't have a permanent job, preferring to work freelance, choosing the projects he was most interested in.

The Alien Corps

Though an expert in many things scientific, Gareth was a rookie when it came to girls. He had a mild crush on Hickory, which she tolerated but didn't encourage.

"Hello, Gareth—welcome to the hollo-meeting."

Gareth brightened immediately. "So, what's it all about? I'm guessing you have a job that needs doing in some far-flung corner of the Galaxy. Otherwise, Mother wouldn't be here."

Jess bristled. "I'm not your mother, boyo, but I'm not averse to putting you over my knee and giving you a good whack, either. Why don't you hold your tongue and listen for a change instead of being a smart aleck?"

Hickory interjected before Gareth could respond. "All right—that's enough!" Jess and Gareth could trade potshots for an hour if she didn't take control. "I do have a job. It's a big one, potentially dangerous, and I'll be leading it personally." There was silence for a moment. This would be her first interstellar trip since the ill-fated Aquarius mission. Both knew the conclusion to that, though only Jess understood how badly it had affected her.

"Hickory...?" Jess began. "You're back on active service? Are you sure—"

"Perfectly sure." She held up her hand to forestall further discussion. "In fact, I'm raring to get into this one." Jess and Gareth glanced at each other. Neither said a word. Hickory swallowed hard. *They'll stick by me; I know they will.* She briefed them on their destination, describing the indigenous inhabitants, and finished up with their mission objective. "Prefect Cortherien wants us to carry out an assessment of this indigenous miracle worker."

Gareth snorted. "You mean expose him for the fraud he no doubt is."

Hickory's brow furrowed. She snapped, "Wake up, Gareth. You know that's not how we do things in the Corps. If you don't think you can keep an open mind—"

Gareth's shoulders drooped. "Okay, okay. There's no need to get all bossy, boss."

Hickory relented a little. "Look, I realize you're a skeptic." She leaned towards him, emphasizing her words. "But we're dealing with a two-thousand-year-old prophecy that speaks to this time frame. We don't know what we'll find on Prosperine. You're entitled to think what you like, but if you want this job, you must put your personal beliefs aside. That's a requirement, Gareth, not an option. Understand?"

This mission was too critical—perhaps the last chance to prove herself worthy of command and earn a return to permanent active duty. The pendant pressed against the skin beneath her blouse. It felt right, as though it belonged there, giving her courage.

Gareth wasn't the only one to question the

existence of a creator, she thought. She, too, had doubts, although, in her heart, she hoped that God prevailed somewhere. But whether she or any of them believed in a supreme being was beside the point. Perhaps Philip's manuscript was a fake, and in all probability, this Kar-sèr-Sephiryth would turn out to be just one more charlatan. Regardless, she was determined to do a professional job. No way would she give Cortherien a second chance to be "concerned for her welfare."

Jess's protective instincts kicked in. "I'm sure he'll be fine once we get started, Hickory. There's no one I'd rather work with on this project than Gareth." She shrugged her shoulders. "He's just behaving like a typical boy."

"Thanks for the support, I think," said Gareth, laughing.

Hickory smiled crookedly. This was typical of the two. "The second part of our assignment isn't the sort of thing we usually get involved with, but it's even more important. There have been incidences of mob violence and anti-government demonstrations in the capital, and the Intragalactic Agency wants us to find out who's behind it." She paused. "Kar-sèr-Sephiryth, the mystic, is Cortherien's priority, but a helluva lot is riding on us coming up with the right answers in Ezekan."

"Could the two issues be connected?" said Gareth.

"You mean a messiah stirring up a revolution? It's possible, but intel suggests other groups could be involved. We'll be working hand-in-glove with Admiral Lace to find the answers."

Jess shifted in her chair. "We're going to work for your father?"

Hickory nodded. "Prosperine is naturally rich in crynidium, which makes it a hot spot for all sorts of adventurers and lowlifes. You would have heard that stocks of the catalyst are running low among the allied planets, and Prosperine has become critical to the Alliance's future. The admiral will oversee the mission, but I'll have autonomy on the ground." She paused and looked at each of them in the eye. "You need to be aware that this will be dangerous for all of us. Questions?" She looked at Gareth, knowing he would be the first to ask.

He cleared his throat. "As a matter of fact, there are a couple of things I'm not sure about. The population is humanoid, although according to the prefect, their DNA is highly correlated with herbivorous dinosaurs. But they look human or near enough human, right?"

Hickory nodded and waited for the inevitable.

"Well, uh, what about sex? The naurs and nauris—that's males and females, eh? Do they have sex for pleasure like us or only when they come into heat? I mean, I don't mind, but I wouldn't want to make a mistake with one of the locals."

Jess raised her eyes, and Hickory burst out laughing. "Gareth, you are an idiot. These girls hatch from eggs! Even you wouldn't want to be making out with them. But just for your information, the reproductive organs of the Avanauri function in much the same way as humans. What's your next question?"

"Ah, well, it's a related question, really. You say their offspring hatch from eggs but do the nauris go into labor, or are they like chickens—plop, and it's out? It's a bit bizarre, isn't it?

Jess snorted. "I'm going to assume that's a serious question, boyo, although I doubt it. Giving birth is way more complicated than you might think. The egg is carried beneath a thin membrane on the pregnant nauri's abdomen. When their time is near, the female moves into a community birthing house where she is cared for by the matriarchs of her family. It takes days for the egg to separate from the mother and hatch. And to answer your next question, yes—it is a painful process."

Hickory raised her eyebrows.

"I was scheduled for a field trip to Prosperine earlier this year," Jess explained. "It was canceled at the last minute, but I attended one of the vid-briefs before we pulled out."

Gareth frowned. "It's...uh, different."

Hickory shrugged. "It's weird, I agree, but they're aliens. We need to get used to it. I've got a feeling we'll come across a lot of strange things on this trip before we're done. Okay, guys, that's it. We leave in two weeks. There will be plenty of time for a full briefing once we get underway. We should all be experts on Prosperine culture and customs by the time we arrive."

PROSPERINE

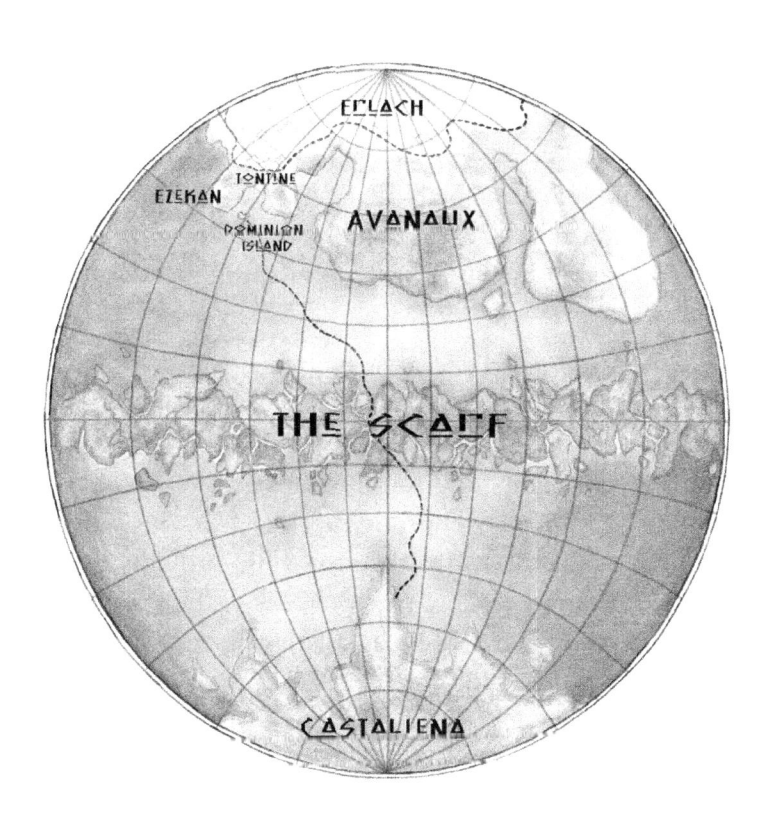

Arrival

The captain's voice resonated in Hickory's quarters. "Commander Lace, Prosperine is now visible in the forward viewing panel if you'd like to take a look."

"About time," Hickory grumbled as she swung her legs off the narrow bunk bed. "Three weeks is too long to be crammed in a spaceship with only seven people and the captain's dog for company." She cursed the admiral for his stubbornness. The Jabberwocky was the fastest transport the Agency could provide, but if they'd waited a few more weeks, the Prince of Wales would have been available. Slower, yes, but infinitely more comfortable.

She showered, fastened the pendant around her neck, and put on the plastiskin uniform of the Alien Corps. Checking her appearance in the mirror, she pushed a brush through her hair a few times and headed for the viewing area.

"Dead ahead, commander," said the captain as she entered.

The Alien Corps

For a second, Hickory felt disorientated. The entire forward bulkhead was taken up with a panoramic view of a dwarf galaxy in Eridanus. Densely packed stellar objects sparkled against a smoky background of interstellar dust, with here and there a dull black splodge of nothingness. *A window to infinity*, thought Hickory, although she knew this was only an image relayed from the ship's sensors and displayed on the curved but solid wall of the ovoid spaceship. Prosperine appeared as a small disc, too far away for the sensors to provide a clear definition yet.

Hickory left the command deck and walked to the multi-purpose mezzanine area that served as a meeting place-cum-resource center. Passengers and crew could relax here, catch up on training vids, or enjoy a drink together.

As she arrived, Gareth was explaining the physics of modern propulsion systems to the junior lieutenant, Jenny Morrison, a pert nineteen-year-old just out of flight academy. The two had been inseparable since the beginning of the voyage.

"You remember the basic theory from your studies, no?" said Gareth. "Think of light as a series of waves. To move at the speed of light, you need to be able to cross from the first wave to the second." Gareth moved one arm like a dolphin swimming until it met his other hand. "Once you get there, the post-light engines kick in to jump the ship from the crest of that wave to the next and then to the next and so on. Scientists call it surfing."

"You're not talking physics again, Gareth?" Hickory rolled her eyes and smiled at Jenny. "He's hard to rein in when he's on his hobby horse."

Jenny flushed and stammered, "No, no. Not at all, Commander Lace. It's all fascinating. It's just, well, I majored in communications. I didn't study faster-than-light theory. But I'd love to know how it all works." She looked through her lashes at Gareth. "And Gar is a great teacher."

Hickory didn't need her empathic ability to know Jenny had fallen hard for Gareth's charm. She placed Jenny's arm through her own and walked her to the roboserver. "Tea?" she asked, smiling. Hickory placed her regular order for Lapsang Souchong and carried the teapot and cups to a table.

Jenny flopped into an armchair and sighed. "I can picture the surfing thing. But I don't get how we reach light speed in the first place."

"That's the hard part," said Hickory, pouring the tea. "Accelerating up to the speed of light to allow the ship to move from the first to the second wave is the key, and it requires massive amounts of energy."

Gareth took over. "The sub-light engines on the Jabberwocky are powered by an s-nuclear fusion reactor. The reactor generates particles with negative mass and propels them through a Crumm

The Alien Corps

Accelerator. The result is that space at the front of the ship is compressed, and the space behind it is expanded. In layman's terms, the energy differential creates a tidal wave of warped space."

Jenny looked from one to the other. "A crumb accelerator?"

"Er, yes," said Gareth, nonplussed. He dipped his finger into his tea and drew an atomic structure on the table. "The fuel source for the reactor is a combination of hydrogen nuclei and the unstable liquid metal crynidium, which was discovered on one of Jupiter's moons sixty years ago.

"It's ultra-rare, and you need to use a lot of it to get to the point where you can switch on the surfboard, but once there, faster-than-light travel takes minutes." He pointed to Prosperine, now a blue disc, on a nearby viewscreen. "The longest part of the journey is the deceleration phase at the journey's end. We wouldn't want to come out of light-speed too close to a planet," he said.

"But how do we avoid crashing into them when we're surfing?" asked Jenny, blowing on her tea.

Hickory nodded. "That's a good question. In reality, it's highly improbable that our flight would take us so close."

Gareth sat at the edge of his chair and nodded enthusiastically. "Correct. The universe is a big place, and there aren't as many celestial bodies clogging it up as you might think. Only about 400 billion in our Milky Way."

"Only 400 billion!" said Jenny, laughing.

Gareth blushed. "I know it sounds a lot, but if you joined them all together, they would take up a tiny percentage of the Galaxy. There's a lot of empty space and cosmic dust in between."

Jess arrived, catching the tail end of the conversation, and emitted a quick, disgusted snort. "I've never known anyone to get so excited by particle physics."

"I figure it's better to know the reason something works rather than take it on trust, Mother. You might be comfortable landing this spaceship without understanding why, but I prefer to know the science." Gareth grinned at Jess's gaping expression. He put his hand around Jenny's waist. "Why don't we continue our discussion over a drink, Jenny? There's no point confusing these old fuddy-duddies by talking about things they'll never understand."

"It's time that boy was taught a lesson," said Jess. "He's getting far too big for his boots."

"He might just be on the verge of learning something new," said Hickory as they watched Jenny and Gareth stroll away arm in arm.

"He needs someone to take him in tow," said Jess, then nodded towards the planet in the viewscreen.

The Alien Corps

"It's beautiful, isn't it?"

"It looks like Earth—a white cloud layer swirling around a sapphire."

"It'll be a lot different on the surface. This place is a radiation paradise. Prosperine's sun has been expanding for millions of years, and the planet has become hot and humid."

"More jungle." Hickory sighed and squeezed her eyes tight to shut out the memories of Aquarius IV. Jess touched her arm lightly.

"We won't see much of that on this trip. The spaceport is built on an island off the coast of Avanaux. Dominion Isle has some wooded areas, but not what you'd call jungle."

Hickory nodded her understanding. According to the vids, the first planetary explorers had found two populated landmasses of significant size. Avanaux and Castaliena were located on opposite sides of the equator, separated by vast, turbulent seas. Travel between them was rare but not unknown.

Castilie and Avanauri natives had similar physiologics, the most apparent difference between them being the darker skin color of the former. Human researchers on the planet adopted the appearance of the Castilie, which provided the Agency and the government of Avanaux with a plausible explanation for the strange-looking creatures now wandering around Ezekan. *I guess it's better than telling their citizens they've been invaded by apes from outer space,* thought Hickory.

The third notable geological feature of the planet was the band of floating islands and reefs, six hundred miles wide, that encircled Prosperine along its equator. Known as the Scarf, the islands mainly consisted of swamps and jungles. Agency intelligence indicated that the further into the Scarf you went, the more inhospitable it became. No humanoids lived there—only insects and lower life forms. *Thank God we don't have to go there*, thought Hickory.

Jess glanced over to the captain seated at the con. "Duty calls. Time I was strapped into my station. See you when we land."

◆◆◆

The *Jabberwocky* nudged silently against the space dock, four hundred miles above the planet's surface. The captain's voice resonated throughout the transport, "Ship is stationary. Gravity and atmosphere are Earth normal. Good luck with your mission, commander. Thanks for traveling with us."

A few minutes later, the door locks released. Hickory led the way through the enclosed passageway to the planet-fall elevator.

The terminal's hollo-assistant greeted them. "Welcome, Commander Lace. Please proceed directly to the departure lounge. Your scheduled bubble-craft are ready for boarding."

The Alien Corps

Three mini-ships awaited them. They settled into the body-length seats and authorized the bio-cocoons to encapsulate them.

Jess signaled their readiness to the ground crew. "Releasing docking clamps for bubble-craft one, two, three. Take us in, boys."

The bubbles dropped one by one, covering the four hundred miles to the surface at almost four times the speed of sound. As they approached their destination, the controllers switched the drive to mooring mode, the bubbles were guided through a central shaft into an expanding Fibonacci spiral, and their speed was gradually reduced to zero.

◆◆◆

All Prosperine was designated a restricted zone, and ships with clearance from the Agency were permitted to land only on Dominion Island. The island was over a hundred miles from the mainland, and the Agency's spaceport was built well away from the main coastal population centers. The port was always busy. Bubble craft from orbiting vessels came and went daily, transporting first-contact experts and cultural attachés back and forth.

Security was high, and the complex was monitored inside and out. At the same time, holographic projections and the screams of wild animals were transmitted throughout the surrounding forest to discourage casual observers.

When Hickory and her team disembarked at the landing module terminal, they were greeted by a young technician whose badge identified him as Ensign Jeremy Strauss.

He saluted Hickory. "We were advised of your imminent arrival only yesterday, commander, but everything's been prepared per Admiral Lace's instructions. Most of the facilities we need, including acclimatization, are housed inside a shielded environment in the outer arm of the spiral. If you follow me, please, we'll get you started."

Their first port of call was the quarantine station on the ground floor. Here, Hickory and her team passed through a decontamination chamber to neutralize bacteria and viruses that might prove hazardous to the Prosperine environment or local life forms. After sixty minutes of blood tests and inoculations, they were given the all-clear and issued with lightweight Avanauri clothing.

From there, the ensign took them to what he playfully called the cosmetics store. "This is the fun part where your human features are changed to resemble those of a Castilie native. Don't worry; it's not as painful as it sounds. The doctors use a combination of polyethylene implants and liposuction treatment. It's like an advanced special effects makeover, and it will look and feel like your flesh until it's removed at the end of your mission."

The Alien Corps

"The fun part, huh?" said Gareth.

"Yes," said the ensign, wearing a huge grin. "The pre-op team will remove your hair—everything except your eyebrows and a strip on your skull, which will be styled in the Ezekan fashion." He laughed. "Strange as it sounds, we've found the Ezekanis are more accepting of a Castilie who wears their hair in a Mohawk style like they do. After the stylist finishes, your skin will be dyed a mottled brown and covered with a radiation screening agent."

That wasn't nearly as much fun as Jeremy had suggested, but it was more agreeable than what was to come.

Hickory, Jess, and Gareth were taken to the operating theatre on surgical beds and connected to devices that monitored their heart rate, breathing, pulse, and blood pressure. Wireless sensors attached to their skulls measured changes in the electrical transmissions in their brains. The monitors were connected via subspace to COLIN, which dictated the subsequent operating procedures and controlled the drone component of the surgery.

The medical team came into the theatre wearing masks and gloves. The lead surgeon introduced himself and his two associates and explained the procedure to the patients: "First, we need to change the appearance of your eyes. COLIN will administer what we call conscious sedation to help you relax and block the pain, but you will be awake during this period." He gestured towards the two men. "Mr. Lampart and Mr. Theophanes will assist in performing the operations.

"After that, all being well, we'll move on to phase two—transforming the functionality of your internal organs that will enable you to survive the Prosperine environment. We'll be using robot technology to help us with this intricate work. I assume you've all been briefed on our friend COLIN's role in these proceedings?"

Hickory paled but nodded. All three had been briefed on the necessity for them to appear, to all intents and purposes, as citizens of Castilie.

She felt her muscles relax as the anesthetic was delivered intravenously. She tried to glance towards Jess and Gareth but could not move.

The surgeons began by removing their patients' eyelashes. They cut the skin, muscles, and fat surrounding the eyelids and then stretched them to make their eyes larger and rounder. The whites of their eyes were dyed tortoiseshell blue, and their irises were covered by a green shield to protect them from the sun's radiation. In Gareth's case, the ridges over his eyes were also enlarged.

About an hour later, Hickory heard the surgeon speak as though through a dense fog, "Phase two will commence in 3…2…1."

The Alien Corps

Thank God they anesthetize us... was Hickory's last waking thought.

While she dreamed, COLIN released a mist of micro medical bots that entered the body through her mouth and nasal cavity. These immediately made their way to the body's vital organs and went into action to expand lung capacity and modify her digestive and immune systems.

When the robots had completed their work, the threesome were brought back to consciousness and taken to a recovery room to wait for the micro-bots to exit their bodies naturally.

◆◆◆

The surgeon, Lampart, held a hand mirror to Gareth so that he could see the changes in his altered face. Gareth pinched his cheeks and squashed his nose. "You guys are true artists," he told the specialist. "How long do these changes last, eh?"

"You'll have thirty-six days before the implants start to break down," said Lampart. "Then, deadly toxins will invade your bloodstream. But that's not so much of a problem because if you don't get back to the base by the thirty-fourth day, your body will have absorbed a lethal dose of radiation, and you'll be dead anyway."

"Oh, right. I suppose it's a fair incentive to finish the job quickly," mused Gareth.

The surgeon grinned. "We can give you a booster any time up to the twenty-eighth day that will extend the life of your maquillage for a further month. If you need to stay on Prosperine longer than that, you'll have to return to Earth for re-humanization before you can go through the process again."

Opposite, Hickory sat on the edge of her bed, still drenched in sweat. Her new feathery curls were plastered to her skull, and the pendant dangled from her neck.

"That's nice," said Jess. "Where did you pick it up?"

Hickory blushed. "It's an ancestral heirloom. My grandmother gave it to me. It was presented to her mother on retirement, and Nonna thought it might bring me luck."

"Really? It's a stunning piece—must be worth a fortune."

Gareth walked over for a closer look. "That is special. What did your great-grandmother do to earn it?"

"I'm still trying to work that out." Hickory had decided to keep the information concerning her great-grandmother quiet for now. Publicly associating herself with such a heroic figure would only aggravate her feelings of inadequacy. It would be her secret. Tucking the pendant into her smock, she sighed. "I don't think I'll ever get used to alien planet arrival.

The Alien Corps

How long do we have to stay here, do you think?"

"Not long," said Gareth. "The differences between Earth and Prosperine are relatively minor. On more exotic planets, the environment can be so poisonous that it takes days for the human biosystem to adapt. Here, we only need to worry about the low oxygen, higher UV, and, of course, the heat and humidity. Luckily, the gravity is almost identical to Earth."

Jess snorted. "This is what you call lucky? You make it sound so simple. Give us an oxygen mask and a pair of shades, and we'll be all right! You forgot to mention that if we walked outside without acclimatizing, we'd be fried to a crisp in a day."

"Actually, according to the specialist I talked with, it would take two days, Mother," he said, grinning at her.

"So, how long?" said Hickory through gritted teeth. "If we don't leave here soon, I'll expire."

Gareth laughed. "A couple of Earth hours, probably. That reminds me—we need to adjust our SIM comms implants to local time and the language mode to Avanauri."

It took closer to three hours for their physiology to adjust to the local conditions before they moved on to the armory.

Jeremy joined them there. "No nukeguns, I'm afraid, nor anything else that can't be found on this planet, but these weapons are the best of their kind," he said.

Hickory nodded. "This is what we trained for."

They examined the range of sidearms provided by the Agency and sanctioned by the Avanauri government.

Gareth looked at the cutlasses hanging on the wall. "Primitive but good-quality steel," he said. He picked up a pair of knives and flipped them into the air.

Hickory and Jess ignored the longbows, crossbows, and the range of spiked clubs, claymores, and spears, instead deciding on swords and lightweight leather tunics decorated with animal teeth.

Jess picked out a long metal saber and simulated cut and thrust moves. "Nice balance," she announced.

Hickory dismissed several blades before she declared herself satisfied with a double-edged longsword. She also placed a hunting knife in her belt.

Dominion Island

As they approached the giant double doors, Hickory had a strong sense of leaving behind the world of science and space travel. On the other side of the doors, she would join an alien medieval society, bringing danger and the risk of personal failure.

She emerged into a hall designed by the Agency and the Avanauri government to provide an aspect of familiarity to the natives whose task it was to interface with the visitors. The curved walls were made of polished black granite etched with silver. Hickory marveled at the creation story represented there. The tableaux spanned the ages from the beginning of the cosmos: the birth of Prosperine and the great and small lights in the sky, all emerging from the womb of the great God Balor. Then came the conception of the first animals, plants, and primitive winged Avanauri. The final panel depicted the modern-day inhabitants and their newest scientific discoveries: steam power and blimp-like flying machines.

P J McDermott

Reception desks, cubicles, and chairs, hand-crafted from polished timber, were strewn around seemingly randomly. Frosted glass windows high above them had been thrown open to admit the fresh air and natural light. *Looks like a cross between a medieval church and a Fabergé egg,* thought Hickory. *Impressive.*

Five Avanauri males approached them. Two held spears with their points upright as symbols of power. All wore ceremonial daggers at their waist. Sparse, downy hair covered their heads, and in contrast to the mottled brown of the visitors, their skins were light in color except for the dark patches around their perfectly round eyes.

Hickory thought there was something strange about how they walked. Stiff and stilted, as though they were afflicted by arthritis. As they drew nearer, other differences became apparent. All wore padded jackets with high collars—the latest fashion, she presumed. These concealed sharply sloping shoulders but couldn't disguise the long, skinny arms protruding from their torso several inches below where a human's would. Five long fingers on each hand extended almost to their knees. Hickory could easily imagine feathered wings attached to those arms.

The officials bowed low and offered the visitors seed cake and a flask filled with pungent liquid. As the leader of her party, Hickory exchanged small gifts to symbolize acceptance of the traditional law. Then, they were formally admitted to Avanaux.

A tall, dark-skinned male waiting on the far side of the hall approached with an outstretched hand. "Jebediah Nolanski, the Alliance's cultural exchange attaché stationed in Ezekan. It's my duty and pleasure to welcome you to sunny Prosperine. I have some transport parked half a klick away. If you're finished, please follow me. We'll get you out of here and take you to our embassy—such as it is. How was your trip?"

"I'm glad to find someone else to talk to." Hickory smiled and introduced herself and the others, then fell into step beside Nolanski. From the briefing she'd been given, she knew he was near retirement age, although his Castalienan markings made him appear younger. He was lanky—over seven feet tall, with a sharp Roman nose and thin lips. "How long have you been on Prosperine?" she said.

"Almost a year, off and on. This is my last term. The brass are sending me home in two weeks for permanent re-humanizing."

"Looking forward to it?"

"Oh, yeah. Been away too long as it is. It'll be good to settle down."

Hickory heard the lie in his voice but ignored it. After a stellar career with the Alliance, it was only natural for him to be apprehensive about retirement.

They emerged from the welcome hall onto a broad pathway with canopy trees on either side growing tall and thick, curving high over their heads like a cathedral. Nolanski kept up a running commentary. "There's a lot about Prosperine they don't put in the guidebooks," he said. "Most of what you see around here is unique to these islands. These trees and vines might look like something out of the Brothers Grimm, but they're mostly harmless—although you need to watch out for the exceptions."

He pointed to a tubular flower sprouting from the center of a leafy plant growing by the side of the path. "This purple giant, for instance, is carnivorous. It will swallow a small bird whole if it gets a chance. Pretty, though, isn't it?" He pushed Gareth's hand away as he reached out towards the flower. "It's not particularly dangerous to us, but its pollen can give you a nasty rash. Best not to touch."

Gareth pulled away hastily.

The variety of life was a surprise to them. They'd expected things to be different, but the flora beneath the canopy appeared more dazzlingly exotic and prolific than any they'd experienced elsewhere. Scores of bright orange shoots stretched high, forcing their way between tree branches and dislodging giant red and indigo fungi that floated downwards like upside-down umbrellas, then collapsed in a puff of spores.

The pink, feathery fronds of a delicate shrub

vibrated to the caress of a light breeze, producing a melancholy, almost hypnotic song. At ankle level, bushy ground cover sported six-inch thorns that jerked back and forth to protect their psychedelically colored blossoms from marauding insects. And, in every patch of ground where the flowers hadn't staked their claim, long golden grasses flourished.

"The twins would be ecstatic. They'd think this is heaven," said Jess. Her eyes were round, and her head swiveled left and right, overwhelmed by the kaleidoscope of color.

"Jess! Stay exactly where you are, and don't move a muscle," said Nolanski. "These long grasses are deadly to humans. Do you see those sharp barbs along the edge of their leaves? One prick and your body would swell up to twice its size. I've learned the hard way to carry an antidote with me just in case a newbie gets stung." He held up a small bottle filled with an orange liquid and grinned. "It's an embarrassing way to die."

Jess couldn't see any barbs but moved away from the grass. "Don't tell me that's a plant," she said, pointing to a giant purple globe covered with coarse hair and sprouting three tendrils twitching like leopard tails.

"Absolutely. Some of the vegetation hereabouts shows signs of sentience and can traverse short distances. In fact, our scientists are studying them to see if they communicate with each other. The stems on that one are covered with a sticky substance, and they catch nearby insects by waving them about, as you can see. Avanauri farmers grow them and harvest the sap, which is used as a glue for housebuilding. Thankfully, none of these plants have learned to walk—as far as I know," said Nolanski with a snicker.

He indicated a trumpet-like flower on a long stem. "That one's even livelier. It's like the pitcher plant on Earth, but it is more cunning in how it catches its prey. It can shoot a sticky ball of spit up to a distance of ten feet away to paralyze crawling insects and small animals. And then it extrudes a tentacle and hauls back its victim to decay around its roots."

"Oh, wow!" Gareth watched nervously as the flower head turned to follow them. Small, multi-winged insects buzzed around his head, and the air was rich with perfume. "Those flowers sure have a strong smell," he mused.

"Actually, it's the flies that secrete the scent. We think it's their defense against the plants—a sort of aromatic camouflage," said Nolanski.

Gareth inspected a bright orange worm as it crawled slowly up the trunk of a nearby tree. He jumped back in shock when it reared up and spat at his face.

"Judas Priest!" exclaimed Jess.

Hickory reached out quickly and hauled Gareth

The Alien Corps

away from the tree.

Nolanski laughed. "Not to worry, son, it's only mildly caustic. Here." He handed him a handkerchief. "It's called a Veruignis - a Firespitter by the locals. That's its defense against any inquisitive creatures who get too close. Ah, here we are." A clearing materialized out of the forest. At the far side, a group of large herbivores were grazing peacefully.

Jess drew in a sharp breath and pointed. "What are those?"

"Our transport," said Nolanski. The Avanauri term for them is yarrak. I call the big one over there, Brutus."

"Is it...is it tame?" asked Gareth, still dabbing at his cheek with the handkerchief.

"Yes, most of the time. Yarraks are more intelligent than dogs, and Brutus has a friendly nature. In the wild, a bull yarrak is a very territorial animal, but they're more docile in captivity. Some rich Avanauri use them to travel between cities and as work animals—they haul logs, plow fields, grind corn—you name it, they do it. They're not quick runners because their legs are too short and dumpy, but by heavens, they're strong!"

The beast Nolanski had pointed to snorted and lumbered across the field towards them. It appeared twice the size of a fully-grown Clydesdale, but that was the end of any resemblance to a horse. Brutus's massive body was hairless, and it had no tail. The uniformity of its predominantly pink skin was broken by undulating gray stripes, and its enormous bulk was supported by two stout legs at the front and two shorter ones at the rear. Overly large eyes stared at them from above a narrow mouth containing two rows of solid and flat molars ideal for grazing.

Brutus slowed and approached them tentatively, swinging its long, curved neck back and forth. The yarrak stopped six feet from the group, its nose quivering like a South American tapir.

Nolanski gathered the reins dangling from the beast's muzzle and led it over to where several wooden wagons were lined up. He stroked Brutus's nose, backed it into the harness, and fastened the straps. The yarrak looked over its shoulder as the others climbed into the cart. Nolanski gave a flick of the reins, and the vehicle lurched forward.

Gareth and Jess chuckled as they were tossed around on the seat, but Hickory was too busy trying to hold on to be amused. "What about wild animals—anything we should be wary of?" she asked. She'd heard something crash through the brush, but when she turned around, it had gone.

"This whole area is looked after by the G.A., so anything big has been cleared out, though there are plenty of snakes and a variety of wild pigs hereabouts. What you heard just then was probably a pig, or it

The Alien Corps

might be the holographic security."

Nolanski pointed into the distance. "There's a cobbled road up ahead that leads out of the forest. From there, it's mainly dirt track all the way to the coast—about twenty miles." He nodded to a watchman as they left the clearing, then turned to his passengers and grinned. "It's going to be a bumpy ride. This cart is genuine Prosperine—strong enough, but they haven't yet gotten the hang of passenger comfort. You might think the Alliance would provide something better for us, but you know about the technology embargo. The Agency tries to minimize the impact of our presence here, although, despite their best efforts, some low-tech equipment does make it through."

"Smugglers?" said Hickory, thinking as she took another jolt of how sore she would be by the journey's end.

Nolanski nodded. "The main culprits are a group calling themselves the Dark Suns. We've been trying to catch up with them for months, but they're slippery. They do a roaring trade, mainly in soft goods and small luxury items, for which they extract a king's ransom in precious gems and metals. Talking about soft goods, you might appreciate some cushions in the trunk at the back."

Hickory gratefully accepted the cushion Jess passed to her. "We were briefed about crynidium being found in some parts of the planet. My understanding is this information is classified, though."

"There are few secrets on Prosperine where money and power are involved," said Nolanski darkly, flicking the reins.

They continued their journey in silence, except for the rumble of the cart and the thudding of Brutus's feet as he plodded along. The arrivals center was located on the highest peak, and it was downhill all the way to the sea. Now that she was sitting on something soft, Hickory found the swaying of the cart and the dappled light in the forest hypnotic, and she closed her eyes.

◆◆◆

The trumpeting of the yarrak woke her several hours later. A dragonfly, the size of a sparrow, hovered a few inches before her face, and she flapped at it, startled. She heard Nolanski snigger.

The forest thinned out, giving way to scrub and tall grasses. In the distance, she could see large herds of animals grazing on the hills.

The humidity was lower once they were out of the forest, and the temperature was kept down by a stiff breeze blowing steadily into their faces. By the time Nolanski pulled over beside a stream, they were ready for a break and keen to get out of the wagon and stretch their legs. They sat on a bank beneath the spreading branches of a squat tree and ate from the ration packs they'd been given at the terminal.

Gareth pointed to the herbivores. "There's a lot of those grazing types around—yarraks, right?"

"Those ones are wild yarrak. There are few predators on this island big enough to worry them, and, of course, the Avanauri are pretty much vegetarian," said Nolanski.

"Vegetarian or vegan?" asked Jess.

"In between, I suppose," said Nolanski, considering. "But not because of any moral or religious beliefs. Their digestive system just isn't designed to process much except vegetable matter. They're fond of naturally occurring foods like nuts, seeds, honey, and dairy products, but red meat is deadly to them. We discovered early on that red blood cells in meat corrode the lining of their stomachs. Over time, if they ate enough of it, they would actually die of starvation.

"They won't eat fish either for the same reason, except for some types of soft, bloodless sea stars that are not strictly fish anyway. They love mollusks and shellfish, especially crabs— they love crabs. There's a big fishing industry hereabouts, though." He swallowed a mouthful of water.

Hickory raised her eyebrows inquisitively.

"They dry and crush the fish for fertilizer. With

such a small arable farming area, the local farmers plow in a lot of manure, which helps them harvest three or four crops a year. That wouldn't be possible if it weren't for the abundance of fish and kelp."

Their guide explained that the soil on the plains was too poor to support much except the native goldengrass, a drought-resistant reedy plant essential to the Avanauri culture. "The grasses produce a cellulose-based fiber that's spun into yarn—"

Abruptly, Hickory leaped to her feet and drew her sword.

"What is it?" hissed Gareth. He glanced about quickly, searching for the danger.

Jess and Nolanski took up positions on either side of the commander.

"Not certain," said Hickory. "Something big—hiding—there." She pointed her sword at a thicket of trees and brush about forty yards away.

"You sure it's not a pig?" said Nolanski. "Some of those mothers are pretty big."

"I'm sure—" she began, then stopped, transfixed. A chittering sound grew in intensity and then rattled into silence.

"What the heck is that?" said Jess.

"I don't think we should wait around to find out," said Gareth, drawing two long knives from his belt.

"Too late!" cried Hickory. "Close up. Stand your

ground."

There was a swish of grass, and two monstrous heads emerged from the thicket.

"Violators." Nolanski's breath came unevenly. "Bad luck bumping into them."

Half as tall as Hickory and black as soot, they inched towards the group, muscles rippling and shoulders hunched like panthers stalking their prey. The two carnivores stopped twenty yards away, raised their heads, opened giant maws, and screeched. Yellow eyes on opposite sides of their heads swiveled to assess the humans. They snuffled at the strange scent through a single nostril high on their snouts.

Gareth crouched to face them. "At least there's only two of them."

Nolanski cringed. "Not for long, I suspect. Violators are pack hunters."

The leading animal made a decision. It pared back its lips to display viciously curved teeth. Saliva dripped from its mouth as it snarled and snapped at them. Its partner stalked purposefully towards the group of people.

Built for speed in attack, thought Hickory. The creature raised its head and let out a howling screech, then charged.

Instinctively, Hickory sprang forward to meet the leading predator. The longsword felt powerful in her hand as she heaved it overhead, poised to strike.

Jess ran straight at the second creature, aiming to stick her blade through its chest.

Startled by the sudden attack from these unknown foes, the animals reared and twisted aside.

Hickory swept downwards, narrowly missing the beast. The momentum of her attack caused her to stumble, and she fell heavily to the ground.

The point of Jess's sword pricked the second creature as it veered away, barely scratching its flank.

Hickory hardly registered how incredibly agile the beast was before it charged her again. She leaped to her feet and spun away from an outstretched claw, then slashed upwards with her sword, opening a cut in the beast's side.

Looping her weapon overhead with both hands, she swung it downwards in an arc, half-severing the creature's head from its body. Blood gushed from the wound, and the Violator collapsed, kicking its hind legs in a death spasm.

The second creature leaped at Jess before she could rally and clamped its jaws on her arm. The weight of the attack forced her to the ground.

The beast crunched and ripped at her, tearing away chunks of Jess's protective clothing. Frantically, she smashed it on the nose with the pommel of her sword. The beast released her arm and lunged at her neck.

The Alien Corps

Jess did the only thing she could think of. Holding the beast off with one hand, she thrust the other into its mouth. She grabbed hold of its tongue and wrenched.

Just then, two more creatures crashed through the bush towards the group. Gareth screamed a warning, "Jess, look out!" and raced to meet them. The first brute leaped at him, and he swung both his knives in to meet the sides of the animal's head. His aim was true, and the blades pierced its eyes. Instantly dead, the weight of the creature forced Gareth to the ground, but he pushed the animal to one side and struggled to his feet.

He dashed towards Jess and was bowled over by the remaining Violator. The massive jaws of the animal clamped onto the back of his head, forcing him into the dust. Warm saliva drooled over his face, and the beast's putrid breath stank in his nose.

He felt a stabbing pain as the Violator's teeth pierced the skin on his skull, and then the pressure vanished.

"Up, Junior. Quickly!" Hickory heaved the carcass from his body and pulled him to his feet.

"I owe you one, boss. For a moment, I was sure I was lunch."

Hickory had already left him and was running to Jess's aid. Jess sat on the ground, cradling her injured arm. She was saturated with the blood of the wounded animal, which was jerking in agony by her side. She gasped with relief as Hickory rammed her blade through the Violator's head.

"You ripped its tongue out?" Hickory stared at the gory object still in Jess's hand. She realized her friend was in pain. "Never mind. You can tell me the story another time." She took her arm and felt gently for shattered bone. "You're lucky. You'll have some painful bruising, but nothing seems to be broken. Do you think you can stand? We need to sterilize these wounds."

Nolanski leaned down to help Jess up, but she shrugged his hands away.

"What the hell! Why didn't you help me when I needed it? That thing would have killed me." Her legs were trembling as she staggered to a rock and sat.

"You okay, Mother?" asked Gareth. "I tried to get to you, but the big doggie wanted to play."

"Boyo, you are an idiot!" she said, then she laughed with relief.

Hickory glanced around the area as she attended to Jess's arm. "We need to hurry. No telling how many more of those things are around here." She stared icily at Nolanski.

"I didn't know," he said, shaking his head vigorously. "I mean, I knew about them. I just didn't realize they'd be on this part of the island. Look, Jess, I'm sorry I didn't come to your aid, but I'm a diplomat,

The Alien Corps

not a fighter."

"More like a coward," mumbled Gareth under his breath.

Hickory gave him a warning look. "Zip it, Gareth."

Nolanski turned to hitch up the wagon. "We've still twenty miles to go before we reach Llandabra. We need to get moving. As I said, other Violators will be here soon—they normally travel in packs of ten or more."

❖❖❖

Two hours later, they came upon a settlement. A waist-high earthen wall enclosed a dozen or so crude dwellings made from wood, grass, and mud. "We should be safe now. Violators tend to keep away from the villages." Nolanski nodded to a few naurs standing in the shadow of the gate. All wore gray rough-spun clothing, with hats pulled low over eyes that swiveled to follow them. Nolanski continued to smile but didn't slow down.

Gareth swung around in his seat. "Hey, hold up a sec! Can't we pull over for a few minutes? I want to take a closer look at a Prosperine village."

Nolanski shook his head. "Number one, it wouldn't be polite to enter the village without an invitation, and number two, they're afraid of us. I doubt they see many dark-skinned naurs this far from Llandabra. Don't worry, son, there will be plenty of opportunities to meet the locals when we reach the bigger towns. The folks in these remote villages are the Prosperine equivalent of the Amish. They like to keep to themselves and have little experience dealing with foreigners."

"They're some kind of religious sect?" Hickory asked.

Nolanski shrugged. "Could be, but I don't think so. That sort of monkish garb is normal for farmers hereabouts. They'll all belong to the same family group, and for some reason—whether religion or politics—they've chosen to live in isolation."

"It must be a hard life," said Hickory, frowning.

"Very tough. Avanauri society is based on a clan system. Sometimes, you get four generations all living in the same camp."

"Don't they have problems with inbreeding?"

"They do," agreed Nolanski, nodding. "Each clan revitalizes the gene pool by intermarrying with nearby groups, and on islands like this one, they enforce strict mores on births inside the clan. Females—the nauris—move in with the naurs' families. The occasional aberration is dealt with ruthlessly."

"No wonder there's so few of them," muttered Jess.

Hickory sensed hostility from the primitives, but it was unfocused, filled with resentment and

The Alien Corps

hopelessness. An image of a group of naurs swallowing lumps of flesh came to her. The folks here were starving, forced into eating meat, and it was driving them mad. She probed deeper but could find no angst towards her or her party. She wondered whether food shortage was widespread amongst the Avanauri community; it would explain the reports of disquiet on the streets they'd read.

When they reached Llandabra a few hours later, her question was at least partially answered. This was a thriving town, the largest on the island, with a native population of several thousand.

"The town population swells to nearly double, depending on how many ships are in the dock. The number of strangers visiting the seaport has surged over time with no signs of slowing down," said Nolanski. "Many local traditions have been relaxed, and as a result, the perimeter wall has fallen into disrepair."

They passed through the gates, and the road changed from dirt to crushed rock.

"At one time, every city, town, and village in Avanaux would have been surrounded by a stout wall to keep out intruders. But with the number of people passing through this place in recent years, it became a barrier to trade," said Nolanski.

The ambassador pointed out the rainwater harvesting system that captured precious water from landscaped areas and rooftops. "The rainwater passes through a filtration system into underground storage tanks, away from light and heat. Some of the Avanauri engineering works are remarkably sophisticated."

Most buildings they passed were the traditional low-rise oval design they'd seen on the ship's vids. Others reflected the expanding trade in the region and were more spacious, with two and three-story structures. All had tall windows that faced the sun to the east, and these modern buildings incorporated either a private vegetable patch or fruit garden on their roofs.

"Avanauri have become very skilled at intensive farming and make use of every available hectare. They'll grow enough in nine months to see them through the rest of the year when the weather makes it impossible to work the soil. Those large buildings over to the side are silos for storing grain and nut crops. Fruit, legumes, and vegetables are dried and held in vaults located underground."

Brutus trumpeted as they passed an open-air enclosure with stalls where some yarraks were being cleaned, watered, and fed. Those not scheduled to leave today could be seen wallowing in a giant mud puddle.

They arrived at the dock area and dismounted, tying Brutus to a hitching post. Trawlers, crabbers, and other kinds of fishing and passenger sailboats

The Alien Corps

were moored alongside a wooden jetty. Nolanski pointed to a ketch that bore twin masts raked sharply forward, with long spars carrying furled sails. "Seabird is our transport. She should be leaving for Ezekan in a few hours."

A lively crowd had gathered around the owner of a smaller fishing vessel selling baskets of flying fish and assorted seaweed. The crowd glanced casually at the travelers passing by but didn't pay them any attention.

Gareth grinned with delight when a young naur waved to them. "Avanauri kids don't seem all that different from the humankind," he said.

Hickory couldn't agree but kept her thoughts to herself. While their faces were humanoid, and they each sported two arms and two legs, that was as far as the similarities went. Many native people wore loose clothing revealing short necks and sloping shoulders. However, the absence of a flexible waistline caused them to bend from the tops of their long legs and made them so alien to her eyes.

They passed several young adults with children clinging to them, tails wrapped around their parents' waists. Jess glanced back over her shoulder and tugged at Gareth's sleeve. "Did you see? Isn't that amazing?"

Nolanski explained. "Those four are only a few days old, but the Avanauri considers them to be in their second development stage. Stage one lasts about seventy days. That's when the embryo grows inside a protective shell attached to the mother's abdomen. I've never seen that stage—you rarely meet a pregnant nauri on the street, to be honest. After seventy days, the egg is released, and a proto-baby hatches out. That's what you see here. Their tail-like appendage acts like an umbilical cord. It latches onto the parent and enables the infant to extract nourishment. After a few months, the child moves to solid foods, and the tail separates and withers away."

"Fascinating," said Jess.

"Bizarre," said Gareth.

Several young nauris passed by, whispering at the appearance of the strangers. Each wore faint markings on their necks, indicating they were approaching puberty. On the journey to Prosperine, the travelers had learned how to differentiate the nauris by the color flashes that started at their eyes and extended to the base of their necks. Dark purple signified the females were of marriageable age and hence of interest to unattached naurs. As the nauris grew older, the markings turned orange and later to brown when they matured beyond childbearing age.

Jess remarked that she found it difficult to tell one Avanauri from another. "Apart from the color flashes, they're almost identical in size and shape. As far as I can see, there are no fat or particularly skinny ones,

The Alien Corps

and their eyes are the same bright blue."

Gareth raised his eyes heavenward. "So, they all look the same to you? Bit of a stereotype, isn't it?"

Jess's mouth gaped open and shut firmly, but the cultural attaché spoke before she could find an appropriate retort.

"Actually, it's a matter of getting used to it," said Nolanski. Once you've been on Prosperine for a while, you'll be able to recognize individuals. Still, there's less variation here than among humans."

"That's what I'm saying!" said Jess. She stuck her tongue out at Gareth, which caused some of the onlookers to become agitated.

"I'd be careful with the tongue, Jess. Mating ritual!" said Nolanski, sniggering.

Jess's face glowed, which caused even more excitement.

"We'd better get you on the boat before you start a riot," said Gareth.

Ezekan

The coastal settlement of Harbor Town was on the left bank of a vast river delta. As the Seabird approached, Hickory watched several groups of nauri working along the estuary, filling baskets with silt from the flood plain and loading them into carts harnessed to Yarraks. Other workers drove the laden carts to a wooden structure on the edge of the town. Hickory looked quizzically at Nolanski.

"The river sediment contains high levels of nutrients, and when it's combined with crushed mountain rock and humus from marine plants and fish, it makes for a very rich soil. That's what they're doing in the shack—it's a primitive factory. Every night, workers haul tons of this stuff to the agricultural areas in the west and northern parts of the country." Nolanski passed his spyglass to Hickory. "You can see the city on the far side of town."

Lying more than a mile inland, the city of Ezekan sparkled like a jewel as they approached from the sea. Avanaux's capital sat perched on top of a solitary volcanic plug jutting vertically from a hummock of

The Alien Corps

grassland. This rocky peak, the mountains in the background, and the city walls all seemed made of the same white stone.

Hickory focused the spyglass on a broad track that snaked up the steep embankment and led to the city gates. Close up, the walls resolved into massive blocks with glittering black flecks reflecting the sun's light. Banners and flags fluttered atop towers and steeples, visible above the outer wall. "Impressive. Is the plateau a natural feature?" she asked.

"It's called a lava neck. Left behind after the planet's ice age scraped away the surface of an extinct volcano. Most of the mountains seem to have a high concentration of extrusive carbonatite—extremely rare on Earth."

They approached the wharves, and half a dozen sailors scrambled aloft to furl the sails. The ship slipped neatly alongside a jetty and was made fast to a bollard.

"I didn't realize Harbor Town would be this big," said Hickory.

Nolanski replied, "About twenty thousand naurs and nauris live here. Sailors, shipwrights, merchants, fishermen, factory workers. It is a thriving market and the biggest seaport in Avanaux. Traders come here from the far eastern reaches of the continent to do business in Ezekan."

The main street meandered along the bank of the

river delta. It was paved with crushed blue stone, and they decided to walk through the town. Nolanski hitched Brutus to the wagon, and the yarrak followed placidly behind them.

Makeshift shelters made from wood, reeds, and natural fibers lined one side of the road, protecting the goods on display. Shoppers crowded around long tables, baskets, and pots laden with fabrics, foodstuffs, and other produce for sale.

The whole place seemed to be buzzing. Musicians plucked stringed instruments, funambulists performed graceful gymnastic feats, and conjurers and other entertainers drew enthusiastic crowds. Patrons spilled onto the street from packed taverns. At the same time, naurs and nauris of all ages solicited custom from doorways along the main thoroughfare.

Gareth and Jess walked together, taking in the atmosphere. "Except for the fact this is an alien planet filled with weird-looking aliens, we could be in Rhode Island," said Gareth.

"Remind you of home, does it?" said Jess, laughter in her eyes.

"To tell the truth, this is nothing like where I was raised. But I did have a boat moored in Newport. I can imagine the waterfront being similar to this in the nineteenth century."

"I'd never have taken you for a sailor," said Jess.

The Alien Corps

"I wasn't. When I was sixteen, my parents bought me the *Pride of America* to reward me for finishing top in the national school competition. I only took it out on the water one time." He waved away an insistent young naur trying to entice him into a shop.

"Your parents must be very wealthy to spoil you so much."

Gareth shrugged. "My father is a news magnate, my mother is a socialite, and I'm their only son. They did their best to turn me into a spoiled brat." The smile left his face. "Damn near succeeded too."

Jess looked at him quizzically. The work on Gareth's features during acclimatization made him hard to read, but a shadow lurked in his eyes.

He exhaled a long breath. "I invited some of my classmates out to the launch for a celebration party. There was one girl I had a crush on. Her name was Carole. I think she quite liked me, too. I organized a live band, some roving entertainers." He gestured at the jugglers and magicians they passed. "These guys would have fitted right in. We all drank too much alcohol." His words sounded clipped, forced out.

He paused, staring at some revelers who were the worse for wear. He shook his head. "All the kids were having fun, and then an argument broke out. I can't even remember what it was about. So stupid, really. There was a lot of name-calling and a scuffle. Someone pushed Carole, and she hit her head on a guardrail and fell over the side. She went straight down.

"A couple of us dived overboard while the others called the coastguard. We searched for ages but couldn't find any sign of Carole. That was the last time I set foot on the *Pride of America.*"

"God, how awful. That poor girl. Who pushed her, do you know?"

Gareth answered hastily. "No, no. It was an accident, but I always wonder, you know, if I could have done something to prevent it." His head drooped.

"Listen to me, boyo. You can't take responsibility for every rotten thing that happens in your life. Some pain can never be forgotten. You just have to learn to tolerate it." Gareth grunted. "I guess. Thanks, Mother."

Hickory glanced over her shoulder. "Looks like sex is a commodity in Prosperine just like every other planet," she said. As they passed, several young naurs stared with interest at her brown skin.

One of the nauris called out to Nolanski, lowering the top of her garment to reveal impressive bright purple and blue flashes. Nolanski coughed and dragged his eyes away from the display. "More so in Harbor Town. In the capital, they're stricter about things like prostitution," he said.

Hickory caught a disturbing image of interspecies

sex from him, and she wondered whether Nolanski made a habit of visiting these quarters.

"Hey," said Gareth, craning his neck. "What's going on over there?"

Up ahead, an unruly crowd had gathered in a semicircle, shouting and waving their fists. Their anger was directed at a young nauri standing with her back against the wall of an inn. She cringed away from the hostile mob, trying to avoid being struck. One of her eyes was already swollen, and blood trickled from her mouth. The closest naurs and nauris pushed and shouted insults at her. One slapped her face, and another spat at her. She sank to the ground and wrapped her arms around her knees, trying to protect her belly.

"We should keep moving. We can't get involved in domestic problems," said Nolanski.

"Domestic …?" Jess could barely speak. "What do you mean? That poor girl is being beaten!"

Nolanski's brow furrowed, and he shook his head. "Listen. You're obviously good folks, but you've only just arrived here. Maybe you should take some time to understand the local culture before getting on your charger."

Jess looked at Hickory, who shook her head. "Wait," she said. She'd spotted a naur making his way forcefully through the crowd.

"Let her be." The newcomer spoke firmly, yet his voice resonated across the square. "Why do you pass judgment on this nauri? None of you are any more deserving in the eyes of Balor than she. All should lie prostrate and beg his forgiveness."

Hickory climbed onto the cart to get a better look and was joined by the other three. Peering over the shoulders of the crowd, she saw the naur position himself between the angry mob and their quarry. Other than his height—he stood almost seven feet tall—he seemed much like the naurs he faced, pale-skinned, with heavy brow ridges and no facial hair except for his eyebrows. But unlike most of the others, his entire head was shaven. His blue eyes swept along the rows of onlookers, seeming to challenge them to respond, and finally settled on the ringleader.

The opposing naur took a step forward, his hands clenched and eyes flashing. "She is a whore!" He repeatedly jabbed a finger at the nauri. "Beyond Balor's forgiveness. She corrupts the innocent. She deserves to die." His whole body shook with his anger.

The nauri's rescuer faced him unblinkingly and spoke, "Who are you to say who should die and who should live? Many who die do not deserve death. Can you give them life? No? Then do not be so quick to say who deserves death and who does not, lest you invite Balor's judgment on yourself."

The Alien Corps

Hickory whispered to Nolanski. "Is this the one we're looking for?"

"Kar-sèr-Sephiryth, yes, I think so—or one of his disciples, maybe."

Gareth's head swiveled to face him. "You think so?" he said. "Don't you know?"

Nolanski clenched his jaw and turned away.

Guardsmen had been alerted to the trouble and, armed with staves, made their way through the crowd. They ordered the mob to disperse.

The ringleader spat on the ground and shouted at the guards to arrest the nauri. "Everyone knows this one is corrupt, diseased. She should not be offering her body for money."

"Go home, Dharba. You've had too much strong wine. Do as I say, or you'll spend the night in jail." The guard encouraged him on his way with a tap on the head from his stave.

As the crowd dispersed, the nauri rose to her feet, holding her arms wide, her palms facing her rescuer and her head bowed. She mumbled something inaudible. He smiled, took her hands, and drew her into his arms. "Tarisa sèra Happon, do not be afraid. No evil will come to you. Now go to the temple and give thanks to Balor." The nauri reluctantly surrendered his hand, then hastened away.

Hickory stretched her neck, trying to keep sight of

the enigmatic hero, but she lost him in the crowded marketplace.

Nolanski took the reins and urged them to sit in the cart. "We were lucky the guards came along when they did. Otherwise, we would have been caught up in a riot," he said as they got underway.

"I think the Teacher, if that's who he was, had things pretty much under control," said Hickory.

"You don't know these people like I do," he replied. "Usually, they're placid, yes, but when they get worked up, they're uncontrollable. It sounded like that guy had a personal grudge to settle. Maybe he caught some disease from her. They're not a forgiving race when it comes to losing face."

Hickory nodded. Nolanski was the expert. Still, it was a revealing encounter. The tall naur, whoever he was, had shown remarkable fortitude. "You're right. We should take advantage of your local knowledge."

Nolanski, somewhat mollified, pointed to a cigar-shaped airship flying overhead. Vapor trailed behind it as it moved sedately across town. "That's a good example of how rapidly the Avanauri are evolving. They invented the air yacht three years ago, and the design is constantly being improved. Right now, they are only capable of short flights, and their steering is unreliable. But engineers are experimenting with steam-powered propulsion. It won't be long before they develop a sound understanding of aerodynamics. Then there'll be no stopping them. Machines like these will allow them to travel to Castaliena, perhaps even around the planet one day."

As they approached Ezekan, the sun sank low on the horizon, and Prosperine's twin moons moved higher. Soon, the entire sky was ablaze with pulsating sheets of emerald, pink, and yellow. A thin ribbon of silver rippled slowly across the heavens and sank behind the mountains.

"I've seen the northern lights in Iceland," said Nolanski, "but I have to say this show beats it hands down."

"Stunning ionization for sure," said Gareth. "There must be massive amounts of charged particles emitted by the sun. How often does an event like this take place?"

"Every evening for nine months of the year. You get used to it, son. We better get moving. The gates will close in an hour or so."

The highway bustled with travelers coming and going from the city. Most walked, some rode yarraks, and a few drove wagons of varying sophistication, raising clouds of dust as they entered the main thoroughfare. Hickory shouted to make herself heard over the clatter of wheels, the stomping of feet, and the continuous chatter of the Avanauri. As they drew near the city, the road became more crowded, and the pungent odor of yarrak excrement intensified.

They reached the massive wooden gates as the sun was setting and passed under a stone lintel resting on twin pillars at either side of the opening.

Hickory wondered aloud what the inscriptions signified.

Nolanski explained. "Exaltations to the One True God and a warning to enemies and non-believers that passing this portal will lead to a terrifying and prolonged death. Not to mention their souls will suffer the torments of hell for all eternity."

"Charming," said Gareth. "Makes you feel really welcome."

"If you're a citizen of Ezekan, it helps you feel secure."

"When you say 'God' and 'hell,' I take it you're not talking literally," said Gareth.

"Of course not," said Nolanski, smiling.

Hickory caught a flicker of annoyance from Gareth. Nolanski had been deliberately patronizing since the attack by the Violators on Dominion Island and had become worse since Harbor Town. She'd have to talk to Gareth about keeping his cool.

Nolanski continued. "Balor is roughly equivalent to the Earth concept of God, but the idea of heaven or eternal damnation is unknown to these people. 'Good' citizens are rewarded by being granted another life on Avanaux. Those who fail in this one merely cease to exist."

They led Brutus through the entry and into a tunnel that zigzagged through the thick external walls. *Pretty effective defense,* thought Hickory. *Tough for an enemy to fight their way through here.*

If the smell had been strong before, it was overpowering in the enclosed space.

Nolanski hurried them through as quickly as the crowds would allow. After a hundred feet or so, they thankfully exited into fresher air.

The outer ramparts of the city were separated from the inner wall by a dry moat crammed with crudely built huts, ragged tents, and a flea market selling everything from second-hand clothing to medicinal cures and bootleg grog. Most other travelers dispersed at this point, but Nolanski guided his party through the shantytown, across a bridge spanning an open sewer, and finally through a second gate into the city proper.

After a steep uphill climb, they turned off the main road and negotiated a maze of narrow streets until they arrived in front of the embassy precinct.

Nolanski fished a key from his pocket and unlocked the gate into the compound. "You can relax now. This is Alliance property leased from the government. Here, you can be yourself. All the employees are Ezekani, of course, specially selected by the Avanauri leadership. They can be trusted to keep your secrets from everybody but their employers—under pain of death." He laughed. "Not much happens here that the Prosperine Senate doesn't get to hear about within the hour."

They dismounted, and Nolanski called out to the young naur leading Brutus away, "Kyntai, make sure you give him a good feed and a scrub-down. He's had a long day."

The boy smiled, bobbing his head back and forth as the yarrak snorted and stamped. "Of course, Master Nolanski. Brutus is my favorite. I will treat him well."

Nolanski led them upstairs to their rooms, suggesting they wash and rest before meeting him for dinner in the patio area.

◆◆◆

Hickory threw her bag on the bed and glanced around. The room was spartan, with a grass mat on the floor and a painted wooden icon fixed to one wall. She studied the painting with interest. It was a portrayal of Prosperine's Supreme Being, Balor. The god, she recalled, had four aspects to his nature: omnipotence, retribution, mercy, and peace. She wondered which one this represented.

Half a dozen earthen pitchers filled to the brim with steaming hot water stood alongside a round stone tub in one corner of the room. Hickory noted the drainpipe leading from the bath to an adjacent cubicle containing a rudimentary toilet system. The bed and a beautifully crafted table with two chairs were the only other concessions to civilization. There was no communication system and no electronics. Smoking oil lamps set at intervals around the walls provided light, and an open fire would afford heating in winter, she thought. She bounced on the straw mattress. *Not bad. Comfy enough.*

The room was large, with wide folding doors leading onto a veranda. She went outside and leaned on the railing. The solar wind had dispersed, and the sky was clear of the ionic disturbance. The silvery moons shone brightly, giving Hickory an excellent view of the city. Centuries ago, when feuds were commonplace, each family unit built their homes within protective enclosures. This meant Ezekan had developed like a honeycomb of roads and alleyways. Dirigibles dotted the sky above, some in use but most anchored to rooftops. *It looks like flying machines are the latest status symbol here.*

Hickory watched, fascinated, as green and crimson sparks swirled high into the air from communal bonfires. The colorful display was due to the copious amounts of nuclear fission products the trees absorbed over their lifetime before being harvested for firewood. The light from the flames reflected off the temple to Balor—a magnificent structure constructed from carbonatite that twinkled and sparkled in the night air.

According to historical records, the place of worship was ancient, dating back more than eight hundred years. To Hickory, the temple looked like a four-sided pyramid with a smooth, flat top, as though it had been severed by a giant scimitar.

Other buildings were three and four stories tall, with spires that reached for the clouds. Flags and banners representing the city's ruling families were draped over the turrets of administration buildings in the city's center. Hickory could see guards silently patrolling on top. Watchtowers, marketplace stalls, lodging houses, and taverns proliferated—another sign of the city's rapid evolution.

Hickory inhaled deeply. Her senses were awash with the sweet aromas from exotic fruits, herbs, and vines that grew over rooftops and hung from window boxes in riotous colors. In the distance, she could see a sizeable grassy area surrounding a sparkling silver lake with an ornate fountain in the middle spouting high into the air. On the far side of the lake stood a low hill with a sprinkling of trees covering its crown like a bad haircut.

After a hot bath, Hickory slipped the emerald-encrusted crucifix over her head and donned the poncho that had been left for her on the bed. She walked into the patio area in time to hear Gareth and Jess quiz Nolanski about the Avanauri.

"Is it true they are a warlike people? Apart from the

The Alien Corps

walls and that one incident in Harbor Town, I haven't noticed any signs of aggression. Overall, they seem quite a friendly bunch," said Jess.

"On the whole, you're right," said Nolanski. "Most of the common people, most of the time, are fairly reserved and like to keep to themselves. The walls are a relic of the past. Centuries ago, when the warlords of the Erlachi became powerful and greedy for land, the Avanauri clans banded together in cities like Ezekan. There hasn't been any conflict in Avanaux for five hundred years, but old habits die hard, I guess."

"The Erlachi? Who were they?" queried Gareth.

"Erlach is a country beyond the northern ice mountains. Look here," Nolanski said, spreading a map on the table. "It's made up of six regions, see? Each one is governed by a hereditary warlord. These six warlords pay fealty to the royal house of Erlach, which has been in power for millennia."

"Yes," said Jess. "Over a thousand years ago, the Erlachi army led by Albetios I of Vistiore invaded the southern parts of the continent. They laid waste to much of the countryside before the legendary warrior, Connat sèra-Haagar, united the naurs and nauris of the South and led them to a famous victory. Even after all this time, she's revered by the Avanauri as a hero."

Nolanski looked surprised that Jess would know this. He nodded his agreement and continued. "There are statues of her everywhere, usually carrying her magical sword by her side. She was the one who founded the modern system of confederated states. Since then, every major population center in Avanaux has had its own regional government, and each one sends a representative to the Senate in Ezekan. The Senate is responsible for establishing Avanauri-wide policies. Trade regulations are a good example—prices are set centrally, and trade routes are guarded by a police force paid for by all."

"So, the police have authority throughout the country?" said Gareth.

"Not for everything—only in specific roles agreed by the Senate. Rural Avanauri still hold to their traditional tribal customs. If one of their own gets into trouble, it can be an all-out war between two families until justice is seen to be served. That's clan justice—an eye-for-an-eye type of thing—not legal redress. There are regional peacekeepers, of course, but most disputes seem to get settled before they step in."

Hickory took a chair opposite Gareth and poured a glass of cold water from a carafe. "There are some beautiful buildings in the city. Some of their temple architecture is stunning," she said. "What can you tell us about their religion? I understand they're obsessive about their beliefs. Does all of Avanaux worship the same deity?"

Nolanski pulled a face. "As I told you before, one or two underground cults practice different beliefs,

The Alien Corps

but I don't know much about them. I don't involve myself in their business, so I'm afraid I won't be of much help there."

Hickory thought it strange the ambassador wasn't better informed. "I'm assuming you've been fully briefed on our mission. You do know this religious leader, Kar-sèr-Sephiryth, is a person of interest to both the Corps and the Alliance?" She rested her arms on the table and looked through narrowed eyes at Nolanski.

Nolanski nodded. "Of course, but—"

"We'd be grateful for anything you can tell us about the Avanauri religion."

Nolanski sighed. "The official doctrine preached by the Temple is that those who do good works such as helping the poor or donating to the priesthood will earn credits with Balor. If you earn enough credits, you're rewarded with a second existence after you die. As I said, those who fail in this life just cease to exist. The Avanauri don't believe in an afterlife."

"I haven't seen any graveyards hereabouts. What do they do if they don't bury their dead?" said Gareth.

Nolanski pursed his lips. "The average lifespan of a naur is fifty five Earth years. The dead are never mourned. If the passing is a painful one, his friends will rejoice because the pain has ended, and if he did not live in accordance with the law of Balor, then their relatives will not speak of him. The common Avanauri believe the essence of their being departs with death. There are no souls and no graveyards. Everything is recycled, and that includes the dead." He shrugged his shoulders.

"It may be environmentally friendly," said Gareth, "but it sounds gross. Exactly how are the bodies recycled?"

"It's not so bad as you might imagine. Every village has a recycling factory. Essentially, this is a vat or a silo containing plant material, worms, soil animals, various fungi, and other organic and inorganic matter. They use a windmill structure to keep the mixture turning over. It takes less than twelve months until the finished product can be used as fertilizer—that's five times faster than a body buried on Earth."

"Does this Kar-sèr-Sephiryth character preach the same philosophy as the Temple or something different?" said Jess.

Nolanski walked over to a cabinet and unlocked it. He took a slim leather pouch from a drawer and placed it on the table. "I've put together this portfolio for you. Everything we have on him is in there. It's not much, but it's what we have." He spread his hands apologetically. "I'm sorry I can't be of more help, but I don't get involved in their religion."

Gareth snorted loudly. "Dangerous, is it?"

"Shut up, Gareth," said Hickory. She flicked through the notes briefly. There was a list of the

The Alien Corps

miracles Kar-sèr-Sephiryth had allegedly performed, complete with witnesses and dates. A second page listed the locations he was known to frequent. One of these was the "People's Corner," which was within the boundary of the park she'd spotted from her balcony. She handed them across for the other two to read.

"And, there's this." Nolanski passed her a black and white snapshot of a tall individual dressed in long robes addressing a group of listeners. The subject seemed to be staring at the camera the instant the image was captured.

"Kar-sèr-Sephiryth?" Hickory asked and passed the photo to Gareth.

"Yes. Taken from our orbiting space station. It's the only print on the planet, and I'll destroy it as soon as you've all had a look at it. Can't risk it being discovered and having the natives worked up over sorcery."

Hickory took the photograph back from Jess and stared at it. There was something about the way the naur held himself—a dignity and self-assurance that set him apart and seemed to make him taller than those around him. His perfectly round eyes were, like all Avanauri, surrounded by dark pigment. The naur in the photo appeared to be the same one they'd seen in Harbor Town.

"These witnesses," Jess said, tapping the list. "How

reliable are they?"

"Solid citizens, every one, but their stories vary. I'm afraid they won't be of much help except to provide background," said Nolanski.

"I'd like to talk to them, nevertheless," said Hickory. She placed the photo inside the folder and handed it to Jess. "Now tell us what you know about the political regime."

Nolanski stared at the folder and then looked at Hickory, his mouth slightly open. He rubbed his forehead with one hand. "Yonni-sèr-Abelen is the High-Reeve. That's what their head of government is called. He's a tough character—"

"Come on, Jeb, you know what I mean. Is he corrupt? Does he have the full support of his government? What's his weakness?"

"Corrupt? They're all bloody corrupt, but he comes from an influential family with powerful supporters, so he gets away with it. His only weakness, if you can call it a weakness, is his preparedness to deal with the Alliance. That's seen in some quarters as a betrayal of the Avanauri traditional law and religion. I wouldn't say he has the full support of his cabinet on this, no. And they're the only ones with the full story of our presence here." There was a sheen of perspiration on Nolanski's forehead. His eyes flicked to Jess, Gareth, and back to Hickory.

"So, is he generally liked—by the people?"

The Alien Corps

"He's been in power for decades. I'd say most common Avanauri hold him in awe. He has the backing of the Temple. But there are rumblings from extremist groups unhappy about the rapid modernization taking place, and they've been demanding a return to the old ways."

"Rumblings?" said Gareth.

"Yeah, you know—rallies, people complaining, attacks on property—that sort of thing. It's called rumblings." A vein throbbed in Nolanski's neck, and he clenched his fists.

Hickory ignored the mounting frustration. "That's been very useful, Jeb. Thank you. Just one last question. Is it safe to walk in the city? Tomorrow, we'd like to discuss the Teacher's miracles with some of these witnesses."

"The locals are polite and pleasant, to your face at least. Around a hundred people from Earth wander the streets of Ezekan every day. The citizens are used to seeing these occasional visitors from Castaliena walking around. The authorities have set severe penalties for anything more than rudeness by the locals. Make sure you follow the conventions, especially when you first approach them."

Jess took over. "Our SIMs will translate the Avanauri language accurately for us, and they've been preset to transmit rudimentary Avanauri to reflect our identities as travelers from Castaliena. This is adjustable, of course, but we should keep it on the default setting unless we're on embassy grounds."

"I agree," said Nolanski. "You don't need to worry about breaking cover with our staff here or those government officials in the know. For anyone else, always keep your story in mind, and you'll be fine. Keep clear of any religious gatherings for now—just in case. They can get a little heated. And if you see a scuffle, please ignore it. I don't want to have to fish you out of jail."

They ate a light meal and turned in early.

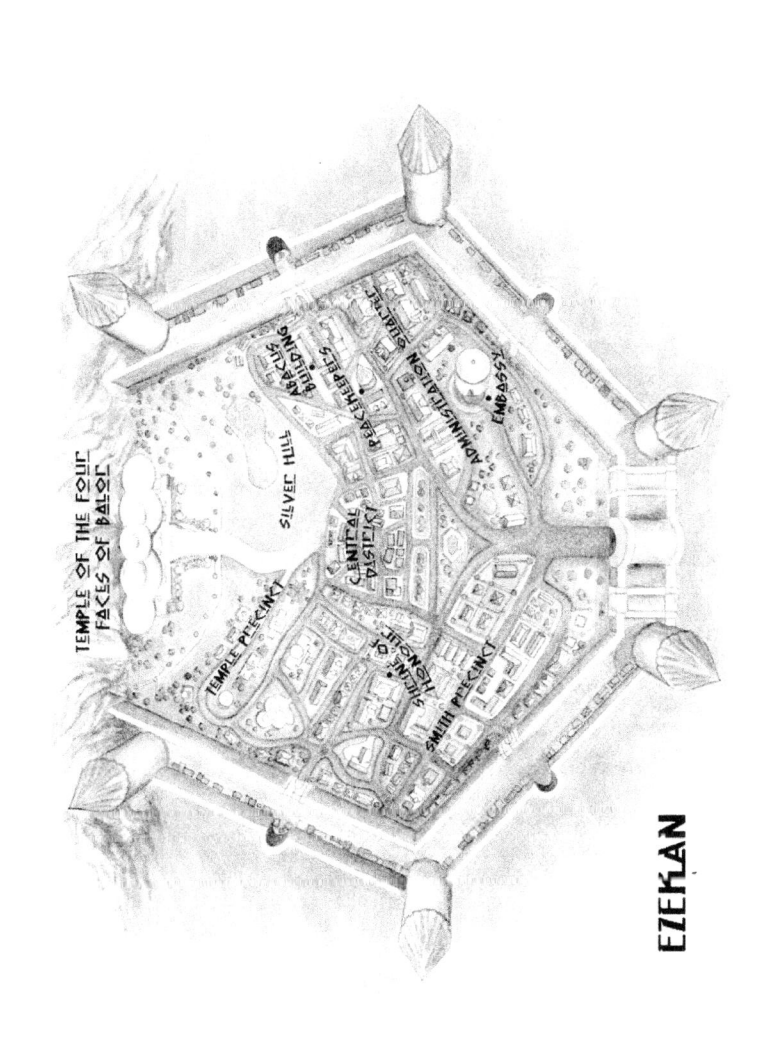

EZEKAN

TEMPLE OF THE FOUR FACES OF BALOR

SILVER HILLS

ABACUS BUILDING

SHANTIES

PEACEKEEPERS

ADMINISTRATION

EMBASSY

CENTRAL DISTRICT

TEMPLE PRECINCT

SMITH PRECINCT

HOUSE OF SMITH

Eyewitness

BY the time they woke, Nolanski had gone. He left them a map of the city with his favorite eating spots highlighted. His note suggested that young Kyntai, the stable hand, would be handy if they wanted a guide. The boy seemed delighted to be of help and capered around like one of his animal charges.

Hickory consulted the list of witnesses. "Kyntai? We need to see Sabin-sèr-Adham, the weapon-worker. Do you know this person?"

"Yes, mistress. Everyone knows Sabin. His forge is in the smithing precinct. It is not far."

When they arrived at his workplace, Sabin-sèr-Adham was hammering at the blade of a sword. A row of weapons leaned against a table, awaiting his attention. The naur was naked from the waist up, and his sloping shoulders and arms bulged with muscle, making him stand out even amongst his fellow smiths. Despite this, his avian ancestry showed in his exaggerated pigeon chest and short legs.

Hickory remained four paces away with her eyes lowered until he indicated they should approach.

Smiling, he greeted them with the standard salutation. "The blessings of Balor be upon you. I am Sabin-sèr-Adham, weapons master. Call me Sabin if it pleases you."

Hickory returned the formal greeting and introduced her partners and herself. "You know each other, I think," she added, indicating Kyntai.

The smith nodded to Kyntai, then addressed Hickory. "What can I do for you, good folks? If you have blades that need sharpening, I'm afraid you'll have to wait a few days. It seems everyone is looking to have their weapons mended, and they all want it done immediately. If you need an edge put on your swords urgently, Ferrier-sèr-Corrine, two streets back, will do a decent job and charge a reasonable price." He wiped his brow, peered at Hickory under his muscular arm, and looked away hurriedly. "Pardon my rudeness, my dear. Many visitors from your country pass by on the street, but none come as close as you are now. It is a wonder to meet travelers from beyond the Scarf. Can't say as I'd want to go on such a trip myself, but I have a few friends who tell me they'd like to see Castaliena."

Hickory smiled back at him. "No offense taken. My companion's sword requires the skill of a weaponsmith, but there's no hurry. We are here on a pilgrimage."

Her SIM was working perfectly. It translated the blacksmith's speech and transmitted it in English to the audio center of her brain. The process was so fast, it was as though he'd spoken in English. The reverse was similar—she thought in English, and her SIM translated the words into Avanauri. The SIM then sent the appropriate phonetic vibrations to her vocal folds, and the words emerged from her larynx. She thought that hearing herself speak a different language, one she understood without having to think about, would take a bit of getting used to. "We came to Ezekan to find the one known as the Teacher. We hear he has much wisdom to share."

Jess handed her sword to Sabin, who examined the blade and placed it against the table with the others. "Fair enough. You can collect it in two days, young miss." He nodded to Jess, then turned to Hickory again. "So, you're looking for Kar-sèr-Sephiryth? He is a marvel; there's no doubting that. He offers much in the way of good advice."

Stepping alongside Hickory, Jess smiled sweetly at

the smith. "They say he performs miracles."

"Perhaps," said Sabin, drawing his eyes from hers. "I saw him do one strange thing. I cannot give you an explanation, so perhaps it was a miracle. I can tell you what I saw if you are interested."

Jess nodded enthusiastically, and Sabin continued. "He was speaking at the hilltop in Silver Park—he's often around those parts. I went, along with many others, to hear what he would say. A young girl came rushing up to her mother in the middle of his teaching. Her arm was sliced open from her elbow to her wrist. Blood was everywhere, and as you can imagine, the girl and her mother were in a panic. Nobody could hear the Teacher speak. He walked up to the girl and took her arm in his hands, and as Balor is my witness, she was healed."

Sabin shook his head as though he still couldn't believe what his eyes had seen. "The mother washed the girl's arm, and there wasn't a scratch on her. Now, I know what you think, mistress, but I've seen many a wound in my time, and I swear the blood was pouring from a deep cut when I saw her first and then not a mark." He picked up the weapon he'd been working on and thrust it into the forge. "Miracles, aye," he said, shaking his head.

Hickory thanked him and said they would return in a few days for the sword. They walked down the road apiece, discussing what the forge worker had told them.

"Pretty impressive if what he thought he saw actually happened," said Jess.

"It's a big if, though," said Gareth. "The holes in his story are so big, you could launch a spaceship through them. Any cheap magician could pull off a stunt like that with a couple of willing stooges planted in the audience."

"So you say, boyo, but Sabin is no fool. If he says the girl was gravely wounded, I believe him."

Gareth snorted. "You'd believe anything, Mother—"

"All right, pack it in," said Hickory. "I'm fed up listening to you two bickering." She glared at them. "Let's see if we can find a miracle that is not so easy to counterfeit." She scanned the list. "Kunja-sèr-Elalel. He's a peacekeeper stationed at the entrance to the government administration building. Apparently, he and about a dozen others saw Kar-sèr-Sephiryth exorcize a demon from a madwoman who was wandering the city half-naked, screaming about the end of days."

"Why did they think it was a demon rather than her being plain crazy?" asked Gareth.

Jess said, "In the early centuries of Earth, madness was thought to be caused by possession. It's probably the same here."

The Alien Corps

"Yes, but you're both missing the point," said Hickory. "The woman's name is Yamu-sèra-Jahini. She has no previous connection to the Teacher, and she is supposedly now sane and spends her time worshiping at the temple. How can madness be cured with the snap of a finger?"

"Why don't we split up?" said Gareth. "You and Jess can go to the temple to interview the nauri, and Kyntai can take me to see Kunja-sèr-Elalel."

"Fine, but don't get into any trouble. Keep your mind on the job. Remember why we're here."

They arranged to meet back at the consulate for lunch.

◆◆◆

The peacekeeper, Kunja-sèr-Elalel, said he'd known Yamu-sèra-Jahini for ten years before the illness came upon her. "She was a modest, caring young nauri, very attentive to her family, and engaged to be married to a guardsman. I didn't see it happen, but her father told me the demon took her without warning, throwing her to the ground one day. She could not speak; her eyes turned white, and her mouth filled with froth. People were afraid to touch her because of the demon."

His chin dropped to his chest, and he stared at the ground. "I am ashamed to admit she lay there all that day and the next. I saw the crowd standing about her just after it happened, and I passed her by. She was raving, slavering at the mouth and shouting vile things. From that time on, she refused to eat or wash." He screwed up his nose at the memory. "I'm not a superstitious man, but the way she looked at me, I could see the wickedness in her eyes." He shuddered.

"What happened when she met the Teacher?" asked Gareth.

"It was ten days later. The Teacher was speaking in one of the smaller temples in the administration quarter when she walked in. I saw her throw herself at his feet, pleading for help, and then the beast started to shake her around like a plaything, and she was cursing and swearing.

"The Teacher put his hand on her forehead and stared into her eyes. He said something like, 'I see you, Yamu. Be at peace, for the demon is with you no longer.' Something like that. I swear to Balor, it was as simple as I say. She wept and thanked him, and he told her to go to the temple and pray."

Gareth thanked the naur and left him to his peacekeeping duties.

Kyntai asked about demons—had he ever seen one? Gareth switched his SIM from pidgin to standard mode, the better to communicate with the boy. "Many strange and wonderful things in the universe can't be explained, but I have yet to shake hands with a demon," he said.

When they reached the main road, a crowd pushed

The Alien Corps

up around them, all heading in the same direction, and Gareth and Kyntai found themselves swept along. "What's all the excitement about?" Gareth asked. Many in the crowd were angry, waving fists in the air and shouting. Gareth grew alarmed when rocks were thrown by some onlookers into the crowd, and when one caught Kyntai above his eye, he pushed out of the throng, dragging the boy after him.

"Let me see." Gareth examined the cut, which had already stopped bleeding. "I think it's okay, but you might have a black eye," he said, then laughed at Kyntai's expression. The boy, of course, wore two permanent black eyes. "What was all that about?" Gareth asked, looking after the mob.

"Kar-sèr-Sephiryth is teaching at Silver Lake," Kyntai replied, breathing hard. "Some in the crowd are looking for a miracle, but others declare him to be a sorcerer. I think we should stay away." He bit his lip.

"You think there might be trouble?" said Gareth, glancing sideways at him.

"The city protectors are sure to be there, but you are a stranger, and those with dark skin are not always welcome." His ears colored in embarrassment.

◆◆◆

Hickory and Jess located the Shrine of Honor in a park just north of the Smith precinct. The shrine was surrounded by shrubbery and well-tended gardens. It had been built in a similar style to the Temple of the

Four Faces of Balor but without its grandeur.

Hickory whispered to Jess, "We've got company. Across the park to your right, behind the large tree. Don't make it obvious; I don't want to scare him away." She raised her voice. "According to my notes, the Shrine of Honor replaces an earlier monument that fell into disrepair. It commemorates the fallen heroes of the war with Erlach."

She turned her head and glanced casually at the stalker, who immediately turned away.

Jess quickly hid behind a bush while Hickory walked swiftly towards the entrance to the shrine.

Their stalker looked around in time to see Hickory disappear through the doorway. As he hurried to catch up, Jess grasped the naur by his arms. He struggled and lashed out at Jess's face, but she took him to the ground with a rugby tackle. "Why were you following us? Who are you, and what are you up to?" she said, pinning him against the grass as Hickory arrived.

"Nobody—I'm nobody, and I wasn't following you. Let me be!"

Jess glared. "All right, nobody. Tell us what you're up to, and perhaps we'll let you go. You've been watching us since we left the embassy compound, admit it. Don't think to lie."

"Please! Don't hurt me—I'm nothing—nobody. I

The Alien Corps

was paid to watch you, no more."

He tried to shake himself free, but Jess tightened her grip. "Tell me your name," she said.

"Mirda-sèr-Sidhartha! My name is Mirda; I am Mr. Nolanski's personal servant. He told me to follow you. I'm supposed to report back on your travels. Please, let go!"

"Nolanski!" Jess said, turning to Hickory. "Why would he do such a thing?"

"I don't know," said Hickory. "Maybe he was concerned about our safety."

Mirda nodded vigorously. "He told me to send a message to him in Harbor Town if you got into trouble."

Hickory hauled the naur to his feet. "I don't think you meant any harm, but you're lucky you weren't seriously hurt. Don't try to follow us again."

"But, Mr. Nolanski—"

"No buts—I'll sort things out with Nolanski. Do you understand?"

Mirda didn't look happy, but eventually, he nodded.

"What's your boss doing in Harbor Town?" Hickory figured she knew but wondered whether Nolanski's indulgence was widely known.

The naur drew his head even further into his

shoulders, if that was possible, and wouldn't look at Hickory. He began to shake.

"How often does he go there?" she asked, but Mirda remained mute.

"What's going on?" said Jess, puzzled by Hickory's questions and the naur's response.

"I think I know, but this guy's too scared to say more," said Hickory. "You can go now." She motioned to Mirda, and he gratefully hurried away.

Hickory looked after him thoughtfully. "Let's finish what we came here to do and go find Gareth."

◆◆◆

Gareth found it difficult to convince the boy to take him to Silver Lake. Kyntai stubbornly insisted it would be too dangerous and instead suggested they visit the morning market in the square before heading back to the embassy. They wandered amongst the stalls, attracted by the pungent aroma of cooking spices. They sampled small servings of exotic vegetable dishes and perused the stands selling clothing and footwear. Gareth bought some of the sweets Jess said she'd liked so much at dinner the previous night. And then they came across the loopus.

The fluffy domesticated animal fascinated Kyntai. To Gareth's eyes, it was not unlike a long-haired rabbit with enormously long ears. He promised the youngster he could have one if he would take him to

The Alien Corps

see the Teacher. The boy squirmed and wrestled with his conscience, but the temptation had proved too great.

Now, Gareth and Kyntai crouched at the edge of the tree line atop the grassy knoll. A mere fifty yards below them, Kar-sèr-Sephiryth stood amidst a sizeable crowd. Gareth looked on, fascinated. From what he could tell, there appeared to be three distinct factions gathered there. The close followers of Kar-sèr-Sephiryth were easy to pick—those were sitting at the Teacher's feet and hanging onto his every word.

The largest number of listeners lounged on the grass, eating and drinking as they watched. Gareth figured they were here for entertainment.

The third contingent was more difficult to spot. Gareth could hear them, though. They were scattered throughout the crowd in twos and threes, all calling out variations of the same theme. "Who are you, Kar-sèr-Sephiryth, the son of a poor farmer, to tell the priests and scholars what is true and what is untrue?"

Organized activists. This could get a little hairy. Maybe Kyntai was right to be worried. Gareth began to rethink his wisdom in coming here with no one to help him in a crisis but the boy. Hickory would be mad at him if he got in trouble, but he decided getting a close look at Kar-sèr-Sephiryth was worth the pain.

The Teacher's voice rose clearly above the hubbub. "Can any man, priest or scholar, divine the true meaning of Balor's word? Only one sent by He can know the truth."

The answer created bedlam amongst the agitator faction. Even the neutral spectators jumped to their feet, shocked at the Teacher's claim that Balor had sent him. Many of those watching shook their fists at Kar-sèr-Sephiryth and shouted insults. Others spat on the ground and punched at their thighs, crying out and shaking their heads. Some, terrified by the crowd's reaction, hugged their children to them and fled.

Gareth couldn't drag his eyes from the Teacher, who stood calmly amid the storm. His words were almost identical to those the Christ in the bible had used to a similar question from his detractors. *It must be a coincidence,* he thought, *or… or…* His logical mind sought answers but found nothing.

One naur, stouter than his brothers, picked up a clod of earth and made to throw it at Kar-sèr-Sephiryth. He hesitated as the Teacher's gaze locked onto his.

Kyntai tugged at Gareth's sleeve anxiously. "We must leave. There will be trouble here, and there are no peacekeepers. We must go now." He tucked the loopus safely under his shirt.

Gareth reluctantly stood up, but it was too late. "Not only does Kar-sèr-Sephiryth blaspheme, but he consorts with devils and foreigners," the thick-set ringleader shouted. "We don't want their kind here."

He threw the clod of earth at Gareth.

Gareth avoided the missile but was struck on the temple by a flying rock. He crumpled to the ground.

Kyntai bent over his inert body and sought to revive him.

Led by their vocal ringleader, a mob of naurs brushed him aside and bundled Gareth away through the crowd. Kyntai shouted in protest and struggled to hold on to the nearest assailant but was knocked over by another of the gang wielding a wooden club.

Holding the back of his head, the boy struggled to his feet. He looked around futilely for his pet. With a sob, he pushed his way through the still-restless mob and followed the kidnappers at a safe distance.

Imprisonment

Consciousness returned like a crab scuttling sideways, clattering over wet rocks, slipping into pools of darkness, and then emerging hesitantly as the dawn breaks. Gareth groaned. The ground where he lay was hard and cold and wet. His head throbbed, and his stomach churned. He had the unsettling thought that he must have emptied his bladder. He tried to rise but found his hands and feet were bound. He struggled to loosen the ropes, but there was no feeling in his fingers. He pulled himself up to a sitting position and tried to remember what had happened. There'd been trouble at the lake. Kyntai had yelled at him to leave. After that, his mind was blank. He hoped the boy was all right.

Where am I?

A single smoking torch mounted on one wall cast a flickering light over his surroundings. He was being held in a large prison cell. Wooden cots, most in disrepair, indicated at least a dozen naurs had been confined here at one time. Brick walls on three sides curved high overhead like a cathedral, while thick

The Alien Corps

iron bars made up the fourth wall.

He recoiled as a rodent-like creature with pale, wrinkled skin and a long tail scurried across the floor and sat in front of him, whiskers twitching inquiringly. Gareth shouted, and the beast disappeared into a dark corner. Instantly, he regretted his action. Except for the rat, he was alone.

No sooner did the thought enter his head than he heard movement coming from outside his cell. He struggled to his feet and peered through the bars. "Hello? Who's there? Speak to me—are you the one who put me in here? I demand to be set free!" His voice echoed hollowly. "Look, whoever you are, you've made a mistake. I shouldn't be here."

A maniacal cackle was his only answer. Gareth crawled caterpillar-like to the back of the cell and rolled into a ball, shivering in the scrubby light.

It seemed like only minutes later, he awoke. His head was clear, although it still hurt. He was shocked at his earlier outburst. He'd forgotten his SIM was set on parity. Anyone who heard his fluent speech would immediately realize he was not from Castaliena. Quickly, he reset it to default mode.

He heard the rasp of rusted metal on metal, and a gleam of light fell on the floor outside his cell. He propped his back against the wall and waited.

Three shadows approached. The leading one fumbled for a key hanging from a ring attached to his belt and unlocked the door, swinging it open to let the others enter.

My jailer. As the figures approached, Gareth guessed one to be a high-ranking Avanauri. He wore a brocade jacket over a clean white shirt, open at the neck, and held a handkerchief to his nose. The other visitor was darker, shrouded in a hooded cloak.

The brocade jacket signaled to the jailer, who approached Gareth and cut loose his bindings. He felt a stinging sensation as blood coursed through his unblocked veins, and he rubbed his wrists vigorously.

"What's going on? Are you one of that mob on the hill? Why did you bring me to this place?" he said, looking from one to the other.

A guttural voice answered him from beneath the hood. "Be quiet. I will ask the questions, and you will answer them, shrelek! State your name and the position you hold within the Intragalactic Agency."

Gareth was taken aback. *Who are these people? What do they know of the IA?* He shook his head and frowned. He assumed a blank look and shook his head slightly as though he was uncertain of the alien's question. "I am Castalie from the Southern Ocean. My name is Kronen-sèr-Varquar, and I am here on a journey of discovery."

"You lie!" The individual behind the hood hissed in anger. "You have come here at the behest of your Agency. What is your mission on Prosperine? Tell me

The Alien Corps

or you will suffer greatly." The figure threw back his hood and glared at him.

Gareth was too stunned to speak. The stranger was neither Avanauri nor human. If he were asked to describe what he saw, Gareth would have said that the creature's head was like that of an enormous soft-shelled turtle. Its skin was like tessellated basalt, it had no forehead, no chin to speak of, and its mouth was a slit. A long snout twitched between two small protruding round eyes.

Gareth cowered. *Bikashi! What's a Bikashi doing here? This is bad, very bad.* He glanced at the naur who seemed unfazed by the revelation. There was little point in carrying on with his deception. Whether in disguise or not, all Bikashi knew an Earthling when they saw one, and this naur obviously knew more than an ordinary citizen should.

The alien pointed a scanner at Gareth and grunted. "Castalie do not wear implant technology, Earthman. If you do not tell me what I wish to know, you will be put to the rack. Co-operate, and I will grant you a quick death."

His speech was harsh to Gareth's ear, adding to his fright. He'd never run into a Bikashi before, but he knew the history well. Everything about this one confirmed the tales of horror he'd heard. "Wait, there's no need for that—it's quite simple. Yes, I am an Earthman. My name is Blanquette, and I work freelance for a private organization called the Alien Corps. They sent me here to find a preacher named Kar-sèr-Sephiryth."

"More lies! You have one last opportunity to cooperate. Otherwise, the information we seek will be extracted from you—painfully."

"I *am* cooperating. I'm speaking the truth." Sweat broke out on Gareth's brow. *Why don't they believe me?* "We were invited here by the Avanauri authorities. You're the one who shouldn't be here. When the Alliance finds out—"

The Bikashi snarled, but Gareth continued regardless. He faced the Avanauri and stabbed his finger at him. "You're some kind of official, aren't you? Your leader asked the Corps for help. You realize you're consorting with one of the most villainous and corrupt races in the known universe?"

The Bikashi's small round eyes remained fixed on Gareth, then turned abruptly to the Avanauri. "I shall leave him to your devices. Inform me when he is ready to talk."

The naur signaled to the jailor. "Bind him." He watched the Bikashi disappear into the gloom, then turned to Gareth. "I fear you have made Vogel angry. That was not wise, Gareth Blanquette." He smiled thinly. "You have guessed correctly. I am indeed a politician of sorts, but perhaps different from what you imagine. I have no love for this government that would barter our faith and traditions. And for what? For money—pah!" He spat at Gareth's feet. "My friend Vogel provides an invaluable service to the people of this land."

Gareth was scornful. "You have no idea who you're dealing with, do you? The Bikashi will say anything and do anything to get what they want. They were ejected from the Galactic Alliance because they couldn't be trusted, and they always demand their pound of flesh, with interest."

The naur pushed his face close to Gareth and spoke through clenched teeth. "The Avanauri government can't be trusted! They are led by fools and sycophants who give credence to meaningless customs and the trappings of worship. They ignore the wishes of the one God and introduce naur-made laws in his name."

He took a step back, then continued more evenly, "Balor does not require idols and the adoration of images; indeed, he abjures them. Abiding by the law passed down to us from the first naurs is all that is required. Nothing more, nothing less."

Gareth bit his tongue. The last thing he wanted was to get into a dispute over religion with a fanatic. "What about the Bikashi? How does he fit into this?" he said.

"Vogel has proven his worth many times over. He will receive his reward when the Pharlaxia rules, and your Alliance and all other despots are banished from this land."

Gareth knew there was only one thing the Bikashi would want from Prosperine. "You must believe me. They are desperate to get their hands on your crynidium," he pleaded, his eyes wide with anxiety.

"Vogel wishes to prevent your empire from gaining further advantage over the Bikashi people. He has no interest in claiming the silver liquid for himself."

Gareth shook his head and barked a laugh. "You can't believe that. As soon as the Alliance leaves this planet, the Bikashi armed forces will fly in and walk all over you. You don't know what you're letting yourself in for. The Bikashi are without mercy! Please listen to me. I'm not your enemy. I can help you."

"You do not understand, Earthling. The crynidium means nothing to me except what it can bring to my country. Our leaders feed the people superstitious stories of it being given to us by Balor."

He laughed mockingly. "The Bikashi have promised to help rid Avanaux of these fools and the priests who support them. They have failed our people and do not deserve to rule. When I become High Reeve, the Bikashi will receive a just share of the crynidium, and I will administer the remainder for the good of all the people of Avanaux."

There was nothing Gareth could do. He said wearily, "So, the Bikashi give you weapons and gold, and in return, you give them the most valuable substance in the universe. And, consequently, you will take over Avanaux by force, and they will have the means to wreak havoc throughout the civilized planets." Gareth shook his head.

The naur signaled to the jailor. "Send for the interrogator."

◆◆◆

Kyntai burst breathlessly through the door, searching for Hickory, Jess, or *anyone* to tell his news. He broke down and sat on a chair with his hands over his head, sobbing, not knowing what to do.

Two hours later, Nolanski found him there. While trying to extract a coherent account from the boy, Mirda arrived with the news that Hickory and Jess had discovered him.

"In the name of all that's holy," said Nolanski, "I give you both one simple job to do minding these people, and you make a hash of it. Kyntai—stop crying, you stupid naur, and tell me what happened."

Between sobs, Kyntai related the story of how he and Gareth ended up at Silver Lake. "The naurs put Gareth in the back of a wagon and covered him with blankets. I followed them until they reached the peacekeeper complex, and then I ran back here."

"The peacekeepers took him?" said Nolanski. "But why would they arrest the little shit?"

"Excuse me, master, but I do not think these naurs were peacekeepers. I saw the insignia of the Pharlaxia party on the neck of one of the naurs," said Kyntai.

Nolanski's eyebrows shot up. "You're sure it was their mark? You saw it clearly?" He tried to locate Gareth on his SIM with no success. Cursing, he questioned Kyntai further about what he'd seen, then called Hickory and Jess. He quickly explained that Gareth might have been arrested, and they needed to reach the city jail as soon as possible. Nolanski told them to stay where they were. He and Kyntai would pick them up on the way.

Hickory and Jess waited impatiently until he pulled up in the cart thirty minutes later. "Jump in. Kyntai can give you his eyewitness account on the way."

"Idiot," said Jess when Kyntai finished his tale. "I knew he was desperate to see this Kar-sèr-Sephiryth. This is just so typical. I hope to God he's okay."

I hope so, too, because he won't be when I find him. He's disobeyed a direct order. I could court-martial him for this," said Hickory. *Damn fool. Why couldn't he wait? He might have jeopardized the whole operation. I specifically told him to stay away from Kar-sèr-Sephiryth.* She asked Nolanski about the mob—the ones Kyntai had referred to as Pharlaxians.

Nolanski shifted uncomfortably in his seat. "The Pharlaxians are right-wing extremists—political activists—one of three or four anti-government cliques operating in Avanaux. But I can't think this is their work, despite what Kyntai might have seen.

"The Alliance does its best to stay out of local politics, and personally, I've had no trouble with the Pax or their followers. Their leader is an ascetic who goes by the name of Ecknit—at least, that's what he's known as in public. He's gathered support by capitalizing on widespread dissatisfaction with the temple priests. He accuses them of being greedy and corrupt and holding too much sway over the state, which is probably true enough.

"Ecknit and his lieutenants practice strict observance of the Book of Balor. Their manifesto is to re-align the common law to their religious beliefs—a return to the 'good old days' before the Erlachi wars. Some people are so stirred up about the self-indulgence of the temple clergy that they don't see the irony in this."

"So, you don't think these Pharlaxians would see some advantage in kidnapping a Castalie citizen?" asked Jess.

Nolanski shook his head. "They are capable of it, sure, but I don't see why they would. I suppose a rogue group might have done this. The Pharlaxians have a militant arm made up of independent cells operating on a classic 'Chinese walls' footing, so the actions of an individual cell can't be traced back to the parent group. Some of these are armed and ruthless."

Hickory ground her teeth. She wanted to lash out, but she held her temper. *Why didn't he tell us this last night? Is this guy deliberately trying to obstruct the mission, or is he just stupid?* Either way, she still needed his help to find Gareth, so she nodded encouragingly. "Sounds like they're well organized. How many followers do they have?"

"Hard to say. The Pharlaxians are a minority group in the city but probably have much more support in country towns. They're well-connected and have sympathizers in key positions across the country. They may even have infiltrated the government, which would be why they've never been held to account for some of their more outlandish activities. There's one other thing…" He paused, rubbing his chin.

"What?" Hickory grabbed his arm and forced him to face her.

"Other than a handful of highly placed naurs in the government, nobody is supposed to know about your mission here. If the Pharlaxians have penetrated the inner sanctum..."

Hickory felt the blood drain from her face as the implication sank in. "They may not be interested in the Castalie, but they might see some advantage in kidnapping an Earthman," she finished.

Jess shook her head. "No—I don't believe it. Why

would a bunch of anarchists take Gareth to the Peace Compound?"

"There are rumors the Pharlaxians have wormed their way inside the law enforcement administration. I know the Chief of the Peacekeepers, Josipe-sèr-Amagon. He's a government appointee and as straight as they come. If Gareth was taken to the Peace Compound, one of his senior naurs might have turned rogue."

Jess glared at Nolanski, her nostrils flaring. "Why the hell didn't you tell us about these Pharlaxians last night when we asked about political unrest?"

Nolanski shrank from her anger. "What d'you mean? I did tell you." His face turned ashen, and he blinked rapidly.

"Rumblings! You called it rumblings."

◆◆◆

Josipe-sèr-Amagon was less than happy to admit them and could not shed any light on Gareth's whereabouts. "There was a disturbance at Silver Lake earlier today, but my guards tell me it was all over by the time they arrived. They didn't have cause to arrest anyone."

Hickory was about to protest, but Nolanski got in first. "Josipe, surely your guards found some witnesses?"

The Chief bristled. "Of course. Look, I don't doubt

your colleague has been kidnapped. I assure you I do not take this lightly. It is a grievous crime, punishable by death, and the perpetrators will be dealt with." He looked at Hickory and Jess. "I'm sorry. I do not have great hopes for your friend being found quickly, but I will investigate further and let you know of any progress. It may be a simple matter of ransom." He ushered them out of his office.

Jess was fuming. Once outside, she turned on Nolanski. "That was a brush-off if ever I heard one. Why didn't you insist on searching his prison? We know Gareth was taken there."

"Ezekan prison is a rabbit warren. There are hundreds of cells located on several levels beneath the ground. Josipe would never take us down there. It's quite likely he has some Avanauri locked up that he doesn't want anybody to find out about. I know him, though. He's embarrassed that some of his police have been running a covert operation under his nose. If Gareth is down there, he'll find him. The only thing to do is to go back to the Embassy and wait."

Neither Hickory nor Jess liked the idea, but they couldn't think of a better option. They tried to contact Gareth on his SIM every few minutes but received no signal, which suggested that his device was either inoperative or that Gareth was out of range. They didn't like to think of the third alternative, which was that the device had stopped working because Gareth was unconscious or worse.

Jess sat on the edge of her chair, clasping her hands. "Can you sense anything at all?"

"Not a thing," said Hickory gently. She squeezed Jess's shoulder. "Normally, I can sense images from at least a mile away, three if I link to my SIM. So far, there's nothing. Maybe the ionosphere is interfering with my empathic reception." Hickory thought this unlikely, but at least it seemed to give Jess some hope.

They spent two days of frustration, hanging around the embassy until a message arrived from Josipe-sèr-Amagon asking them to meet him at the hill overlooking Silver Lake.

Murder

Hickory touched the gem-encrusted crucifix around her neck, seeking to draw strength from it. Then, she drew a deep breath and forced herself to objectively examine the body on the grass. There was no doubt it was Gareth. The young man had been cruelly tortured. His mohawk was torn out in patches, and his hands were bloody and swollen where his thumbs and fingers had been crushed. The toes on his feet were missing, and burn marks covered his torso. Both dislocated shoulders lay at an unnatural angle while his eye sockets were bloodied and empty.

Jess sank to her knees and cradled Gareth's head in her arms. She rocked his body back and forth as though sending a baby off to sleep. "Why him?" she asked over and over. "Why Gareth? He was just a kid."

Hickory raised Jess to her feet and held her tightly, feeling her shudder with sorrow. Her heart ached as she murmured words of comfort and brushed the tears from Jess's eyes.

The Alien Corps

Josipe-sèr-Amagon was standing, grim-faced, a few feet away, speaking to Nolanski in a low voice. "I am sorry, my friend," he said. "It is a tragedy. We will find whoever did this thing and bring them to justice. You can rely on it." His gaze darted to Hickory and Jess as they approached.

"Was it...was it Pharlaxians?" asked Jess, the stress evident in her voice.

"It has many of their hallmarks, certainly. But see here." He knelt beside the corpse and gently turned its head. "What would make these marks? I have never seen this before."

Hickory released Jess and bent to look. There were two circular blotches about the size of a small coin on Gareth's temples. They were red and blistered. The significance of the marks swept through her. She stood, struggling to keep the shock from her face. "No, I don't recognize this," she said after a long pause.

The Chief looked at her thoughtfully, then shrugged. "I will have our physicians examine them. Perhaps they will be able to shed some light on this mystery."

Nolanski glanced at Hickory, then said. "If you don't mind, Josipe, I think it best if our people do the postmortem."

◆◆◆

Hickory and Nolanski sat opposite each other at

the dining table. Through the open windows, the nightly aurora was in full swing, but it didn't lighten the mood in the room. Hickory pushed the food around on her plate and spoke little. Her mind was ablaze with the image of Gareth's body at the park that afternoon. She looked up as Jess joined them.

Jess's eyes were no longer red, but her mouth was set sternly. She took a chair beside Hickory, nodded to Nolanski, and glanced at the empty seat beside her. "My apologies for breaking down earlier—it was the shock of seeing him like that, but I'm better now. Have you decided what we're going to do?"

Hickory placed her hand on top of Jess's. "There's no need to apologize, Jess. I'm finding it hard to believe he's gone, too. It's all right for you to feel angry and sad. Gareth was young and vibrant—full of life, with so much to look forward to. His death is a tragic waste, and finding him mutilated like…"

Jess squeezed Hickory's hand. "He teased the life out of me by calling me 'Mother,' but the truth is I loved him like one of my own." She spread her hands. "How could this happen? I mean, what was the point? Who would do such a thing?"

Hickory's brow darkened. "Good questions—all of them. I don't have the answers, but I swear I'll find out before I leave this place."

Nolanski coughed. "I don't mean to be unkind, but this is the risk we all take when we come to an unknown planet, isn't it? The boy didn't take the time to get to know the customs of this place. He was brash. He might have unwittingly insulted someone or some group—"

Hickory broke in angrily. "Did you actually look at the body? Nobody goes about torturing people because they insulted them!"

Nolanski looked instantly remorseful.

"And another thing, you saw those blotches on his temple, didn't you?"

"Blotches?" said Jess, shaking her head uncertainly.

"Whoever did this used thumb screws and toe-wedging equipment, and I'd guess his shoulders were dislocated when he was suspended from a strappado. Those are all primitive instruments to force confessions or extract information. They're typical of the methods employed by security forces or terrorists in a culture in transition like Prosperine's."

Nolanski nodded his head. "Josipe has quite a collection, but I don't—"

"The marks on his temples were inflicted by something altogether different. I'd be willing to bet they were left by an electronic device used to short-circuit his implants and prevent Gareth from calling for help."

Jess rose slowly from her chair. "That means—"

"If the ones responsible for this know about implant technology, they can't be local. We're looking for someone from off-world."

Jess sat back, stunned. "Gareth was tortured because an off-worlder thought he knew something. Who would do...?" She shook her head. "About what?"

"I don't know specifically, but it must have something to do with our mission here. We need to talk to the admiral."

Nolanski nodded somberly. "I didn't think it was the Pharlaxians. Gareth could have run afoul of smugglers. Some of those groups, like the Dark Suns, have the technology, and they can be vicious—especially if they think their operation is in jeopardy. Perhaps the autopsy will tell us more."

"Perhaps," said Hickory. "I want to talk to the admiral and find out what we can do about it. I won't let Gareth's death go unanswered."

◆◆◆

Admiral George Lace leaned forward, his elbows resting on the table. His perfectly manicured hands formed a steeple in front of his face.

Hickory felt a warm flush creep up her neck. She couldn't rationalize whether this was caused by recent events or because her father's holographic image had joined the meeting.

The Alien Corps

When the light barrier was finally broken, scientists turned their minds to solving the communication delays resulting from the vast distances and flight speeds that were now possible. The time interval over several light years had reduced to no more than a few seconds.

The admiral appeared to be listening intently to the conversation between his lieutenant James Brandt, Nolanski, and Jess, who were exploring the possibility of smuggler intervention in the Alien Corps project.

"Commander Lace," he said, interrupting Nolanski in mid-stream. "You're certain it was Gareth. Could you be mistaken?"

Hickory noted the look of annoyance on Nolanski's face and answered, "I'm pretty sure, admiral: same build, same height, same coloring. I think we need to acknowledge he's gone." She looked at Jess. Nothing good could come from providing false hope.

Nolanski nodded his agreement. "I don't have the full autopsy results yet, but the SIM implant has been validated as Gareth's. The DNA analysis will confirm it."

The admiral looked at Hickory for a few seconds, then gestured for Brandt to push on.

"All right, let's look at the likely perpetrators. There are three alien species we monitor regularly on Prosperine," Brandt said. He turned on a video hologram showing footage of the suspect groups.

"The Saturnine Raiders originally came from the Vindicine region. They migrated to Prosperine three hundred years ago after their homeworld entered a nuclear winter."

The video showed a group of naurs sitting around a campfire in a country settlement. There was nothing remarkable about the people except that the children had no tails.

"They brought what they could with them, but it was precious little. They had to resort to piracy and smuggling to keep them going. And, as you can see, fifteen generations later, they've pretty much assimilated into the local population. Occasionally, we come across a few cases where the original genes are strong. Normally, these would be culled at birth, but some escape this fate."

Nolanski interjected. "There's a community of a hundred or so throwbacks in the hinterland, but they're a sorry bunch. I doubt they would have the technology or the desire for this kind of thing."

The video switched to a second group of aliens, and Brandt continued. "The Dark Suns are a different proposition. They are more sophisticated and numerous than the Raiders and live in temporary camps dotted around Avanaux. Picture them like a guild or a loose association of professional thieves and adventurers originating from nearby star clusters and operating all over the galaxy. Unlike the Raiders, the

The Alien Corps

Suns have no intention of settling here. They have space travel technology and come and go, running the Alliance's blockades pretty much at will. They steer clear of the Avanauri, except when they're looking to trade."

From the video, the Dark Suns were an eclectic mixture of races: short and tall, fat and thin, broad and narrow, with black, white, red, or green skin. The one unifying feature was that each wore a dark, circular tattoo on one side of their face.

"On Avanaux, they deal mainly in luxury items in exchange for precious metals and jewels," said Brandt. "This is the mob Jeb has been trying to eradicate for a while now. The Dark Suns could well be involved in something like this."

Hickory glanced at Nolanski. His arms were folded, and he stared stony-faced at Brandt.

"The third group we call, appropriately enough, 'the Invisible.' We have no video of them, but they seem more likely prospects to me. They arrived on Prosperine ten years ago, fleeing the law in the nearby Epsilon sector. They're a band of warriors operating throughout the sector who lend their muscle to the highest bidder. They work by night, and their specialty is murder and assassination. The last we heard, they were not in Erlach, but it wouldn't surprise me to see they were working with a political group like the Pharlaxians."

Even though the admiral was a holographic image projected across light-years, Hickory could feel her father's presence, watching silently in the background. "You think that's where we should look first, then?" she asked Brandt.

The admiral rapped on the table and spoke, jolting Hickory. "James, what's the probability one of the non-aligned planets is involved?"

Brandt nodded. "It's certainly possible, sir. We know the NAP regularly patrol this sector of space, but I don't have any intelligence to indicate they're working with the Pharlaxians."

"If they are, they wouldn't stop at murder to upset the Alliance's plans," said the admiral.

Hickory turned to face her father. "Why would they kill Gareth, though? The Alien Corps isn't actually working for the Alliance," she said. "Are they?"

Her father said nothing, which only strengthened her belief that he and Cortherien had a secret agreement, but now wasn't the right time to pursue it. "How do I find the Pharlaxians?" she said, surveying the attendees.

The admiral nodded and said tersely, "James can help with that. He's in charge of planet security until I return from Earth." He shuffled some documents lying in front of him and looked up. "Gentlemen and Jess, thank you for your attendance, but time is short, and I'd appreciate a few minutes alone with my daughter."

Brandt saluted and left the room with Nolanski and Jess, who glanced anxiously over her shoulder.

The admiral and his daughter faced each other across a gap of a billion miles geographically and almost as far emotionally.

"The Alien Corps is not working for the Alliance," said George Lace, shaking his head. "The Corps was called in because you people are the experts in handling complex religious situations. We don't have a clue what this guy's agenda is, this Kar-sèr-Sephiryth."

"And you're worried how he might impact your interest in the crynidium? Just what deal did you strike with Prefect Cortherien?" said Hickory.

"Hickory, please don't be naïve—the Alliance and the Corps often work together for the greater good. We both have similar aims—seeking to bring unity of purpose and meaning to humankind's existence."

Hickory smiled wryly. Her father had a way of twisting things to suit his own ends. But she now knew there was an arrangement between the two organizations, one she should have been told about. She wondered what that agreement contained and whether it had any bearing on Gareth's death.

"One thing I don't understand. I know you

desperately want the rights to the crynidium, and you would go to any lengths to prevent one of the non-aligned planets from getting their hands on it." She held her hand up as her father started to protest. "Please, sir, let me finish. Until now, you haven't allowed any planet to become a member unless their social development is comparable to the existing Alliance planets. Do you really need the crynidium so badly you would waive that rule?"

Her father looked at her over his hands, his elbows resting on the table. He sighed. "You see conspiracies where none exist. Earth and some of our allies indeed have a desperate need for faster-than-light fuel. Our stocks are low, and it would be disastrous if something were to rob us of this opportunity. But no, we're not so desperate as to break our primary rule. When Prosperine is ready to join the Alliance, she will be welcomed with open arms. We estimate that will be around five hundred years from now."

Hickory snorted, nodding her head. "And in the meantime?"

"In the meantime, we continue negotiating with the Prosperine authorities." He held his arms wide, palms open, as though this was the obvious course of action. "What did you think? That we would take the crynidium by force?"

Hickory knew there was no point in "negotiating" if the government continued to consider crynidium as sacrosanct. "*Negotiating?* You mean trying to destroy their traditions and religious beliefs?" A breakdown in the people's faith in Balor would certainly accelerate a decision in the Intragalactic Alliance's favor.

"All this speculation is beside the point," said the admiral. "We both have a job to do." He paused and nodded, then smiled. "It's good to see you again, Hickory, even if you don't trust me. You look more like your mother every time I see you."

She could feel tears at the corners of her eyes. "You don't see me often enough to say that. You couldn't even be bothered to visit me when you were in town last time. Why didn't you?"

Hickory had concealed the hurt caused by her father's indifference from everyone, including herself, pushing it so deep she refused to acknowledge it. He'd never spoken to her about her mother. His simple comparison made her feel like a child again, confused by his aloofness and desperate for his approval.

His face was sallow and lined, and there was sadness in his eyes. He looked older than his years. Then he pressed his lips together, and Hickory saw his heart harden. "I really didn't have the time. There are always too many things to do." His chin came up, and he straightened his back. "In any case, you've been doing pretty well without me all these years."

"You don't seem to mind catching up with Michael." The words escaped unbidden, and she felt the poison on her tongue, bitter and slimy like the aftertaste of vomit. Instantly, she wished she could take her words back.

Her father's eyes fell. "Mike is a different kind of person. You've always been the confident one. He's six years younger and much less sure of himself. Mike, well, needs me—you don't."

She felt her lungs constrict, so she could hardly breathe, hardly force the words out. She swallowed hard. "That is so unfair." She shook her head slowly and brushed a tear from her cheek. She gritted her teeth, angry again. "And you know it's not true. Why don't you just admit you don't care?"

"I do care, Hickory."

Hickory looked at her father, but she only saw the admiral, dispassionate and remote. "How could I think anything different?" She spat out the words. "If you cared even a little, you would have made some sort of effort. You …you abandoned me when I needed you most." She sniffed and swallowed. It was stupid; she was too emotional, but it was hard to accept that he didn't love her but did love Michael. In her heart, she'd harbored a glimmer of hope she'd got it wrong, that there was a reason. She searched his face, looking for clues, but could neither see nor sense anything.

"Hickory, you have work to do. I suggest you get on with it."

His image snapped out of view, and she was alone.

Dark Suns

Nolanski didn't show up for breakfast the following morning. Hickory had hoped to learn more about his extra-curricular activities in Harbor Town, but Gareth's tragedy left little room for thinking about anything else. *Time enough for that later. There are more important things to attend to.* She looked at Jess, sitting opposite, head bowed, picking skin from a finger.

Jess glanced up and said, "You think Prefect Cortherien and the admiral have a hidden agenda?" said Jess.

Hickory sighed. "The Alliance wouldn't let anything stand in the way of a good trade. And the Vatican must be becoming desperate—it's almost a century since the Corps was set up, and they don't have much to show for it. The Prefect would dine with the devil to bring Philip's prophecy to life."

Jess shivered. "You don't think Cortherien or your father could be involved in Gareth's death, do you?"

Hickory saw the pain in her eyes. "That wouldn't

make sense, Jess. Why wait until we reach Prosperine? No, Gareth's death was opportunistic. If he wasn't so desperate to see the Teacher, I think he would be alive today."

Jess poured two coffees and offered one to Hickory. "Was Nolanski able to give you any further leads on the Pharlaxians?"

"Nothing concrete, but James Brandt passed this to me after our meeting." She unrolled a scroll and spread it on the table. "Government forces discovered this at an abandoned stockade in the desert last month. They think it may have been a training camp for insurgents. Whoever they were, they left in a hurry and ditched a lot of their kit—including this map."

Jess leaned over the parchment. The schematic of the Ezekan city precinct showed several locations marked with an infinity symbol. "I assume when the security forces visited these places, they were empty too?" she said.

"Right. But as Nolanski told us earlier, this mark is the Pharlaxians' calling card." She jabbed at the map. "Followers have it tattooed someplace on their body. It's supposed to be hidden from the casual observer, but Kyntai said he saw it on the neck of one of the people who kidnapped Gareth. Brandt believes the mark is part of the identification protocol when two cells meet. I asked Nolanski, but he says he doesn't know anything." Hickory paused, sensing Jess's doubt. "What's the matter?"

Jess shrugged, and her mouth curled down. "I don't know what or who to trust anymore, Hick. There's something not right about Nolanski. He really didn't like Gareth, did he? I want to believe him, but ..." She took a deep breath and slowly released it.

"I feel that too. Nolanski is good at hiding it from me, but he's definitely holding something back."

"Why, though? Surely we're on the same side?"

Hickory nodded her agreement. "I think so, but it makes sense to be cautious, especially since we don't know what political games are being played. Our best plan is to locate somebody wearing this symbol, even though it may prove difficult."

"Nolanski said the Pax were interested in Kar-sèr-Sephiryth, and not in a friendly way, either. His sermonizing against mystical symbols and ancient dogmas has rubbed them up the wrong way. They don't take kindly to revisionist views on their religion," said Jess.

"Yes, that's how I understand it, too. Cortherien told me as much when he briefed me." Hickory thought for a moment. She'd already decided to keep a close watch on the Teacher to see whether she could find a way to infiltrate the Pharlaxian cult. It was something she could better achieve on her own. "Jess, I want you to stay here at the consulate. I need someone I can trust to relay messages to the admiral and to suss out any information or equipment I might need—without asking questions. Will you do that?"

Jess sighed with relief, and Hickory relaxed. Since they'd found Gareth's body at Silver Lake, Jess had been emotionally burnt out— incapable of much more than making a cup of coffee. She was putting a brave face on it, and Hickory felt she would recover in time, but right now, Jess didn't need the added stress of having to chase down Gareth's killers.

"Just tell me what you need me to do," Jess said.

"The first thing is to transform me from a Castalie into an Ezekani citizen. I need a new look."

◆◆◆

With Kyntai's and Mirda's help, the maquillage specialist sent by her father achieved a miraculous transformation in Hickory. Her entire body was now Avanauri white. Her face and neck were decorated to resemble a well-born native woman, and her brow ridges and cheekbones were more striking than before. She liked how the speckled purple coloring encompassed her eyes and then followed the curvature of her cheekbones onto her shoulders.

Hickory put on a tailored cloak with padded shoulders and an ultra-high collar. Looking in the mirror, she didn't recognize the haughty, high-born Avanauri female staring back. Kyntai and Mirda expressed satisfaction and went on to teach Hickory some of the more esoteric customs omitted from her vid-briefings.

By late afternoon, Hickory was as ready as she was ever likely to be and set out alone for the city. She took an apartment at a hostelry just outside the central district. Mirda had told her the Crossed Swords had a reputation for being the favorite haunt of rogues and undesirables. She rented a private room with a balcony on the first floor as befitted her adopted status, then took the file she'd brought with her and started to read.

Brandt was apologetic. Little was known of the Teacher's life until two years ago when he barged into a Senate meeting, demanding an end to the government's use of orphans as low-paid labor. A memorandum from the office of the Chief Peacekeeper was attached. This recommended that Kar-sèr-Sephiryth be considered a medium-security risk to the state. His description had been issued to all guards with orders to report any suspicious activity.

Copies of half a dozen official reports were attached to the file. Hickory scanned these but found nothing helpful. At the bottom of the last page was a note in Brandt's handwriting: *Sorry there's not more to give you. The Teacher seems to appear without warning and disappear just as quickly. My sources say he spends a lot of time traveling around the country—some suggested he'd even been as far as Castaliena. However, I'd take this last with a grain of salt.*

The Alien Corps

There was a knock on her door. Hickory opened it to find a young nauri standing outside with her head bowed, waiting to be acknowledged. Hickory nodded and smiled encouragingly at her.

The nauri's face shone. Orange flashes tinged with blue indicated she was not yet of childbearing age. "They are serving hot food downstairs, Johan-sèra-Anna, should you wish to dine," she said.

"Are there many in the hall?" said Hickory, closing the door behind her. "Many naur, some Castalie, other strangers, but there is room for you."

Hickory paused at the entry to the serving room, her senses assailed by the smoky atmosphere, the clamor of customers, and the aroma of herbs and spices drifting from the kitchens. Hickory chose an empty booth where she could sit against the wall and observe. The place was almost full. Most were naurs crammed around wooden tables, eating from communal plates and drinking ale and wine. She spotted two Castalie pretenders sitting quietly near the exit.

An elderly nauri sat beside an unlit open fireplace in the center of the room, playing a stringed instrument and singing a strangely haunting melody. Mirda had said such artists were honored guests in local hostelries. They would reprise war songs dating from the times of the Erlachi and reputed to have been composed by Connor-sèra-Haagar to spur her troops into the final battle.

Hickory signaled the nearest server. He brought her a steaming pot of freshwater crab and vegetable stew, poured some liquid from an earthenware bottle, and left it on the table. Hickory sipped cautiously. The drink was pleasant but strongly alcoholic, she suspected.

She dipped some hard bread into the stew and put it in her mouth. *Not bad,* she thought, breaking up some of the chunks with her spoon. *At least I can be sure it's not yarrak.*

Hickory relaxed and poured a second cup of the brew as she became accustomed to the setting. The tavern's guests were enjoying their meal and conversing in a friendly fashion. She was feeling pleasantly mellow when a heated argument broke out at a table on the far side of the room. The naur incurring the wrath of his fellow diners was short in stature but sharp of tongue. He wore a dusty brown jacket with matching leggings and had the look of a recently arrived traveler from the country. His adversaries—four of them—each wore richly decorated coats beneath their outer cloaks, proclaiming them to be wealthy merchants.

The biggest of the four drew a hunting knife from his belt, struck the table with a thunderous blow, and roared at the little fellow, "You do not belong here, *Biletung!* But if you do not leave now, we will make

The Alien Corps

sure you remain in Ezekan forever."

A scornful grin spread over the traveler's face. "It'll take more than you to make sure of it."

The merchant jumped to his feet and aimed a fist at the smaller one's head.

The traveler swayed out of harm's way, then overturned the table, scattering plates, food, and wine over the other three merchants.

Nearby patrons hurriedly abandoned their meals and clustered by the walls to watch the fight's progress, cheering each move by the underdog.

By this stage, all the merchants were brandishing knives. They voiced a tremendous roar and charged. The first ran into a straight-arm block. His knees buckled, and he fell, hitting his head on the floor. His adversary stepped to one side and sent a second antagonist on his way with a chop to the back of his neck.

Hickory raised her eyebrows. This unlikely warrior moved with the speed and agility born of years of practice.

The remaining two opponents hesitated and decided on a more cautious approach. They moved apart and circled, hoping to attack from either side. One flew at him from behind and held him in a bear hug, pinning his arms to his sides. The other grinned and holstered his knife. He pummeled the naur's unprotected stomach with both fists.

Hickory rose to her feet, instinctively wanting to help the underdog. A tall, dark figure barred her way and shook his head. "Let Saurab have his fun. There's no point in you getting hurt," he said, sitting at her table.

Hickory resumed her seat slowly, thankful for the stranger's intercession. It would have been incredibly stupid to draw attention to herself by intervening in the fight. There was no need, anyway. Saurab had already broken loose.

Ducking under the merchant's reach, Saurab seized his arm and forced it upward behind his back, then placed his boot on his rear end and heaved the naur into the face of his companion. Both antagonists fell heavily against the table and sank to the ground. Saurab flourished a wicked-looking curved knife and advanced. The four attackers scrambled to their feet and fled through the exit.

The landlord went over to Saurab and whispered something to him. The small naur laughed and tossed a bag of coins to the elderly troubadour whose song he'd interrupted. Replacing the weapon inside his jacket, he approached Hickory and her new acquaintance and pulled up a chair.

"Who the devil are you two?" said Hickory. They were the oddest-looking naurs she'd come across since arriving in Avanaux.

"I'm Saurab. This one's Jakah," said the victorious fighter, jerking his thumb at his partner, "and I need a drink. Hope you don't mind?" He poured a cup from Hickory's flask and quaffed it, sighing with pleasure. "That's better. Nothing like a good fight to give you a raging thirst."

Hickory peered closely at Saurab. He seemed like any other naur in the room, albeit a small one—except for the almost invisible circular shadow on his cheek. Her head jerked back, and she felt her skin tingle. *Dark Suns!* She fumbled for her knife.

Saurab grinned and winked at her. "You won't need that. You know who we are, and we know you."

She kept her hand on the handle of her knife. "I suppose I shouldn't be surprised. What's your business around here?"

The one called Jakah showed pearly white teeth and turned to his friend. "I told you she was smart," he said, facing Hickory. "We came here to talk with you. We believe you can help us with a small problem we have."

Saurab poured himself another cup and said, "We've been following you since you left the Alliance compound, Commander Lace. Although we almost didn't recognize you under your new get-up."

Hickory relaxed her hold on the knife and postponed the obvious question to give herself time to think. Instead, she said, "Who were those four, then?"

"My guess would be a Pharlaxian posse sent to rough us up. They were too well dressed to be common thieves," said Jakah.

Hickory looked around the room, but nobody seemed to be paying them any heed. Brawls were likely a common enough occurrence in the hostel. She was worried, though. If the Pax had seen through the disguise of the Dark Suns, how safe was she?

Strictly speaking, it was against the agreement with the government for her to masquerade as an Avanauri citizen. "How did they recognize you…you look like local naurs to me," she said.

Saurab scowled. "I hope so. These disguises cost us a year's profit. Somehow, they got the impression that I was a heretic from the east trying to muscle into their operation. It might have been my accent, but my guess is they were tipped off by the competition—probably that mongrel, Nolanski."

Hickory was flummoxed. "Nolanski? Jeb Nolanski?"

"The very same. He's been trying to get rid of us for months."

"Rubbish! The Alliance doesn't go in for those sorts of shenanigans."

Saurab leaned over the table. His lips were white. "You know nothing, Earthling! We've been cramping his action. Nolanski's been hoarding crynidium and selling it to the non-aligned planets—yes, the NAP—for months."

Hickory choked off a laugh. "I don't believe you. Nolanski's worked for the company for twenty years—more. He's Alliance through and through." But despite her words, Hickory felt uneasy. She sensed the smuggler was telling her the truth.

Jakah seemed less excitable than his partner. "All true, but he retires in a few weeks with a pension and nowhere to go."

"Nowhere to go? Why wouldn't he retire to Earth?"

"Nolanski developed some unhealthy habits not long after he arrived here. He started frequenting the whore district in Harbor Town, experimenting with cross-species sex. He met a nauri there—Kalichia is her name—quite a beauty by Prosperine standards, I hear, but depraved. I believe they fell in love, as you humans call it. The rumor is they have spawned a child."

"That—that's not possible!" said Hickory.

Jakah lifted an eyebrow. "Impossible or not, it happened. They say the child is poorly and won't live long, but Nolanski believes he can save it."

Hickory quickly put the pieces together. This was why Mirda-sèr-Sidhartha had been so nervous when questioned about Nolanski being at Harbor Town the other day. "So, he needs money to get his lover and their child away from Prosperine to somewhere they can find the right medical care?"

Saurab's savage laugh cut through her. "We wouldn't be concerned about his extracurricular activities if he weren't such a two-faced *kartog*. Ripping off the locals and, at the same time, doing his best to put us away. He's a phony as well as a hypocrite." His face was dark.

Hickory thought he would be a dangerous person to have as an enemy.

Jakah saw her concern and said, "Don't worry about Saurab. It's a personal thing. He and Nolanski were partners until Nolanski got greedy and decided he didn't want to share anymore. The Earthman double-crossed him. Led him into a trap with the Pharlaxians and left him for dead. Those four," he said, nodding at the doorway, "came here to try and finish the job. They'll be back with help soon enough." He began to rise from his chair. "Best if they don't see you talking with us."

Hickory's mind was in a whirl. *Nolanski and the Pax, together?* The two Suns might be the best liars on Prosperine, but she would have detected some dissemblance. She held Saurab by the arm. "Wait—what can you tell me about my crewman, Gareth Blanquette? Do you know anything about who might have killed him?"

The Alien Corps

Saurab shook his head and removed her hand gently. "Don't know, and it's not our problem, Earthling. We're going to have to leave now." Jakah withdrew a folded sheet from inside his jacket and pushed it over the table to Hickory. "If you want to learn more about the Pax and perhaps your friend's death, this might prove useful. We will meet again, Earth-girl. Watch out for Nolanski." The smugglers left the room without looking back.

Hickory made sure she wasn't being watched, then unfolded the document under the table. On it was written one sentence: *Abacus Building, Administration Center – 9.00 tonight.* ∞

Pharlaxians

Hickory sat on the bed in her room, mulling over her conversation with the two Dark Suns. In retrospect, Nolanski's attempts to incriminate the group in Gareth's death seemed transparent. At the very least, he was trying to deflect attention away from his connection with the Pharlaxians. She felt some sympathy for the man's plight but wondered at the same time if his involvement with a nauri was the real catalyst for his treachery. *Why did he allow the pregnancy to come to full term? He had to know his career and his pension would be in jeopardy if he was found out. Was he in love with Kalichia—was such a thing even possible between two such different species? Did they so desperately want a child together?*

She checked the time on her SIM. Three hours remained before the meeting began. Feeling drowsy, she allowed herself to slip into a light slumber.

The self-recriminations rose unbidden. Hickory's brow creased as she sought to push the thoughts into the background, but they persisted.

The Alien Corps

Who are you to judge others? You killed your own son, you callous bitch.

"No, I…I was barely eight weeks pregnant at the time."

And you sacrificed your son's life to protect your career.

"I was young and foolish, too desperate to right a wrong. I didn't understand the harm I would do to it."

To him! To him! And you didn't tell Jacob. Didn't give him a chance to accept his son.

"Jacob was a self-centered monster."

No more than you.

"I needed to track down Crxtor Aliaq's killers. I was to blame for losing him in the first place."

Is being a Lieutenant in the Alien Corps so important to you?

"Lives depended on me. I was the only one who could track him down."

He was only eight weeks old. You had a duty of care.

"No one else would have found them. I was the only neoteric on the planet. I had to go."

And then you lost your child.

"Swamp fever caused me to miscarry."

And you lost your son.

"I lost my son!"

Hickory woke abruptly. Her head throbbed and

sweat covered her brow. She wiped it dry with her sleeve. This was the first time she'd dreamed about her miscarriage since leaving Earth. And it was different this time. This time, she'd fought back.

After she'd returned home from Aquarius IV, she'd found the time and space to grieve the loss of what might have been. She knew her response to the mess she'd found herself in on the planet was a normal one, but even so, she regretted her actions in chasing the killers so single-mindedly and felt the miscarriage weigh heavily on her.

She contacted Jess via her SIM and told her about the meeting with Saurab and Jakah and their claims concerning Nolanski. "I don't know for sure it's true—only that they believe it is, but it adds to our suspicions he's up to something. Jakah wasn't putting on an act, either. He hates Nolanski. Jess, I want you to nose around and see what you can flush out. There may be nothing to it, but if there is—"

Jess completed Hickory's thought. "He could be mixed up in what happened to Gareth. That mongrel!"

"Let's not get ahead of ourselves. You run a trace on Nolanski's finances; I'll go to this place tonight and see what I can find out."

"Be careful. It might be a trap. You could be being set up."

"I will. Let me know if you learn anything new."

The Alien Corps

She disengaged and checked the time. *One hour to go.* She decided to walk to the location on the map and look around.

◆◆◆

Hickory gathered her cloak about her and slipped quietly into the deeper shadows as she headed to the rendezvous point. Few people were out and about—a quartet of city peacekeepers patrolling the dark streets and an occasional night reveler weaving their way between watering holes.

At this time of night, the city took on an eerie quality. The occasional gas lantern outside the public buildings provided little illumination. Ezekanis turned in early and got up with the sun, she realized. *Makes it easy for groups like the Pax to do whatever they have to do.* She kept to the shadows opposite the Peace Compound.

A little further on, she crossed the road, then turned into an alley and paused to check her map of the city. *This must be the place. It's strange that it's so close to the peacekeeper headquarters. They must be confident they won't be discovered.* She padded softly along the alleyway, noting the sign above the doorway of the meeting place as she passed. *Looks like an empty shop front.*

A few blocks further on, she stopped inside a portal that gave her a clear view of the area. She didn't have long to wait. A stranger stopped outside the Abacus

P J McDermott

building and looked around furtively before knocking.

The door opened a crack, and a face peered out. The newcomer exchanged words with the doorman and then drew open his shirt to reveal his chest. The doorman nodded, and the stranger disappeared inside.

The Pax arrived in ones and twos, and all underwent the same procedure. Some bared their chest, others an ankle or a thigh. Hickory guessed the newcomers were displaying the secret symbol. *Brandt was right. They all have a different password, and it has something to do with where the tattoo is located.*

She figured it had to be simple because the guard didn't need to refer to a checklist. A naur walked up to the entrance and removed a sandal. The symbol was on the sole of his foot. Hickory strained to hear. *Ootfit*, she heard, and he was passed through.

A few minutes later, another Pharlaxian approached the door. He rolled up his sleeve. Hickory thought the word he spoke sounded like *oramfit*. She realized she'd heard wrong when the next naur also rolled up his sleeve and said clearly, "orearmfit."

Suddenly, she had it. It was a variation of Pig Latin code. First, you take the initial letter of the body part where your tattoo is and move it to the end of the word. Then, you add two secret letters to the end to form the code word.

The Alien Corps

She waited for the next cult member to arrive to double-check her analysis, then walked up to the doorway and revealed the symbol on her left breast. "Reastbit," she said.

The guard smirked. "Nice mark." Hickory grinned back, her azure flashes on display. "And where do you have yours?"

He nodded to the entrance. "Perhaps I will show it to you later tonight."

Hickory snorted as she brushed past him. "It's probably too small to see." The guard laughed as he pointed to a door further down the corridor.

The room was lit by candles placed in nooks along the walls, and there were no windows, only darkened ventilation shafts that disappeared into the shadows of the ceiling. A large gathering of naurs and nauris sat cross-legged on the floor in a semi-circle. Their attention was focused on a figure dressed all in black who was conversing quietly with two others.

Good. It looks like the meeting hasn't started yet. She sat at the rear of the crowd and tried to raise Jess on her SIM. She soon realized it wasn't possible. The thickness of the walls and the central location of the room would prevent any signal from getting through.

The speaker turned to face the audience, and his two associates took up a position on either side of him. "Avanauri of the sacred order of Pharlaxia." He opened his arms wide and paused. "It is fitting you are here tonight. I am Ecknit. I welcome you and urge you to keep our covenant. Do not talk to your neighbor at this time, save as necessary to carry out the commands of our Creator. Soon, we will stand unshackled and united as brothers, but until then, we must remain strangers, even to each other.

"The time is near when we will return Prosperine to the rule of our forefathers. Balor is a jealous God, and for too long, he has watched his people harnessed to the yoke of the false law of Ezekan. The book of Balor tells us how believers must live." Ecknit raised a heavy tome above his head and shook it. "'Beware strangers claiming to be my children. They are less than the beasts in the fields, even though they walk on two legs.' So says the Book of Balor."

He passed the book to an associate and raised his voice. "Many monsters walk with two legs in the streets of Ezekan, brethren. Beasts have fallen from the celestial realm in the guise of Prosperine beings to pillage our world!"

Hickory could sense the crowd warming to the speaker. Some held their hands in the air; others called out, "Balor is great!" She wondered how long she would last if they realized a monster on two legs was in the room with them. She glanced around and saw the guard looking at her. *I hope I'm not going to have trouble with that one,* she thought before realizing there was another in the room whose eyes were not on the

The Alien Corps

speaker.

The figure stood near the guard, a hood obscuring his face. She felt it was male, but she couldn't be sure. He was surveying the room as she had been. His head turned towards her, and he started as their eyes met. His hand came halfway out of his pocket, and he pushed it back quickly. Hickory reached out empathically and felt a mental barrier go up as the figure turned and hurried out the doorway.

Her pulse quickened. The hooded figure's glove shielded the hand from her view, but she'd glimpsed the wrist covered in scales. Cautiously, she moved towards the door.

Ecknit stopped speaking. His eyes fixed on the departing alien, and then they flicked around the room.

Hickory lowered her head and felt his gaze pass over her without stopping.

There has to be a connection between these two. She decided to wait. The speaker gathered his robe about him and pointed his finger at the group. "As evil as the fiends on two legs are those amongst us who harbor them. Those who speak blasphemy; those who lie." His finger stabbed out again and again.

"And the most evil of all is he who seeks to put aside the words of Balor and replace them with foulness. The one who seeks to abandon our way of life and would see Prosperine damned by consorting with shades and wickedness. This evil one would break our holy covenant with the God of our fathers." His voice rose to a shrill note. "What should we do with such a one?"

The audience, as one, climbed to their feet and pumped their fists above their heads. They shouted out in rage, "Kill him! Burn the heretic! Death to the revisionist!"

"Aiaiyee!" cried Ecknit, "Kar-sèr-Sephiryth is he, of whom it has been written, 'One will come amongst you, and his words will be as venom blended with honey.' Our fathers foretold his coming long ago, but the hour is at hand when the infidel will choke on his own vomit! Who will join me in this righteous war against the evil one?'

He smiled with satisfaction as he saw all in the room thrust their fists in the air, clamoring to claim the honor. "Brethren, you are soldiers of Balor. All who die in his name while rooting out the heretics from this land will live in the palace of our God for eternity. Blessed are you, for your every desire will be provided for. This has been revealed to me."

Ecknit urged his followers to leave in silence and seek out and destroy the followers of the evil one wherever they were found. He singled out three devotees. "You will remain behind after the others depart. We have much to do."

The meeting broke up, and Hickory shuffled out

The Alien Corps

amid the crowd to avoid the attention of the partisan who'd admitted her.

She knew the rules. Local politics were none of her concern, although she hated to see religious bigotry, especially when it preached hatred and violence. Her mission was to investigate the Teacher, Kar-sèr-Sephiryth, which would be problematic if he was killed before she had a chance to talk with him. But, as the Pharlaxian leader, this Ecknit would surely know something about Gareth's death. She couldn't let this opportunity slide.

The sky was overcast, and a mist covered the ground. The last of the brethren disappeared into the night. Hickory waited until she was sure they'd gone, then scrambled over the wall surrounding the house, climbed onto the roof, and waited.

She considered the hooded alien. *Scales—at least on his hands. NAP obviously, but what—Ortagan, Gerbik, Bikashi, Tzernube?* A lot of NAP were scaled to some degree or another. Some members of the Galactic Alliance even had scales. *I hope I get another chance to find out who this one is.*

A short time later, the three devotees emerged with Ecknit. He embraced each, and they went their separate ways.

Hickory prowled along the rooftops and followed the black-robed leader at a distance. Ecknit glanced around several times, but Hickory found little trouble avoiding his scrutiny. Where the lane met the main road, she sprang down to street level and trailed him at a distance. He was headed toward the central district, she thought. *It could be the government buildings or the detention center.*

Then, the Pharlaxian abruptly changed course and swerved into Silver Park. Hickory quickened her pace when he climbed the stairs and disappeared into the Temple of the Four Faces of Balor.

Conspiracy

Hickory closed the temple door quietly behind her and looked around. Her first impression was one of austerity. There was no gold paint, glitter, or colorful murals here to distract the eye of the worshiper, only shades of grey. The temple was clean, precise, and built on a grand scale into the side of the mountain to emphasize the spiritual nature and permanency of the creator. A domed roof stretched high overhead. On the far wall, a tableau carved out of the mountainside depicted the four faces of Balor seemingly caught in the moment of emerging from the rock.

A series of broad steps led down to a giant iron fire pit set on a dais a few yards before the sculpture. Flickering flames sent shadows dancing across the carved images, enhancing the supernatural aura. A few supplicants lingered, supine on mats, praying to their God.

Halfway along the left wall, a grotto dedicated to

Connat-sèra-Haagar had been hollowed out of the rock. The heroine held a double-edged sword aloft while the dead and dying enemy lay before her.

Hickory spied Ecknit sitting on his haunches in front of the grotto. His arms were outstretched, and his head lowered as though inviting Connat-sèra-Haagar to bring the double-edged sword down on his neck. She wondered whether the Pharlaxian dreamed of having his hands on the weapon's hilt in another life.

Hickory crouched out of sight with her back against the wall and established a SIM link with Jess. The connection was scrabbly, but she managed to update her partner on progress. She asked whether Jess had found anything on Nolanski.

"Not much, but then if he's really on the take, it's not going to be obvious, is it? I'm… a search of Earth banks. If he's saving for his retirement, that's where… And Hickory, please be… If… aligned is involved, it could mean serious trouble."

Hickory signed off. One of the worshipers had risen to his feet and was moving towards Ecknit. He stooped as he shuffled forwards, which kept his face in the shadow of his hood, but Hickory was sure this was the alien from the meeting. She wasn't so sure about what she should do. She wanted to hear their conversation, but could she get close enough without being seen? Would they recognize her from the

The Alien Corps

meeting? She could confront them, but to what end? While she was considering her options, the door opened, and a tall figure entered.

Nolanski! She could scarcely contain her excitement. "Jess?" she transmitted again. "I don't think you need to chase up any more bank accounts. Nolanski's here."

"You're… ing! He left here half an hour ago, saying… a meeting with the Chief Peacekeeper," said Jess.

"Well, unless Josipe-sèr-Amagon arrives soon—which wouldn't surprise me—I think he must have his venues mixed up. Jess, see if you can round up the Chief—tell him I think we've found Gareth's murderer."

Hickory followed a safe distance behind Nolanski, flattening herself against the wall and edging towards the grotto. She strained to hear the words over her thumping heart. Ecknit was speaking.

"There was no outsider, save you, present at tonight's gathering, Vogel. You imagined it. You are beginning to see ghosts at every corner."

The shrouded figure expelled a long hiss. "I see no ghosts. It was a mistake to take the boy. Now, his friends will look for him and may interrupt our preparations."

"You're damn right, it was a mistake!" thundered

Nolanski when he reached the other two. "What were you thinking, Ecknit, to kidnap an Earthman in the first place? And tell me how you thought killing him was a good idea?" He grabbed the Avanauri by the throat and forced him against the mural.

Vogel, with seemingly little effort, pulled Nolanski's arm away. "Let him speak."

The Pharlaxian adjusted his jacket, fury written plain on his face. "I do not answer to you, *Biletung!* If you lay hands on me again, I will see to it you are flogged." He pulled a handkerchief from his pocket and waved it under his nose. His features became impassive again. "It was an accident. Vogel thought he was a spy sent by the Alliance and a threat to our joint operations. I ordered the Inquisitor to make him talk—find out what he knew. But the boy proved stubborn. He insisted he was not from the Galactic Alliance but was sent by some religious corporation to study Kar-sèr-Sephiryth. He died slowly but told us nothing. I ordered his body taken to the hill as an example to others."

Hickory felt her anger rise but kept her breathing under control. *An accident? Gareth was tortured to death because of a misunderstanding?*

"What others?" said Nolanski. "Surely you didn't mean to draw the attention of the I.A.? And what was your part in this, Vogel? Don't tell me the Bikashi were innocent bystanders."

The Alien Corps

Vogel stared at the Earthman from under his hooded lids before he replied. "I neutralized his comms chip—that's all. I left the interrogation to Sequana. But this is all pointless. The important thing is our arrangement is in jeopardy."

Hickory felt confused for a second until she realized Sequana and Ecknit were one and the same. Her heart beat furiously. She now knew who was responsible for Gareth's death. All three were working together on something important, but what? Could it be crynidium theft, or was there something else?

Her concentration was broken by some nearby worshipers who were muttering and gesticulating at her. *What the …* She realized her furtive posture was causing some angst among them and decided it was time to get out of there. She wasn't quick enough.

Vogel heard the disquiet and stepped out from around the corner to see what the fuss was about. He glared at her in surprise. "You!"

Hickory turned to run, but the Bikashi grabbed her arm and pinned her against the wall.

Nolanski sighed. "Hickory. You just couldn't let it rest, could you?"

She straightened, assessing the trio. Nolanski and Sequana alias Ecknit, she thought she could handle, but the Bikashi looked dangerous.

Vogel reached towards his belt, but Sequana held him back. "You cannot. This is a sacred place. The spilling of blood is proscribed on penalty of death."

Vogel growled and shook free of Sequana's grasp, but he slid his dagger back into its sheath.

Hickory pleaded with the Earthman. "Nolanski. Give yourself up. You're not like this lot. I promise you'll get a fair hearing. You won't be implicated in Gareth's death."

"I'm sorry, my dear. I've worked too hard and taken a lot of risks to build my little nest egg. I'm not inclined to give it up, and even if I wanted to … well, that's a story for another time. But the question is, what do we do with you and your partner now? Where is Jess, by the way? I presume she now knows your situation and is taking the appropriate action?"

He turned to his accomplices. "The peacekeepers will arrive at any moment. Any ideas on how to get out of this?"

Vogel shook his head in disgust. "The problem is yours, Nolanski. The IA will be all over this planet within hours. I will not sacrifice myself for no reason."

Sequana's eyes flared, and he no longer looked an effeminate fop. "You will not abandon us, Vogel. We have all committed to this course because we need each other. The future of the Bikashi race and of Avanaux depends on the success of our mission." He coughed violently, raised the handkerchief to his nose

The Alien Corps

again, and sniffed. "Besides, you promised me more of this wonderful perfume."

Hickory sensed the Pharlaxian's discomfort. He was an asthma sufferer, and the Bikashi provided medication to douse the handkerchief.

Vogel dismissed Sequana with a snort and started towards the exit. At that moment, the temple doors burst open, and Chief Josipe and his men rushed in and fanned out.

Vogel hissed in anger and charged. He almost made it to the door but was dragged to the ground by half a dozen peacekeepers. They ripped off his hood, and his thin lips peeled back, revealing snarling, pointed teeth and a quivering proboscis.

The peacekeepers sprang back in alarm. "Demon!" screamed one and turned to flee.

The Chief smacked the frightened trooper hard across the head and snarled louder at his men to bind the fiend. "If you let this monster escape, I will flay the skin from your body and feed your carcass to the violators. Bind his hands and legs. Quickly now, or by Daloi—"

A dozen peacekeepers immobilized Vogel and tied a rag around his mouth. The alien struggled, but the fastenings were taut and resisted his efforts.

Sequana had managed to slink away, but Hickory held Nolanski fast, and she could tell by his sardonic smirk and slumped shoulders that he was resigned to his fate. He'd rolled the dice and lost. There was no point in him either fighting or fleeing—he was too old to fight and too well-known to get away. She saw Josipe-sèr-Amagon approach, looking grim.

Shaking his head, Nolanski admonished himself. "Typical. What will Kalichia say?" He raised his arms in submission.

The Chief pulled Nolanski's arms down to his sides. Sadness and disappointment battled with the anger on his face. "Nolanski, my friend," he said. "Today is a sad day for both of us, but I fear it will only become worse for you. I am arresting you for larceny and for conspiring to unseat the lawful government of Avanaux. There may well be other charges."

Hickory stared at the man she'd trusted, then turned away. "Jess? Call Brandt at the spaceport and tell him to send a team over here. Actually, tell him he might want to deal with this one personally."

"Have you got them all?" said Jess.

Hickory looked around. Sequana, alias Ecknit, had disappeared, taking his chance to flee during the capture of Vogel. "We've got Nolanski and the alien. He's a Bikashi—better let Brandt know that too. I guess Prosperine's secret hoard of crynidium isn't secret anymore. The admiral is going to have to rethink his strategy. The Pharlaxian has disappeared.

Let's hope we've put his plans to eliminate Kar-sèr-Sephiryth on hold, but somehow, I doubt it."

Teacher

Kar-sèr-Sephiryth reminded Hickory of an African gazelle: long limbs, ramrod-straight nose, and large soulful eyes that gave him the appearance of wisdom beyond his thirty years.

Jess whispered to Hickory, "He looks the part."

They settled themselves amidst the Teacher's followers gathered on the steps of the government building. Hickory thought the Teacher's choice of location curious. Perhaps his aim was to challenge the powers that be or sway them to his ideas. More likely, it was a message to his followers that Prosperine's rules and regulations held no authority over him.

He'd been reading from the Prosperine holy scrolls, and now he put them aside and addressed the crowd. "Know for certain Balor has already set the day and the hour of Prosperine's ruin. Then will the ground buckle and heave, and the air be consumed with fire, and the unbelievers and the righteous will both perish in terror and agony. Beg Balor for his forgiveness now, and believe in me, then you will be numbered amongst the just and will be with my father always."

Some in the crowd turned aside, muttering. Everyone knew they could hope for another lifetime on Avanaux if they were virtuous in this one. Talk of everlasting life was madness. Others, although confused, sought clarification. "When will this happen?" asked one. Another said, "My wife is a good woman, but she does not know you. Will she be counted among the just or the wicked?"

Kar-sèr-Sephiryth spread his arms wide to encompass his followers. "My brothers and sisters, listen to what I say: in the Book of Balor, many signs foreshadow the end of time. Before that day comes, Prosperine will be a shining light for many. My brothers will spread the word throughout the whole of creation. In the last days, the lights of heaven will be extinguished one by one until all is dark. When that time arrives, Balor will descend from the firmament riding a shining chariot and will gather the faithful to him. He will make three lines, one for those who are damned, a second for those who have lived a righteous life, and the third line will be honored and sit at the table with my father. Those are my true disciples."

A vision of the end of the universe, thought Hickory. It wasn't an uncommon theme in many civilizations. She personally had listened to another version of the

P J McDermott

apocalypse in her previous mission, and several others had been documented. All were proven to be conjured up by the creative minds of beings who were less than divine. She waited until his audience quieted, then put the test question devised by COLIN. "Teacher, why doesn't Balor reveal himself to us?"

Kar-sèr-Sephiryth looked to where Hickory and Jess sat and inclined his head, smiling at them. "Don't you know me, Hickory? How can you say, 'Show us the Father?' Even were Balor to appear here in all his glory, many would not believe. I am here. Believe in me."

Hickory felt a tingling sensation at the back of her neck. She couldn't take her eyes off the Teacher, and her mind raced. *How could he know my name?* She struggled to think clearly. Someone must have told him. *But who, why? Does he realize I am an alien? He must know.*

Jess tugged her arm, and Hickory patted her hand. "It's okay, Jess," she whispered.

The significance of the Teacher's reply wasn't lost on Hickory. Of the fourteen previous investigations by the SPRA, the Teacher's answer represented the closest to the biblical account of Philip's questioning of Jesus.

Kar-sèr-Sephiryth waited, an enigmatic smile playing on his features.

Hickory took a deep breath. "Teacher," she said,

The Alien Corps

"you say Prosperine will be a beacon for many. Where, then, are the many? Are there other lands we do not know of that also worship Balor?"

Kar-sèr-Sephiryth let some sand run between his fingers and then looked to the heavens. "Do you seek to test me then? For the sake of those others you serve, I will say this. The children of Balor are as grains of sand by the sea. The lights in the sky are many, Hickory, and my Father knows the name of every one. There are many lands and many peoples. Some already know the Father; some have yet to know him."

For those others you serve…? Another clue. It wasn't difficult to believe this naur knew there was life beyond Avanaux and also that Hickory reported to a higher authority.

Though his followers might not understand the meaning, they hung on his every word.

Kar-sèr-Sephiryth rose to his feet and walked towards the two Earthlings. He gazed a few moments at the pendant around Hickory's neck, then cupped Jess's face in his hand and looked at her with compassion. "I am sorry, Jessica-sèra-Jayne. You have lost a good friend but fear not. He showed much bravery in the face of great terror and evil. Be at peace, for Gareth grieves not."

Jess flinched. "How can you know these things? How do you know my name? What right do you have to speak about Gareth like this?" She looked confused and frightened.

"Do not be afraid. All will be revealed in time." He placed a hand on Jess and Hickory's shoulder. "You are knight commanders of Balor. You know not your power." He held their eyes for a moment, then shading his own against the sun, he gazed into the distance. "The followers of Sequana are near. I must be gone before they find me. I will see you again before this chapter is finished." He beckoned to his supporters to follow and then walked swiftly away.

"Well," said Jess, "what an experience. Look at me—I'm shaking like a leaf. You know I'm not a believer, but that guy could convince me otherwise. How come he knew our names? How could he possibly know my mother's name is Jayne? He must know we're not from this planet, too." She shook her head slowly.

Hickory laughed half-heartedly. "It was a shock, all right. It baffled me at first when he said it, but logically, he could have found out from any number of people. Nolanski, for one, or the Chief, or someone from the embassy." She knew it wasn't so simple. It was a stretch to suggest he could discover Jess's mother's name from one of these sources. There were too many unanswered questions. Hickory spread her hands. "I agree he's impressive. The Teacher has more knowledge about a lot of things than your average

The Alien Corps

citizen. For one, he understands that Prosperine isn't the center of the universe. I have to admit, his similarity to the historical Jesus is astonishing."

"Hickory..." began Jess. "When he touched me, it was like a wave of peace surged through me. It was the strangest thing. I—"

"Hush, Jess. Don't read too much into it. He showed a lot of empathy over Gareth's death. You probably felt a rapport with him."

Hickory had also felt the energy emanating from the naur, but she didn't want to think of what that might mean, not yet. She reached out and pulled Jess towards her. "We're both vulnerable at the moment." But she wondered how this Teacher could know so much about them and Gareth.

◆◆◆

James Brandt introduced Alex Mackie. "Alex is our new representative on Prosperine. His first job will be to organize Nolanski's trip home."

Mackie had yet to complete the Maquillage process, so they were face-to-face in the "Half Way House," a small room inside the spaceport created as a temporary meeting place for both Avanauri and Humans.

Mackie's eyes crinkled as he shook hands with Jess. "Call me Mack. It's not a great start to a new job—getting rid of the old boss, is it? But I hope to be of some help to you folks when I get settled."

Jess giggled and then blushed as Mack grinned at her.

He inclined his head. "I've been told the Avanauri like a little color on the face. I can understand why," he said.

Hickory glanced at Jess, surprised by her reaction. It was many years since Jack had died, and not once in that time had Hickory seen her blush at a compliment. Hickory noted the laugh lines around Mack's eyes, the broad shoulders, and the square jaw and decided he could be good for Jess.

"We could do with some help tracking down Sequana," Hickory said. "He's the one responsible for Gareth's death, and he won't stop until Kar-sèr-Sephiryth is dead, too. He's become invisible since Nolanski and Vogel were arrested, but I bet he's still rallying his followers to start a holy war."

"Is he still in Ezekan, do you think?" said Mack.

"I doubt he'd hang around long. There are too many peacekeepers looking for him in the city. I wouldn't be surprised if he's headed upcountry to lick his wounds," said Jess

Hickory nodded her agreement. "James, did Nolanski say anything about where Sequana might have flown?"

"The ex-ambassador hasn't been too cooperative

since his arrest. My guess is he's holding back, hoping to negotiate his way out of this mess. I'm sure he retains some loyalty to Sequana and Vogel. Still, he volunteered that the Pharlaxians have a sizeable training camp in the desert, near Tontine, towards the Ice Mountains.

"He couldn't be more specific, he said, because he hasn't been there himself. Personally, I think he's lying, but he'll only tell us more if we reach an agreement. I'm confident he will eventually tell us everything he knows."

Mack lifted his eyebrows, and his lips parted in a wide smile. "Sounds like a good reason for us to do some desert exploring, Jess. What do you say?"

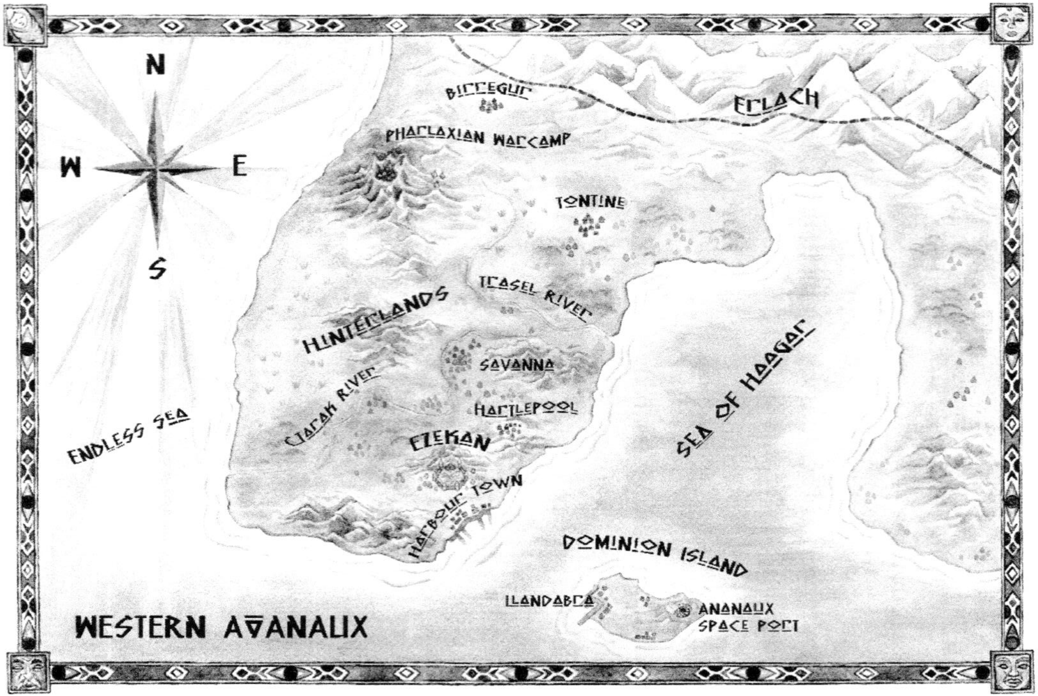
N
W
E
S
BIRREGUR
ERLACH
PHARLAXIAN WARCAMP
TONTINE
TRASEL RIVER
HINTERLANDS
SAVANNA
HARTLEPOOL
CIARAK RIVER
EZEKAN
HARBOUR TOWN
ENDLESS SEA
SEA OF HAAGAR
DOMINION ISLAND
LLANDABRA
ANANAUX
SPACE PORT
WESTERN AVANALIX

Pursuit

Josipe-sèr-Amagon sat behind his desk, rattling a pencil between his teeth. Losing his card partner was disappointing but unavoidable. If Nolanski had confided in him, both might have profited, and Nolanski would not be in IA custody tonight.

He sighed. Perhaps it was for the best. Things were more complicated since the Earthmen arrived, and he did well to keep his wits about him and his hands clean. It annoyed him that the Pax leader had escaped. Sequana would cause a lot more trouble before he was through, but he would deal with it when the time came. He would have enjoyed watching the rebel leader languish in his jail. Instead, the Bikashi was in custody. "Balor!" he swore, then touched his lips briefly in contrition.

Too many had seen the grotesque figure since his arrest. Despite his threats, it was unrealistic to expect his guardsmen to keep silent. Rumors would be flying. No one yet realized the truth—it was almost impossible for a naur to conceive of such a thing. Most believed the rumor he'd spread that the Bikashi was a deformed creature from the Scarf.

Soon, though, questions would be asked, and the truth would be revealed. There were aliens on Prosperine, and the Avanauri people were not the only, nor even the most advanced, civilization in the universe. From there, it was a short step to denial of the Good Book and a sharp decline into anarchy. It could set the country back a hundred years—more!

The pencil snapped in his hand. There was only one option. He couldn't make the Bikashi disappear without incurring the wrath of Vogel's masters. The answers to his questions made it clear that Vogel was a high-ranking official, and should he be disposed of, there would be repercussions, and others would take his place.

On the other hand, if he gave Vogel over to the Earthmen, he would become their problem. That would at least delay things until the politics were dealt with, and afterward, he could spread the rumor that the monster had been put down.

Having reached this conclusion, the Chief wasted no time. He sent the Bikashi to the Alliance spaceport on Dominion Island with an escort of eight of his most trusted troopers under the command of an officer.

◆◆◆

The Alien Corps

Lieutenant Thurle-sèr-Gammons was the son of the Chief's sister. He was a competent officer, considered fair but tough by his troops, although considered somewhat surly by his superiors. He'd received no favors from his uncle to arrive at this point in his career and had accepted he was unlikely to progress past his current rank.

But Thurle hadn't been ignored by everyone. Considered a firebrand and a radical in his youth, he'd been attracted to the right-wing policies of the Pharlaxian main party and often attended their meetings. More recently, he'd come under Sequana's personal tutelage.

Halfway to Harbor Town, the escort was attacked by a combined troop of Bikashi and Pharlaxian yarrak cavalry. Thurle lined his naurs up to meet the charge, positioning himself at the rear with Vogel. He struck and killed three of his own command from behind. The remainder were slaughtered by the charging Bikashi, and Thurle headed off to the Hinterland with Vogel and his troops.

◆◆◆

Jess, Mack, and Hickory discussed the best way forward and decided to split their resources. While Hickory remained in Ezekan to follow up on the Teacher, Jess and Mack would head to Tontine by yarrak, taking on the persona of Castilie explorers seeking trade opportunities.

For the first ten miles of their journey, Jess and Mack passed field after field of cereal crops. The region west of Ezekan was considered the food bowl of Avanaux, producing more than a third of the country's food supply. Hills were covered with fruit trees, while vegetables, fungi, and grains thrived on rolling river flats and valleys enriched by the soil carted in from Harbor Town. It was a pleasant start to their journey, and Jess and Mack exchanged small talk as they went.

The farmlands gave way to vegetation consisting of brushwood and stunted forest growth, followed by savannah—vast expanses of rolling golden grass, home to wild yarrak and other beasts.

The ground underfoot became uneven, forcing them to make several detours to avoid deep crevasses. To their west lay the River Ctarak, impassable by foot or yarrak for most of its journey from the Mountains of the White Cloud to the Endless Sea.

Kyntai had told them there was little point in braving the raging torrent and slippery rocks. On the other side of the river, the savannah soon petered out to sunbaked deserts leading to barren mountains. This area was called the Hinterland, home to violators and other predators.

To reach Tontine, travelers were forced to head north, past the small town of Hartlepool and across the savannah between the Mountains of Valor and the

The Alien Corps

Ctarak until they reached the toll bridge spanning the river.

Jess and Mack rode through the night, crossing the bridge at mid-morning the following day. From that point, there were two possible routes. They could proceed north as far as the Trasel River and hope the ferry was operating. Alternatively, they could detour eastward to the river mouth and travel up the coastline to Tontine.

Jess decided on the ferry crossing, rationalizing this as the path more likely to be taken by Sequana. When they arrived, the barge was moored on the far side of the river. They dismounted and raised the signal flag to alert the ferryman to their presence and awaited his response. "We might be here a while," said Mack, picking a stalk of golden grass and sucking on the stem. "He'll want to wait until he has a passenger or two on the other side to make it worth his while."

"I could do with the rest, anyway," said Jess, stretching. "How long have you been with the Alliance, if you don't mind me asking?"

"I don't mind." He smiled. "I joined as a geologist eight years ago and spent the first three surveying remote star systems searching for crynidium deposits. I met the admiral on a planet orbiting Arcturus. He asked me to do a presentation on my findings." He twirled the grass between his thumb and forefinger, then threw it away.

"That would have been a tough assignment. The admiral can be a scary man."

Mack laughed. "Especially as there was no good news to tell him. I spent half an hour explaining how gamma radiation reflectors and robotic stations operate, with him staring at me all the time. When I'd finished, he said, 'Mr. Mackie, you're no damn good as a geologist, but I think you'd make a fine administrator.'"

Jess laughed at his impersonation.

"I received the transfer order the following week, and I've been with him ever since." He told her it was his perfect job. "Never a dull moment and always something new. I get bored very easily otherwise."

"I hope you don't get too bored working with me," she said

"There's absolutely no chance of that!"

◆◆◆

It took Jess and Mack a week to reach the village of Tontine. Both were tired, stiff, and saddle-sore. They handed the reins of their yarraks to a stable hand, with instructions to provide fresh water, food, and clean bedding for their mounts.

Outside the stable, they glanced around the almost deserted, dusty streets. By Avanauri standards, Tontine was a sizable town with a population of around a thousand. It was the gathering point for the surrounding farmers and boasted a temple, a school, an inn, and a variety of supply stores, plus a marketplace.

It was late afternoon, the sun was a wavering orange ball low on the horizon, and the first shimmer of the aurora was visible high above.

Most townsfolk would be settling in for the night. The inn, though, was crowded. Jess and Mack drew stares as they made their way over to the serving area.

The naur behind the counter nodded to them. "You'll be some of those travelers from Castaliena we keep hearing about? We don't get many strangers around here, but you're welcome all the same. Can I get you something—food or a drink, perhaps? You look as though you've come a distance."

"We've journeyed from Ezekan, and we could do with a cold drink to start with. It's hot as Hades out there," said Jess.

The bartender poured some ale into two beakers, and they drank thirstily. "You speak well for a foreigner," he said.

Jess flushed. "Oh, we've been in your country for several years now. We're almost locals—except for our color!" She and Mack laughed, and the bartender joined in. Jess hurried on. "This looks like a busy town. You must get a few people from the city looking to buy at your market?"

"Used to. But these days, most farmers take their produce into Ezekan. They fetch a better price that way." He leaned over the bar and spoke in a confidential tone. "Tell me, I've often wondered what it would be like crossing the Scarf. They say strange creatures live there. Half-naur, half-plant is what I hear."

Mack laughed. "We've come across some strange sights since we left Castaliena, all right, but nothing so bizarre. No, the Scarf is a thick jungle crawling with insects, and there are some carnivores with big teeth to avoid. But I never saw anything remotely naur-like."

"One day, we will find a passage to Castaliena and visit your country," said the bartender, polishing the bar top vigorously.

"No doubt," Jess said, placing her empty mug on the polished surface. "So, you don't get many visitors in town these days?"

"Not many. There are always farmers in town, of course, and the occasional travelers like yourselves. Once a month, people from the commune up north come here to buy a few essentials, but that's the extent of the excitement." He smiled genially at Mack. "If you're staying tonight, perhaps you would honor us with some tales of your own country. I'm sure the locals would be interested in hearing about Castaliena."

The Alien Corps

Mack looked at Jess. "It would be a relief to sleep in a soft bed if only for one night." She nodded her agreement. They would continue their journey in the morning. Mack turned back to the barman. "Be glad to," he said. "Will anybody from the commune be here?"

"No. They stocked up last week. They won't be back for a while."

◆◆◆

Later that evening, relaxing in front of the fire in the main room, Jess said, "You think this commune might be the place we're looking for?"

"Could be." Mack took a sip from his mug. He'd spent an hour regaling the locals with anecdotes of his imaginary homeland. The stories bore a distinct resemblance to the Folk Tales of Ireland Jess had seen him reading the previous night. "They're keen on their privacy. Anyone curious enough to ride out there doesn't get far before they're turned back by armed naurs.

"And one of the locals I was chatting with said the last time naurs from the commune came to town, one of their group carried a 'magic weapon.' It spat fire when the stranger pointed it at some kind of wild boar that was attacking a child. Scared the life out of everyone who saw it. The pig was none too pleased either, by the sound of it."

"Magic weapon? A gun? Who would have

something like that around here?"

"That's what I thought. Definitely worth having a look at this commune."

They both fell silent for a moment before Mack cleared his throat and said, "Jess—do you mind if I ask you a personal question?"

"You can ask. I won't promise to answer, though." Jess took a sip of her drink. It was a pleasant enough concoction, she thought.

"Are you with anyone right now? You know—is there anyone special?"

She darted a glance at him and just as quickly looked away, giggling nervously. "I've two grown-up kids, and they're pretty special to me, but if you mean do I have a boyfriend or lover, then no." Jess felt the warmth rise up her neck. *This stuff must pack a punch; I'm feeling a bit lightheaded already.* "My husband passed away seven years ago."

Mack looked earnestly at her. "Seven years is a long time to grieve." He paused, tapping his lip and looking up at Jess from below his eyebrows. "I suppose I'd better give you fair notice. I like you, and I think you could get to like me, too, if you give me a chance. I know we're just getting to know each other, but I enjoy being with you."

Jess raised her eyes to see Mack smiling at her. Her heart fluttered rapidly. *Like a little kid.* She hadn't felt

The Alien Corps

this giddy for a long, long time.

It had seemed the sun would always shine for her and Jack. Their love was immune to the vagaries of the real world. Like Cinderella and her Prince, they swirled to the music of an eternal waltz. She'd exulted in the warmth and safety offered by Jack, his strong arms holding her close and his boyish grin igniting a fire in her heart that consumed her. Then he was gone, his light extinguished by a wasting disease that tortured and changed him before taking him from her It was a mercy when darkness prevailed.

She placed her hand on Mack's. "I like your company too, Mack," she said quietly and then laughed. "Listen to me! What did you say was in this drink?"

Throughout their journey to Tontine, Mack had kept his tone light and humorous, a flirtatious preliminary that enticed Jess from the protective shell she'd built around herself. They spent the next few hours talking about their likes and dislikes, the things that were important to them, what made them laugh, and what they had always wanted to do but had never found the time.

Jess talked about her life with Jack and the twins in Australia and about Gareth.

Mack admitted to being divorced with no children. He and his wife had separated after three years of marriage. "She left me for another guy." He saw the look of sympathy and added hastily, "It was a good thing—for both of us, as it turned out. She's in a happy marriage with three young kids, and I've enjoyed the opportunity to spread my wings. I'd never have joined the Agency otherwise."

At the end of the night, they went to their separate rooms. Jess sat on her bed, wondering what she should do. She wasn't really interested in a fling, although that might be fun, too. He was a good-looking, sexy specimen. She flushed at the image that flashed through her mind. No, she had the kids to consider. What would they say if they found out she'd taken a lover? They'd be shocked. She'd never shown any interest in men or sex since Jack passed. Of course, they'd want to meet Mack just to make sure he was a suitable prospect. She giggled to herself. "Damn that ale. I shouldn't have downed that third mug." She waited a few minutes more, glancing at the door. Perhaps she'd got it all wrong. He did have a budding career. Maybe all he wanted was friendship. *Only one way to find out.*

◆◆◆

His eminence, The High Reeve of Avanaux, stood on the balcony of his office in the House of Government and surveyed the city spread out beneath him. In the distance, beyond the walls, the flying machines hovered above Harbor Town, floating silently on a sea of dense, blue mist that covered the ground all the way to the horizon. The fog swirled around his feet, giving him a ghostly appearance.

But Yonni-sèr-Abelen was not feeling particularly spiritual. His ordinarily white face held a dark blush that his friends rarely saw, and his enemies did well to fear. He breathed deeply to subdue the emotion threatening to erupt, then walked inside and addressed the naur sitting at the oval table in front of his desk. "You lost the Bikashi?"

Sweat trickled down the side of Josipe-sèr-Amagon's face. He hurriedly wiped it away. The High Reeve was the most powerful individual on the planet, subject to none and influenced by few. If he decreed it, the Peacekeeper Chief would be incarcerated without trial or, worse, taken out to the desert and left to become an evening meal for some wild Arioch. And no one would ask why.

Yonni-sèr-Abelen spoke in a whisper. "You lost this monster? Why didn't you send a bigger escort? Did you not understand the importance of your mission?" His voice became a roar as he towered over the Chief. "Or is it that you are incompetent and your men are not to be trusted?" He slammed his fist on the desk.

Josipe's words came off his tongue thickly. "Your eminence, I sent eight of my best people with Vogel. They were attacked by a well-armed force of Pharlaxian rebels. According to witnesses, they were assisted by other off-worlders like Vogel. Had I sent twice the men, I doubt it would have made any difference. If I have done wrong, it is in not foreseeing such an attempt to free him."

He did not mention his nephew. Thurle's body hadn't been found with the other guards. Either the rebels took him captive, which seemed unlikely, or he'd defected to the Pharlaxian cause.

The High Reeve bit his lip and turned his back on the Chief. The news alarmed him, but it wouldn't do to show fear. Having one alien escape was bad enough, but the subtext of Josipe's message was the Pharlaxian rogues were in league with more than one off-world alien. "Did your witnesses happen to notice how many Bikashi soldiers were there or which direction they made off in?" he asked scornfully.

"Yes, your eminence. The numbers vary, but my guess is that there were between four and six aliens and a dozen Pharlaxians. The rebels headed towards Harbor Town, and I thought they might be looking for a ship to take them up the coast. I sent my best trackers after them, and they arrived back barely an hour ago.

"They followed the yarrak trail south until noon, and then our quarry veered westwards into the desert. My men lost them two hours later."

"What do you mean *lost* them? Even a half-sighted nauri child could follow yarrak signs, desert or no."

"When I say they lost them, I do not mean they found their tracks difficult to follow. No, they left plenty of signs showing where they passed. But these stopped abruptly at the bank of the Thornton River. My men searched upstream and downstream, but there was no trace of them. They simply vanished."

◆◆◆

Jess and Mack pressed on early next morning, following a path into the hills marked on a handdrawn map given to them by the innkeeper. They made good time, and by late the next afternoon, they'd traversed some forty miles to the other side of the range, reaching the point where the scrubby bush met the desert.

They set up camp for the night beside a dried-up stream and lit a small fire. Mack cooked them a vegetable stew, using the fresh supplies they'd bought in Tontine mixed with an Alliance-supplied protein concentrate. Afterward, they lay on their backs and looked at the stars for a time, making small talk. The night was quiet except for the hoot of a nightjar calling for its mate.

The snap of a twig brought Jess and Mack scrambling to their feet, but they were too late. A figure emerged from the darkness. The tall, slender nauri was swathed from neck to toe in a black cloak. She pointed a curved scimitar directly at Jess. Other warriors appeared beside her. There was nowhere to run. Jess counted at least twenty armed adversaries surrounding them. She blanched when she saw some of them carrying projectile rifles.

The pack closed in silently. Jess and Mack bent their heads and spread their hands to show submission. The circle parted to admit a rough-looking character wearing grubby gray robes with a jagged-edged sword in his belt. He reached out to Mack, gripped his jaw in one hand, and stared intently, twisting Mack's face from one side to another. Then, he did the same with Jess. "Take them. Bind them securely," he said in a gravelly voice.

"Wait," said Mack. "We are but simple travelers. We mean you no harm, nor do we carry anything of value. What do you want with us?" He struggled to avoid being bound, and a naur struck him behind the knee with a stave.

He slumped to the ground, and a second naur kicked him in the stomach. Mack doubled over, retched, and tried to regain his feet only to be laid low finally by a rifle butt to the head.

Jess was horrified by the speed and ferocity of the attack. Blood flowed freely from Mack's head. Another naur kicked him as he lay unconscious on the ground. "No! Leave him, leave him alone!" she shouted, struggling to shake herself free from the grip of the two attackers who held her by the arms. Mack's assailant looked at Jess and hesitated. He turned and spat at Mack, then signaled three others to lift him onto the back of a yarrak.

The Alien Corps

They traveled belly down, strapped to their mounts throughout the long night, being jolted across the desert sands. Jess couldn't tell whether Mack had regained consciousness because his head hung over the far side of his yarrak.

Their kidnappers maintained a steady pace until mid-morning the next day, by which time Jess was dehydrated, and her head felt as though it might split open. Their captors untied the prisoners, hauled them off their mounts, and let them fall slowly to the ground.

Jess pushed herself to a sitting position and looked blearily around her. They were at the foot of a high rocky outcrop, and she could just make out the shadow of a path zigzagging to the top. She heard Mack moan and crawled over to him. His face was pale, and dried blood caked his hair, but at least he was alive. His eyes fluttered open.

"Where am I? What happened?" he whispered hoarsely. His lips and tongue were swollen, and Jess could hardly make out his words.

She looked around frantically. "You there," she addressed the leader, "There's some water in my pack and some bandages. His head needs seeing to."

The chieftain seemed unmoved at first. He strode over and nudged Mack in the side with his boot, then shouted at him, gesturing towards the rocky escarpment. When Mack didn't get up, the chieftain motioned angrily to one of the nauri to bring a drinking bag.

Jess dribbled some liquid into Mack's mouth. He spluttered, then took a long swallow and grinned stupidly at Jess. "I don't know what this is, but it's got one helluva kick to it."

They began the ascent tethered behind their kidnappers. Many times, Mack fell to his knees and was forcibly dragged to his feet. At intervals along the way, Jess saw sentinels sitting motionless on their haunches, their black eyes never wavering from the horizon. She could tell by the purple flashes peeping out from under their sand-colored cloaks that these were young nauri. Several throwing spears stood rooted in the sand beside each warrior, their angry barbed heads leaning against each other. She wondered why all the spearcasters were nauri, then remembered the female of the species had superior eyesight to the male.

They were led into a ravine wide enough to fit no more than two abreast. Jess thought it would be nearly impossible for ground forces to fight their way through. After a short while, their escort swung onto a track that snaked to the top of the ridge. The two prisoners, still shackled to their captors, stumbled over treacherous rock debris until they reached the summit.

Jess looked out over a valley, circular in form and

surrounded by a craggy wall of carbonatite. She realized she was looking at the caldera of a long-extinct volcano, now covered with golden grass and small trees. A sizeable force was bivouacked below, and Jess counted at least fifty large tents and over a hundred grazing yarraks.

The Avanauri tribesmen sitting by their campfires murmured to each other and stared curiously at Jess and Mack as they scrambled down the scree and made their way through the camp.

The company passed through an opening in the cliff face that led to a wide tunnel. It was dim and damp inside, but torches fixed to the wall every fifty feet illuminated the way. The tunnel rose sharply at the beginning and then leveled off, ending fifty yards above the floor of a vast underground cavern.

Sunlight poured from a series of vents on the walls, reflecting off large pools of crynidium and bathing the entire area in dazzling luminescence.

Mack shaded his eyes and whispered, "This is a magma chamber—been here a long time too—look at the size of the stalactites." He nodded at the roof and walls. "This whole area was created from an erupting volcano. When the pressure eased, the lava withdrew, leaving behind this massive cave."

Below them, Jess was astonished to see a sizeable community of soldiers, servants, spouses, children, and other camp followers. Tents, lean tos, kitchens, and other facilities were erected to serve the rebel army. Adjacent to the living quarters stood a blacksmith's shop and a corralled area containing scores of yarraks. A contingent of Pharlaxian men at arms equipped with swords, spears, and shields marched across a dusty training ground next to the blacksmith's premises. Jess thought the place was like a beehive, with the Pax soldiers and their retinue ever on the move.

A massive rock platform stood in the middle of the chamber, high enough to provide a view of the entire cavern or perhaps to allow the surrounding masses to see those seated on the dais.

Their captors urged Jess and Mack to get moving. The path wound slowly downwards, hugging the cavern walls. Groups of naurs and nauris leaned against a wooden rail along the outer edge, watching the proceedings below.

Jess noted storerooms and what she took as officers' quarters hewn into the solid rock. This was a permanent base where the rebel Pharlaxian army and their followers could wait, train, and grow secretly. Shocked, she realized the men she'd seen outside the cavern were a small part of a much larger force.

Their escorts bustled Jess and Mack down a series of crude steps toward the raised dais. Jess inhaled sharply and nodded to draw Mack's attention towards the platform. Sequana, the Pharlaxian, easily

The Alien Corps

recognizable from Hickory's description, sat alongside four other rebel leaders.

Sequana looked up from the document he was reading to listen to the chieftain who'd captured them. He glanced at Mack and Jess, said a few words to the warrior, then put down his quill and motioned for the captives to approach.

"Tell me who you are and what are you doing in this part of the country?" he said, leaning forward and staring intently at them.

"We are Castalie travelers, friend, passing through the desert on our way to the North," said Mack. "We meant no harm. Your captain took exception to our presence and brought us here against our will. We didn't know we were trespassing."

Sequana's features were ugly to begin with, but when he smiled, the scar running from the corner of his mouth to his cheek made him appear cruel. He coughed and raised a handkerchief to his mouth. "My men are instructed to bring me any dark-skinned intruders found on my land, and my land extends for many miles in all directions." He waved his arm around to emphasize his area of interest. "He tells me you resisted and needed to be subdued. That is unfortunate." He waved the handkerchief, gesturing to the guards to untie their hands, then turned to Jess. "What is your business in the North? I am curious. What reason could two Castalie have for traveling three hundred miles across the desert?"

Jess stared steadily at the naur. "We are scholars come from Castaliena to explore your country and learn about the Avanauri people and your customs. We are gathering seeds and roots that we might grow in our own land. We heard of a plant with miraculous healing properties that grows only in the soil around Birregur, and we would like to take samples to examine—"

The Pharlaxian leader cut her off with a wave of his handkerchief. "Some who call themselves travelers from beyond the Scarf have been known to keep evil company. Others are not from Prosperine at all but are demons from another world who come here to steal our treasures. Which are you, I wonder? Bring her here!"

Two guards seized hold of Jess by the arms and dragged her to face him. Sequana gripped her head on either side and pushed his fingers and thumbs roughly against her skin.

"What are you doing?" asked Jess in a strained voice. "You're hurting me."

Sequana released her and addressed his puzzled companions. "Demons have metal inside their heads. You must always do this when you meet anyone claiming to be from Castaliena.

Jess's tone was indignant. "There is no metal in my head! I am, as I said, a visitor to your country. I would

The Alien Corps

have hoped for better treatment from one who is a leader of his people."

Mack emptied his rucksack on a table with a clatter, revealing a collection of jars and pots. He grinned widely. "Already, we have found plants that may produce great wealth in our land."

Sequana took one of the jars, opened it, and poured the contents onto the table. He pushed the fibrous roots around with his fingers. "Weeds," he said. "You are collecting weeds?"

"Not just any weeds. The ones you have spilled onto the table are rare, even in your land. When chewed, they aid digestion and relieve disquiet of the nerves. As well, they increase sexual vigor, or so your priests tell us," said Jess.

"Ha! I would not trust anything those *brickshaks* tell you. You are more likely to be poisoned than cured eating these!"

Jess smiled. "Perhaps we should try them out first on some of our own clerics?"

The Pax leader grunted. "You will eat with me tonight, and we will talk. I would like to hear more about your country. If I am pleased, I will arrange for you to be escorted to Birregur in the morning. Your yarraks will be watered and fed and returned to you before you go. This one will show you where you can sleep." He dismissed them with a wave of his hand.

Their guide led them to a small hollowed-out room containing only a rickety bed, the mandatory painting of Balor hanging on the wall, a basin of cold water, and a rag to dry themselves.

"Just as well the fearless leader knows nothing about implants," said Jess. "I was a little worried there for a while."

"You handled it brilliantly—just the right amount of outrage, but isn't it strange he hasn't placed us under guard?"

Jess shrugged. "He doesn't have to. I imagine there aren't too many black faces around here. We won't be able to go anywhere without him knowing."

Loud shouts and cheers erupted from below. Mack looked through a narrow slot in the wall, overlooking the cavern they'd just left. "Jess, come over here," he said. A band of warriors led a wagon train into the arena. On the back of one cart, a figure grasped the bars of his cage. "Have a look at that prison transport. Isn't that—?"

"Kar-sèr-Sephiryth," finished Jess, her heart dropping. "A Pharlaxian scouting party must have found him."

"Yes, but look!" said Mack, pointing at the leading troopers.

Escape

The soldiers who led the Pharlaxians into the arena wore dark plasteel armor on their bulky chests, arms, and legs. Spiked helmets with closed visors concealed their faces.

"A squad of Bikashi troops," said Jess. "What the hell are they doing here?"

"Yes, and guess who's out front," Mack said. The leading rider sat astride his yarrak with his visor open, surveying the crowd with cold eyes.

"I reckon I know that face—Vogel—the one Hickory had her run-in with. I pulled his file before we left Ezekan. He's an area commander in the Bikashi Shock Pack. This guy's been involved in a dozen guerrilla attacks on Alliance planets over the years."

"The last I heard, he'd been arrested by the peacekeepers." Jess's eyes were wide.

"A temporary situation, it seems. Vogel's troops idolize him," Mack shrugged. "As far as they're concerned, he's a war hero."

"He'll know we're from Earth as soon as he spots us," said Jess.

"We need to get away before he does," said Mack.

"Agreed, but there's something I need to do first. I don't want to put your life more at risk than it already is…" She avoided his eyes.

Mack grinned at her. "You won't get rid of me so easily. I'm in this for the long haul, remember?"

Jess blushed. "We should be all right until the evening meal. If we don't turn up for it, Sequana will want to know why. We need to keep out of sight in the meantime, but I want to find out their plan for Kar-sèr-Sephiryth."

The crowd below was becoming more agitated. They crammed against the cart that held the Teacher, pumping fists into the air and shouting abuse. The Bikashi column pushed its way through and came to a standstill in front of the dais.

"Bring the sorcerer to me," commanded Sequana.

Two soldiers dragged Kar-sèr-Sephiryth through the crowd of hecklers and onto the platform, then threw him onto the floor.

"He doesn't look so good," whispered Mack.

The Teacher's face was swollen, his nose was broken, and his shirt front was stained red. Still, Kar-sèr-Sephiryth was unbowed, and he stared stoically into the eyes of his captors.

The Alien Corps

Sequana glared back but could not maintain eye contact for long. He gripped the arms of his chair and pushed himself to his feet. The rebel leader raised his arms to the assembled crowd. All became quiet, and Sequana's voice echoed around the hall. "My brothers, this is Kar-sèr-Sephiryth, the fortune teller who claims to speak in the name of Balor, now brought before us to receive judgment. You know the tricks this man has conjured to convert the gullible. He professes to heal the sick. He says he can cure the lame and feed the hungry!"

The crowd erupted in laughter.

"All of these are but deceits from a master liar. This one serves the purposes of the enemy, the evil spirits, and the destroyer of our faith. Look at him cowering here, powerless before us." Sequana pointed at the preacher and sneered. "Where are your miracles now?"

Kar-sèr-Sephiryth continued to stare silently at the Pharlaxian.

"Have you nothing to say, master of lies?" Sequana folded his arms and looked over his audience, who cheered him at every turn.

The Teacher's voice was deep and mellow and carried over the crowd to Jess and Mack. "The proof of who I am is not in what I say but in what I do and how I serve Balor."

Those watching hissed and jeered. Sequana

motioned to the captain of the guard. "Take him away and watch him well. We will have some sport with this one tonight."

Jess made for the door. "Stay here," she commanded. "I want to hear what the leaders have to say. It will be easier for one Castalie to mingle in the crowd than two."

"I don't suppose there's any point in arguing with you, is there? Just be careful," said Mack as Jess pulled up her hood and slipped out.

The crowd surrounding the dais had thinned, but the leaders remained deep in discussion. As Jess approached, a few stragglers stared at her curiously but did not approach. She paused at a table laden with fresh fruit and gathered some into her arms. Twenty meters short of the platform, she deliberately stumbled and let a few pieces drop to the ground.

As she stooped to pick them up, Jess focused her SIM on the leaders, straining to pick up their conversation. One of the Avanauri had a hawk nose and was wearing a feathered cape. He rose to his feet and addressed the others. "I do not agree with letting this mystic live a moment longer than necessary. The idea of using him to further our cause is dangerous. He is clearly insane, and no one who is not could believe otherwise."

Another nodded his agreement. "He has a large band of followers—but hardly enough to cause us concern, surely."

Sequana shook his head and spoke with authority. "This naur is a symbol of change, but not the change we would like to see. He represents a future world where the Book of Balor is nothing more than a child's storybook. I can assure you I have studied this man well. He and his followers will become a threat to our cause if they are not dealt with now." He looked into the faces of the movement's six leaders, holding each one's eyes for a moment.

"Am I not Sequana, the one chosen to lead the people back to the ways of Balor? Hear what I say. When we are ready, the imposter will be torn asunder in front of the gates of Ezekan. This will be a sign to his followers that he is nothing more than a simple naur. We will send a warning that such is the fate of all heretics! We must strike terror into the hearts of our enemies."

Jess had heard enough. She retreated quickly to her room and relayed the discussion to Mack. "We have to do something," she said. Jess didn't know why the thought of Kar-sèr-Sephiryth suffering a painful death terrified her so much. In her work, she'd witnessed death many times and had herself dealt out death. *But this is different.* Her nails bit painfully into her palms.

Mack saw the anguish in her eyes and spoke softly. "I'd like to, but what can we do? You know the Galactic Alliance has a policy of non-interference in local affairs."

"That's bullshit," said Jess. "The Alliance is well known to 'interfere' when their best interests are threatened. In any case, this is a good person, Mack. There's something special about him. Whether he's the Son of God or not…" She faltered, then found strength again. "It doesn't matter. I can't stand by and watch him being drawn and quartered."

Mack gripped Jess's arm as she tried to brush past him. "Hold on, Jess. Wait a minute—let's think this through." He guided her to the table and took the chair opposite. "If we're going to do this, we need a plan."

The worry left Jess's face, and she smiled. "You're quite a guy, you know?"

Mack left an hour later to try to find where they were holding Kar-sèr-Sephiryth.

Jess went foraging for the supplies they would need when they escaped. *If we make our escape*. The plan was flimsy, but it was the best they could come up with. If it didn't work out, they would likely both be dead by morning. She wished Hickory were here with them. She would know what to do.

Traders from nearby towns and villages sympathetic to the Pharlaxian cause had been permitted to set up stalls in the caldera outside the main chamber. Jess bought several mid-sized water carriers and a quantity of dried crab and fruits without any questions being asked.

She returned via the stables and checked on their yarraks. They looked well cared for but happy to see her nonetheless. She hid her purchases under some bales of goldengrass in the loft. With a bit of luck, they would go undiscovered until it was time to make their escape.

When she returned to their room, Mack was waiting with information that the Teacher was being held in one of the dungeons below ground level. The guard he'd spoken to was prepared to take them to see him—for a sizable fee. "I told him you were his consort and wanted to attend to his injuries."

An hour later, they made their way to the rendezvous point. The naur waiting for them was huge, with hands like shovels and a ragged scar on one cheek. He fidgeted nervously and glanced around as though expecting to be discovered at any second. Mack pressed some coins into his hand to forestall any change of mind and whispered, "Double this when we're done."

The guard's moist pink tongue darted across his lips at the sight of the gold glinting in his hand. He nodded, then hurried them into the lockup. Closing the door behind them, the guard snatched a torch from its holder and led them down a spiral staircase. The flickering light cast eerie shadows before them, and their footsteps echoed hollowly.

They emerged into a guardroom where two soldiers lounged at a table playing cards. Chains, irons, and instruments of torture hung on the walls behind them. They looked up as the trio approached. Scarface spoke, gesturing towards Jess and Mack. The taller of the two guards nodded and tossed a set of keys to Scarface.

The naur led Jess and Mack along a corridor that led to some holding cells for prisoners awaiting trial or death. When they reached the last cell, Scarface peered through a peephole and unlocked the door.

A steel-barred cage was partly visible in the shadows. Scarface walked a few paces into the gloom, and Mack followed, drawing a short club from inside his jacket, ready to strike. Scarface swung his torch left and right and took another step toward the cage. It was empty. He shouted in alarm.

Mack thrust his club back inside his jacket just as the other two guards came running. They stared wide-eyed around the cell, but no one was to be seen. The soldiers fell into an argument, with the other two accusing Scarface of somehow spiriting the prisoner away.

Jess intervened. "It's not possible," she said. "How could he have bypassed you without you seeing him?"

"Unless you were asleep at your station," said Mack.

The Alien Corps

The three guards looked aghast. Anyone investigating the escape would come to the same conclusion. They blustered that the Teacher must have used magic to disappear, swearing they had always remained awake.

"Look," said Mack. "You might be telling the truth, but I don't think Sequana-sèr-Kira will believe you. If I were you, I'd get out of here, fast."

They stared at one another, and then Scarface made a move for the door, and the other two followed on his heels.

Jess put her finger to her lips. "Wait," she whispered to Mack. When the guards disappeared, she pointed to the cell, and both went inside and searched the walls inch by inch. There was nothing. No sign of any loose stones or any possible means of escape or anything to indicate Kar-sèr-Sephiryth had ever been there.

"Either he disappeared into thin air, or he left by the door," said Mack. "I'm inclined to believe the latter."

"Which means someone took the keys from the wall and let him out," said Jess, pacing back and forth excitedly. "Or he was given a duplicate key before he was put in here."

Mack laughed. "My guess is one of the guards let him out while the others were asleep. In any case, he's gone. Probably halfway to Ezekan by now. I don't think Sequana will be happy when he finds out. We should get out of this place as soon as we can."

"I agree." She nodded quickly. "We've learned as much as we can. We must get back to Ezekan and alert Admiral Lace to the Bikashi presence here."

"We'll need a disguise to pass through the gates and avoid the attention of the lookouts," said Mack.

"I think I know where to find that," said Jess. "I'll meet you in fifteen minutes inside the stables."

◆◆◆

Mack drew his cloak around him and made his way to the shed. It was empty because most of the Avanauri were preparing for the evening festivities.

He saddled his and Jess's mounts, then searched the surroundings for anything that could prove helpful.

A short time afterward, Jess arrived with two ankle-length garments with long sleeves she'd bought from a stallholder at the market. "Put these on. It'll help us blend in."

"And here's my contribution," said Mack, holding out two Bikashi helmets and breastplates. At Jess's astonished look, he explained. "They were hanging up in the next room. The helmets smell, but we won't have to wear them for long."

The guards didn't give them a second glance as they rode past and out of the caldera.

Ultimatum

The High Reeve looked askance at the scrap of paper on his desk. *A singularly uninspiring piece of drivel but dangerous.* He'd questioned the messenger at length but was unable to elicit anything other than a desert rider from Tontine had given him some coins to ensure its safe delivery. The naur was tortured but to no avail. He'd died taking any secrets he might have carried to the processing plant. Yonni-sèr-Abelen regretted the necessity but felt compelled to ensure the messenger kept nothing back.

The letter was signed "Sequana-Sèr-Kira, leader of Balor's chosen people of Prosperine." *Impertinent braggart*, thought sèr-Abelen, then read the message once more. *In the name of our God, Balor, the magnificent… blah, blah, blah.*

He skipped the rest of the self-acclamations, noting only that the author was at pains to point out his close relationship with the Supreme Being.

If the despotic rulers of Avanaux and their priests do not stand down in favor of the Party of the Pharlaxians, Balor's chosen people will wage a holy and vengeful war against you and the demons from the world beyond the heavens come here to steal our treasures.

You have three days from when you read this to decide. Send your response with the one who brought this letter. If I have not heard from you by midday four days hence, the head of the demon spy will be paraded outside Ezekan.

Yonni-sèr-Abelen shifted his gaze to the icon of Balor hanging on the wall behind his desk. The central question was whether this was a minor uprising. If so, he could crush it with his own resources, but if not, a more substantial response would be needed. He pondered the letter and recalled his previous conversation with Josipe-sèr-Amagon. If the Pax indeed were in league with off-worlders, then it was beyond him. He sighed, pushed the icon to one side, and then placed his palm on the sensor pad.

A section of the wooden paneling silently slid to one side to reveal a hidden room. The High Reeve stepped over the threshold, and the door closed behind him. He shivered, fearful of the power of the alien technology that opened locked doors without a key, allowing him to observe his office while remaining invisible to those outside.

The Earthlings had installed this secret room shortly after they arrived so they could speak to their distant scientists. He did not know why or how it worked, but he did know how to *make* it work. He crossed to the bureau and felt underneath for the pushbutton. A small panel slid open on the desk, revealing a screen and a touchpad. Hesitantly, he sat down and placed his hand on the pad.

After a few minutes, the screen glowed to life, and George Lace smiled out at him. "This is an unexpected pleasure, High Reeve. To what do I owe this honor?"

Yonni-sèr-Abelen stifled a gasp. He'd known what to expect, but it was still unnerving. "I have received an ultimatum from the Pharlaxians led by the rebel, Sequana-Sèr-Kira. If I don't stand down my government within the next few days, he threatens all-out war."

The admiral pursed his lips. "That isn't good news, Yonni, but I'm sure you will be able to deal with it."

The High Reeve snapped back, his white face blushing darkly, "I wouldn't have called if it was something trivial!"

"Indeed. I am somewhat surprised. You know our policy of non-intervention in internal matters. That was made plain when we outlined the scope of our support for your administration. But please, continue." His hands formed a steeple, and he tapped his bottom lip, smiling.

Perspiration shone on the High Reeve's forehead. He hated dealing with the aliens, but he had no choice. They were his allies, like it or not, and this was their problem as much as his. Still, he would only tell them what was necessary. "The Pax has enlisted the help of Bikashi soldiers."

Lace's smile faded quickly. He placed his hands on his desk and leaned forward, speaking urgently, "There are more Bikashi? Are you sure? How many?"

"I have received word of at least ten, but there may be more." He didn't want to admit to Vogel's escape because the incompetence of the Chief reflected poorly on all Avanauri. "The one called Vogel, who was in our custody, was freed by a band of Pharlaxians accompanied by Bikashi soldiers."

The admiral's face was impassive, but the High Reeve noted the change in color. "My men were ambushed while transporting Vogel to Dominion Island. We had intended handing him over to you." He paused. "The most worrisome thing is, other than Vogel, we'd no idea these *Biletung* were here at all. There could be a lot more of them skulking in the mountains with the Pax."

Lace didn't respond for a moment, and then he seemed to make up his mind. "Yonni, thank you for your honesty. I need to consider the issues you have raised. I can assure you that whatever we can do, we will do, but I need to discuss this with my superiors. The presence of a significant force of the nonaligned on Prosperine is a complication and something I agree we will need to deal with together. I'll contact you in two hours."

The screen went blank. The High Reeve pressed the pushbutton once more and returned to his office.

◆◆◆

"Hickory, this is as serious as it gets." Her father's image almost bristled with the intensity of his feelings. "I wouldn't ask this of you—especially you—if there was any alternative."

He outlined his concerns about the Bikashi and his fear that a successful revolution by the Pharlaxians would lead to a total fracturing of the Alliance's objectives on Prosperine. "If there were only a few rogue Bikashi to deal with, then maybe we would risk extracting them, but there's at least a squad, maybe a platoon. Worse, we know this Vogel is highly regarded by his superiors, and he is clearly here at their behest. Taking him out of the equation would be messy and construed as an act of war on our part, and we don't want to risk a full-scale conflagration with the non-aligned—not at this time."

Hickory raised her eyebrows and crossed her arms. "Unless there's no other option, of course," she said.

He sighed. "You're right—unless there's no other option. We can't afford to let the non-aligned beat us to the punch on this. The stakes are too high. As it is, I'm not sure whether you will achieve anything by going in. I just don't have any better ideas."

She couldn't detect any dissemblance in him, but he'd always been a master at keeping things close to his chest. She changed the subject. "Have you been keeping tabs on Jess and Mack?"

"We were, but we lost them in the hills south of Birregur. They're too far away to contact via SIM, and our deal with the Avanauri government prohibits the import of alien technology to Prosperine. That includes using orbital surveillance equipment over inhabited areas. They're paranoid, they don't fully trust us, and they are adamant. "We took a risk and put a GPS chip into the heel of Mack's shoe, but the signal is dead. I hope it hasn't been discovered."

"What exactly do you want me to do?"

The admiral let out a huge breath and nodded several times before answering. "Find where the Bikashi are holed up, get a headcount, and figure out what their involvement is. They might be here as trainers or advisers—not combat troops." He paused. "Also, I'm going to send a package to the consulate for you. I've arranged for a leather sword belt to be made with a secret pouch containing a transmitting device. If anyone asks, the belt is a birthday present from your father. The transmitter is voice-activated. You get the information to us, and we will do the rest. And, Hickory, don't get caught."

Hickory wondered what he meant by "the rest" but didn't ask. *Sometimes, it's better not to know.*

She expected him to sign off, but he cleared his throat instead. "When you've completed this mission,

I'd like you to consider spending a few days with me."

She was taken aback but recovered quickly. "A few days with you? Why? Where? I mean—"

"We'll have a debriefing, of course, but it would be good if we could spend some personal time together—get to know each other better."

She was instantly suspicious. "Why the change of heart all of a sudden?"

"I've been mulling things over. Maybe I've been too wrapped up in my work, a little unfair to you especially. If we nullify this threat, we could end up working with each other more often. There are some things we need to talk about. Clear the air and so forth…"

Three days with her father. "I'll think about it," she said.

The transmitter turned out to be an amplifier for her SIM. It boosted its reach by a factor of two hundred. Considering her empathic power, that would mean an effective range of about eight hundred miles. Just powerful enough to contact the *Jabberwocky* in orbit if it was directly overhead, but it only worked one way—she could send but couldn't receive.

◆ ◆ ◆

Hickory was beginning to regret her choice of transport. She'd opted to ride a yarrak named Titus rather than use a wagon on the basis that she would cross the wild outback hills and deserts more quickly. After only two days of being jerked and swung around by the ungainly yarrak, Hickory was stiff and saddle-sore. Still, she thought, as she brushed the dust from the beast's back, at least he was warm and didn't seem to mind her company at night.

She tethered Titus to a nearby tree with enough leaves for him to munch on and lit a fire. The evening light show was beginning, and curtains of green and red danced in the north. She settled down to study the map Brandt had given her.

From beyond the glow of her campfire, a twig snapped, sounding like a rifle shot in the still night. Her head jerked upright, and her heartbeat raced as she saw a figure limned against the aurora. She gripped her sword. She'd been told that bandits were a frequent occurrence this far from Ezekan.

"Fear not," spoke the apparition. "I am but a traveler seeking a place to rest my head for the night. I would enjoy sharing the warmth of your fire and any morsel of food you can spare."

"Come into the light," said Hickory. She rose to her feet and slid the sword from her belt.

"You won't need that, Hickory," said Kar-sèr-Sephiryth as his form materialized from the darkness.

Hickory gasped and took an impulsive step toward the Teacher. "What—what are you doing here?" Her relief was quickly followed by confusion at his

The Alien Corps

unexpected presence.

"It will take some time to recount that story. But, if you put down your sword, I will tell you." His blue eyes sparkled with amusement.

A flush spread across Hickory's cheeks. "Of course." She laughed, embarrassed because her sword still pointed at the Teacher. She led the way to the fire and nodded to a place beside her. "Please, uh, make yourself comfortable." She busied herself to cover up her confusion, pouring hot java and offering dried fruit from her store of provisions. "We have time, Teacher. The night is long."

"Indeed, and it will become darker before the sun rises." He sat and gazed at the fire, then began, "My brothers and I were gathered in the town of Hartlepool, not far from the city. We were discussing rumors of unrest from beyond the Ice Mountains in the North. It seems there are distressing signs the old ways are being revived, and a new warrior-leader has emerged amongst the Erlach." He paused, shaking his head slightly.

Hickory looked at him keenly. *That's the first time I've seen him troubled.*

The Teacher gathered his cloak about him and continued. "I received a warning that a Pharlaxian mob was nearby, apparently looking for me. I intended to confront them, but when the time came, some of my followers became angry and started to argue with the mob. They were in danger, and I did not want harm to befall them, so I allowed my captors to take me. They bound my hands and bundled me out of town in the back of a cart."

The love this naur has for his people, that he would risk his life for them. "Why were the Pharlaxians so keen to take you prisoner?"

"They have some plan for me that requires they keep me alive. Otherwise, I would not be speaking with you now." He laughed.

The sound was like a bubbling, sparkling brook in Hickory's ears. She felt a flutter in her stomach. *Get a hold of yourself, Hickory. You're as bad as Gareth.* The memory of her lost friend jolted her back to reality.

The Teacher continued with his story. "We journeyed without sleep for three days and nights until we reached Tontine. As we entered the village, we were met by half a dozen warriors covered from head to toe in dark cloth—not even their eyes were visible."

He nodded his head, looking grimly at Hickory. "The Pharlaxians who captured me were afraid of these newcomers. They would not look at them nor ride beside them but followed some distance behind for three days until we reached the mountains." He took a long draught from the mug and selected a dried fruit that he chewed on while he spoke.

"The Pharlaxian base camp," said Hickory.

The Alien Corps

"Yes. The leader of the newcomers rode beside me, and we talked about many things along the way. He could not hide his ambitions from me, though he tried. He had a harsh tongue and allowed me to glimpse his face—I think to frighten me—but I have seen its like before and do not frighten easily. You refer to his kind as Bikashi. The leader's name was Vogel." He smiled. "I fear many things in this world, but monsters are not among them. "

The Teacher struck Hickory as someone who wouldn't be afraid of much at all. She had already guessed the soldiers were Bikashi—the same who had massacred the peacekeepers and liberated their leader. Hickory studied the mysterious naur. Other than a few specks of dust on his clothes, he might have just emerged from the temple in Ezekan. She wanted to ask him so many questions—and, she realized with a start that not all of them strictly related to her job. Tentatively, she reached for his thoughts but pulled away before making contact. She experienced an overwhelming feeling it would be vulgar to intrude.

"How did you break free from them?" she said.

"At that point, I did not attempt to escape, although I could have done so easily enough. I was curious about them and wanted to know what they were doing in Avanaux. Vogel evaded many of my questions, but he was eager to understand the Avanauri philosophy on life and death and our ethical ideals.

"This Bikashi is tenacious and believes in the righteousness of his cause, but he was troubled, and he revealed more to me than he intended. He told a strange tale about a Bikashi soldier who defeated his enemy in battle, then tortured him physically and emotionally to near death."

"Typical Bikashi modus operandi," said Hickory sourly. "I don't suppose he offered any rationale or excuse for the cruelty?"

Kar-sèr-Sephiryth raised his eyes from the fire, looked to the stars, and sighed. "He said it was done to obtain vital information—something that would ensure the survival of his species. He asked me whether I thought the soldier's actions were justified. Would Balor condemn or praise him for his deeds?"

Despite her cynicism, Hickory was intrigued. It was a paradox. To what extent could someone knowingly commit evil and still deserve God's forgiveness? Does God consider extenuating circumstances when making His judgment? Prefect Cortherien would say God's love is infinite. He had sacrificed his son to save the human race from eternal damnation. She wondered how the Teacher had responded to the conundrum, given that he might still turn out to be the victim in the story.

"I could offer no answer. Who can truly know the mind of Balor?" They sat in silence for a few minutes,

The Alien Corps

and then he continued, "We arrived at their camp, a stronghold for Sequana's rebel forces, and I was brought before him in chains. He told me his intention was to publicly humiliate and execute me to mark the start of their revolution. I have no wish to be the trigger for a bloody war, although war seems inevitable."

He reached for Hickory's hand and looked earnestly into her eyes. "It is the human condition to wage war, is it not? It is also so on Prosperine. But one day, there will be peace in every heart. This, I believe." His gaze traveled to the pendant around her neck. "That is an unusual necklace. May I see it?"

Hickory handed it to him, and he held it gently in his hands, a smile passing across his face. "Tell me about this."

"It belonged to my great-grandmother and has been passed down to me."

"Ah, yes, but what is the symbolism—what does it represent?"

Hickory's heart pounded. What should she tell him? Perhaps it was a mistake to bring it with her to Prosperine. If she told him the story of Christ, it would contaminate her investigation. "It is a symbol of forgiveness in my world."

He reluctantly returned the crucifix to her. "There is something beautiful and inspiring about this keepsake."

Empathy flooded Hickory. She felt she would weep from the tenderness she sensed. She swallowed and said, "How did you escape the stronghold?"

"In truth, quite easily. One of the guards is a cousin to my first disciple, Jacob. He was caught up in the Pharlaxian cause when he was young but has become disillusioned of late. I convinced him to leave my cell door unlocked."

Hickory was surprised. She suspected there might be more to the story but didn't press. Instead, she asked what was uppermost in her mind. "You didn't, by any chance, come across my friend, Jess? She was headed in the direction you've come from. I've lost touch, and I'm trying to find her."

The Teacher put down his empty mug. "I saw Jess and one other in the Pharlaxian stronghold. Their transport and belongings have been confiscated, but they are in no immediate danger." He smiled. "They have been picking wildflowers and herbs, I believe."

Warmth radiated through Hickory's body. Jess and Mack were alive and apparently unharmed. Maybe they would be able to find a way out of this mess. "Tomorrow, will you show me where to find her?" she said.

"Jess has a good heart, and I would help if I could," replied the preacher. He pulled his cloak around him and lay down, facing the fire. "But, I am weary and must rest now."

The Alien Corps

"One last question, Teacher, please? She leaned forward, touching his sleeve."

"Only one, Hickory?" He smiled at her and lifted himself onto an elbow.

"One for now, then." She grinned and waited until he nodded, then said, "When we first met, how…how did you know my name?" Her heart beat wildly.

His smile faded. "This is what you would ask of all possible questions?"

"For now," she repeated.

He sighed, "Very well. Kyntai told me."

"Kyntai told you?" Hickory's face went slack, and she paled slightly. "When… why?" she spluttered.

"The boy is one of my most attentive students. I saw him with Gareth that day on the hill. Afterward, he came to me seeking solace. It was natural for him to talk about you and Jess, and later, he pointed you out to me."

Hickory let her head drop to her chest. She didn't know whether she should feel relieved or disappointed.

"You should not blame the boy," said the Teacher, looking into her eyes.

"No, no. I don't blame Kyntai for anything." She raised her head, smiling. "That's one less mystery I need to worry about. Thank you."

"Rest well, Hickory."

Hickory would have talked more, but Kar-sèr-Sephiryth fell immediately into a deep sleep. She pulled her blanket around her and tried to settle without success. The naur beside her, by his own admission, had allowed himself to be arrested and then fortuitously escaped from a locked prison. He'd "convinced" the guard to let him go? Then he'd walked through the desert and rough country for days, yet looked as fresh as if he'd been out for a stroll in the garden. He didn't seem to bear any grudge towards his captors or have any concern he might be retaken by them. What sort of being was he? A miracle worker by some accounts, a charlatan by others. It was early morning before she eventually stopped tossing and turning and drifted into a fitful slumber.

Charakai

Hickory awoke late to find Kar-sèr-Sephiryth gone. There was no sign he'd ever been there. She was almost prepared to believe it was all a dream. Almost. She was disappointed because she'd taken the Teacher at his word. He said he would help, and she'd trusted him. She felt let down and irritated at herself for being gullible.

Dog-tired from her sleepless night, it wasn't until after she'd eaten a breakfast of corn cakes and coffee that she noticed the lettering in the sand. It was a squiggle with the word *Ctarak* above it and an arrow pointing northwest.

She climbed aboard Titus and resumed her battle with saddle-soreness, heartened by at least knowing Jess was safe—if she could believe the Teacher.

It was late afternoon, and the sun still blazed in the sky. Hickory sought shelter beneath the spreading branches of a lone tree, fed and watered Titus, and then sat down to eat some of her meager rations. She gazed out over the horizon, shimmering in the heat.

P J McDermott

After the lush vegetation on Dominion Island and the teeming life in Ezekan City, it was quite a contrast to encounter the hot, searing conditions of the savanna. *It's a wonder anything grows here, never mind intelligent life forms.* She closed her eyes for a second and woke in fright two hours later. She jumped to her feet, swinging wildly around, but saw nothing to alarm her. Her heart slowed to normal, and she berated her timidity.

The sun had sunk low in the sky, and the day's intense heat had diminished somewhat. She spotted a dark cloud over a distant rise. At first, Hickory thought it was a mirage, the last vestiges of the shimmering heat rising from the sand, but as she watched, the shadow grew more substantial and spread. *Whatever it is, it seems to be moving quickly—and in this direction.* She took the spyglass from her saddle pack and focused it on the approaching darkness. *A local storm? No. Birds or bats, maybe.*

A high-pitched screech preceded their arrival. Titus huffed and puffed, tugging at the reins that secured him to the tree. His eyes rolled in his head. "Easy, Titus. What's the matter, boy? It's only some birds." She tried to soothe him by patting his trembling nose, but he reared up, shook his head to break the rope, and galloped away.

"What the—" Hickory pursued him but gave up quickly. The cloud was now much nearer and had

The Alien Corps

resolved into individual dots. The dots grew bigger, and now she could see they were neither bats nor birds but reptiles with flapping leathery wings. They circled overhead, and she could clearly make out the long beaks, saw-edged teeth, and sharp claws. Titus's frightened bawling reached them, and the flock veered towards the yarrak.

Titus doesn't stand a chance. He'll be ripped to shreds. Three of the creatures turned towards her. She could sense their primitive minds being readied to rend and tear. *Fresh flesh. Eat. Mine, mine!*

Images of the creatures devouring her while she was still alive flashed through her mind, tearing chunks of flesh from her body and squabbling over her eyes, toes, fingers. Adrenaline flooded through her, sending her heartbeat racing and strengthening her muscles. Primal fear overcame reason, and she ran for her life.

One of the reptiles swooped and clipped her head with its beak. Red-hot pain brought Hickory to her knees, but she struggled to her feet, pulling the sword from her belt as she did so. She ignored the warm blood flowing down her neck and slashed at the creature.

A second attack from the air sent her sprawling in the dirt, and she lost consciousness for a moment. Vague images of the reptiles circling above penetrated her stupor, and she felt something jar loose in her brain. *Is this to be my end?* The fear that triggered her flight evaporated, replaced by a deep sense of disgust. She would *not* end up in some *dinosaur's belly*. A moment's exhilaration was followed by an overwhelming sadness that these beautiful, unique creatures must die so she might live.

Anger followed, flaring up like a long-dormant volcano erupting in a pyroclastic explosion. She felt angry at the reptiles, at her father, at Cortherien, at the Alliance, but most of all, she was mad at herself. Her inner voice screamed at her. *What are you doing in this place? You shouldn't have come here. You're not fit to lead a mission like this. Are you going to lie here and let these monsters eat you? Give up without a fight? Die then!*

In a tiny corner of her mind, she realized her responses were extreme, that her limbic system was operating erratically, but she had no control over her rampaging emotions. Indeed, she welcomed the onslaught of fury.

Guilt, shame, and doubt vanished, but her rage escalated with no definable cause. Burst after burst of dazzling white light struck at her optic nerves. She cried out, blinded.

The pain and her anger doubled and redoubled, one building on the other until she felt she would explode into a billion stars and fill the universe with her hatred and her torment. It hurt. It hurt so much, but she would not stop—could not stop—the surge of power building in her.

What is happening to me? She rolled onto her knees, gripping her head in both hands as the acrid odor of electrical energy crackled in her nostrils. The memories of her mother's anguish lying dormant for so many years now crashed through the barriers erected by the surgeons when she was sixteen and flooded the neural pathways of her brain with a massive positive charge.

Hickory's SIM implant responded by creating a magnetic field that surrounded and penetrated her skull. At that moment, synapses were severed, and new networks were created.

Hickory felt her pain abruptly metamorphose into a fierce, malleable force.

Like a moth in its cocoon, her empathic power battered at its confinement, struggling to grow and be free.

Images of every rotten thing she'd ever endured attacked her mind. Once more, she lived through her mother's suffering and death, saw again Gareth's broken body, felt the desolation of her father's rejection, relived her failed love affair with Jacob and the devastating loss of their miscarried child, and experienced the ache caused by her failures and sacking from the Corps.

Her power wrapped all her negative emotions in layer after layer of reassurance, comfort, and love from her mother, her nonna, the Teacher, Jess, and poor, dead Gareth. And it was enough. The moth emerged fully formed, magnificent in its power, able to compel and persuade and encourage and coax so her will would be done.

"Go away!" she roared.

The nearest flying reptiles stopped in mid-air. Those swarming above the yarrak fluttered for a few seconds as though disoriented, and then all flew back in the direction from which they'd come. Hickory's mind was afire. Her focus remained on the creatures, aware of her control over them.

Come here. She projected her thoughts at the departing cloud and saw them change direction toward her.

Settle. The reptiles landed on the ground in front of her. She knew their minds, pure thoughts of hunger and the joy of flight, and for a second, she was one with them.

We are Charakai.

They were silent now, watching her, awaiting her next command. *Home.* As one, the flock rose and headed off into the distance, shrieking as they went.

Hickory fell to the ground. Her mouth tasted the sourness of bile, and her head buzzed with images and sounds, both real and imagined. She couldn't comprehend what had just happened, but she knew she'd changed, and it frightened her. She needed the medical supplies that had disappeared with the yarrak. *Titus*, she thought, more in despair than expectation, and then she fell into a deep sleep.

◆◆◆

Hickory, help me!

The nuzzling of the beast's snout roused her from the bizarre dream. She'd been lost in a fog so thick she'd been able to part it with her hands, but the faster she shoveled it aside, the denser the mist seemed to become. A distant voice called to her, and she recognized it as Gareth's. She'd tried desperately to find him, but as soon as she thought she was getting nearer, the voice would cry out from another direction.

Titus's tongue rasped at her cheek and brought her to the surface. It was pitch black. *How long have I been asleep?* Images of the Charakai surfaced in her mind, and she knew these were not memories but a distant connection she still maintained with the reptiles.

Hickory shivered, then struggled to her feet. She found the carry bags and rummaged through them for the analgesic tablets, a clean cloth, and the jar of antiseptic ointment. She applied the balm, dabbing at the cut on her head, then swallowed three pills with some of her remaining water.

Before falling asleep, she recalled the mantra she'd learned as a child. *I am calm and peaceful, like the boundless ocean. I am open-hearted and free, like the wind.*

When she awoke the following day, the yarrak was grazing on the leaves of the nearby trees. She stretched her arms and legs and rotated her head, slowly checking for residual pain. The wound on her skull still throbbed, but her head was clear.

She lit a fire to brew some coffee and considered the events of the previous evening. Never had she experienced such an outpouring of psychic suggestion, not even before she'd learned how to moderate the intensity of her empathic responses as a sixteen-year-old. It had flashed through her without her thinking about it in a moment of sheer terror. It was strange how the pterosaurs responded like they did, though. They weren't frightened by her outburst. Instead, they behaved more like soldiers obeying an officer's commands. And the way they'd gathered around her, silent and waiting, was uncanny.

And Titus? Had he responded to her call, too? She didn't think so. His brain was more developed than the others and would be less susceptible. More likely, he'd merely returned to her for the company once the danger passed. *Come.* She tested her theory, but the yarrak stayed where he was. *Titus,* she tried again. The brute cast an intelligent eye in her direction but otherwise remained unmoved.

She wished Jess were here, or Gareth. Poor Gareth, he would have had the answers. He'd always known the solution to every problem. She smiled at the memory, then mounted Titus and set off.

Hickory traveled most of that day and the next. She rode through pasture after pasture of goldengrass and then crossed the Ctarak River at a point where she felt she wouldn't be swept away by its wild currents. Following the Teacher's directions, she turned northwest and that night slept soundly by the banks of the Trasel.

By noon the following day, she'd crossed over the river and was nearing a range of distant hills when she saw a twinkle of light reflecting from the crest of a rocky outcrop. Quickly, she dismounted and lay down, pulling the spyglass from her pocket. It was too distant to make out anything. There it was again! Could that be a signal, light reflecting off something shiny, or the sun reflecting off the rock surface? She couldn't tell from this distance, but it was better to be cautious. Hickory altered her course so she would come to the ridge with the sun behind her.

Leaving Titus at the bottom of the rise, Hickory continued on foot. She worked her way around the side of the hill and climbed towards the peak. Hickory heard them before she saw them—two Avanauri chattering in an unknown dialect. Cautiously, she leaned over a ledge and looked down.

The nauris were sitting in a depression in the rocks, ten yards below her. They were absorbed in a game, throwing stones in the air and catching them on the way down. Every now and then, their heads bobbed up to survey the plains in front of them. Hickory's pulse raced when she saw one was carrying a laser-guided projectile rifle with a polished brass stock. The reflection from the metal was what had alerted her.

How had the Pharlaxians acquired the firearm? It was a blow to think that either the Bikashi or the Black Suns were supplying such weapons. Avanauri scientists were experimenting with explosives and pyroclastic liquids, but Hickory knew projectile weaponry was at least a generation away.

The rifle held by the Pharlaxian was an older model but far superior to the weapons the Ezekan army used. Traditionally, the Avanauri wore long swords or knives in their waistband and carried a longbow on their back. A small group with guns would make short work of a more numerous enemy.

Hickory crept away from the two guards and sat with her back against the bluff. Sequana's camp must be close by. She unclasped the golden pendant from her neck and placed it inside the hidden pouch of her sword belt alongside the transmitter. *If I'm going into the lion's den, I think the crucifix might attract too much attention.*

She crawled on her belly to the top of the ridge and stifled a gasp. A great tent city filled the crater of the extinct volcano below. This was what she'd been sent to find. She scanned the entire area slowly and spied a troop of Ezekani soldiers marching into a narrow cave almost directly beneath her. *Some of the city defenders must have defected.* She estimated the numbers of naurs, yarraks, and types of weaponry in the caldera as the admiral had asked, then attempted to contact Jess. Hickory worried when Jess didn't answer, but she rationalized that if she and Mack were inside the cave, the rock would prevent any signal from getting through.

The sun was low on the horizon. Dusk would be here soon, so she decided to wait, hoping she could slip past unnoticed.

A sudden commotion broke out amongst the troops below. Naurs were shouting and pointing towards the opposite hillside, where a lone figure scrambled up the rocks. "Kar-sèr-Sephiryth! Quickly! After him—don't let him get away," yelled an officer. Many soldiers rushed to obey, while those who remained were intent on the chase, shouting instructions to their comrades.

Hickory slid down the bank of scree to the cave entrance and slipped inside. The Teacher had been as good as his word, she thought. She hoped he managed to evade the pursuit.

◆◆◆

She leaned against the wall and crept along the tunnel, her senses tuned to any sound or movement that might herald discovery. A hundred meters from the entrance, she came upon an opening to her left. She glanced around the corner. It was an empty antechamber. She stepped inside and stopped, startled, as she came face to face with a Bikashi soldier.

He'd been in a latrine cubicle and was just as surprised to see her but slower to respond. Hickory brought her arm up and unleashed a karate blow to his neck. The soldier recovered, partly deflected the chop with one arm, and sent a right fist into Hickory's stomach. She doubled over in pain and staggered backward, gasping for air. The Bikashi followed up his advantage. He lunged and threw his powerful arms around her, applying a bear hug. She could feel her spine being forced unnaturally backward. The soldier was intent on crushing her, and she could smell the sourness of his breath as he grunted with the effort. The pressure on her lungs intensified. She couldn't breathe.

Hickory felt herself begin to lose consciousness. She jammed her forearms under his and reached for his face, forcing it backward. She searched with her fingers for the eyeholes in his mask and squeezed. Her opponent shrieked and let her go. Hickory gasped with relief, then spun to face her enemy. She struck, stiff-armed, at his chin, and the Bikashi's head jolted back, his eyes closed, and he slumped to the ground.

Her head was spinning, and she felt her stomach

heave. She sucked in some deep breaths and leaned over, her head between her knees, and managed to stop herself from retching. *Close, very close. I'm lucky this one was alone.* She wiped her mouth on her sleeve, took a couple more deep breaths, and glanced around. A dirty, half-filled cup rested on a wooden table with half a dozen chairs scattered around it.

She stooped over the Bikashi and checked for a pulse. *Steady. Should be awake in half an hour or so.* Hickory removed his helmet and studied her adversary. *Ugly mother's son. No wonder he wears a mask. Good fighter, though.* She dragged the soldier over to a corner behind the doorway, removed his overgarment, then took some rope from her backpack and bound his hands and feet. For good measure, she gagged his mouth with his own shirt, slowly opened the door, glanced left and right, and stepped into the corridor.

She strode purposefully, wearing the Bikashi helmet and hiding her sword beneath her cloak. Those she encountered moved quickly out of the way to let her pass. She emerged from the tunnel onto a terraced platform overlooking a vast underground chamber. She thought it was like Aladdin's cave—the rock walls were crusted with multicolored stones that sparkled in the light from hundreds of flaming torches.

Enthusiastic applause and shouts of approval rose from the cavern below, and hundreds of Pharlaxian zealots rushed to the barrier wall to see what was happening. Hickory pushed her way to the front. A column of Avanauri troops in full battle armor marched into the arena and snapped to attention in front of a naur seated on a throne. Hickory felt a tightening in her chest as she recognized Sequana. He wore a lustrous silver cape and carried a ceremonial staff in one hand. His features were severe as he inspected the soldiers in front of him. When Sequana rose from his seat and raised the staff above his head, cheers erupted from the watching crowd.

The Pharlaxian leader turned his face upwards, and Hickory instinctively drew back. She collided accidentally with a nauri and bowed low, murmuring an apology. As she moved away, she became acutely aware she was over-tall for a Bikashi warrior. Then she realized all the Bikashi troops were standing in a group, keeping their distance from the crowd. She felt a flutter of panic. *Of course, the troops would want to avoid physical contact with the Avanauri.* Her camouflage now worked against her. She was no longer invisible. She needed to find Jess and Mack quickly and leave this place. *Where would they be?* Were they prisoners or guests, as Kar-sèr-Sephiryth had said? She tried her SIM again, more in hope than with any expectation of success. There was only silence.

Hickory glanced over her shoulder. The nauri she'd bumped into was tugging at the arm of a guard

The Alien Corps

and pointing in her direction. She spun on her heels and kept moving despite the guard's cry of "Halt!" Not knowing where it might lead, she turned into the nearest passageway and broke into a run.

The bola whistled loudly as the weights at each end of the cord spun through the air and wrapped itself around her legs. Her momentum carried her forward, and she crashed to the ground, knocking her head on a rock.

Hickory opened her eyes and tried to push herself onto her knees but slumped to the ground. Her skull felt like someone was beating on it with a club. She'd taken a lot of headshots in the last couple of days, from the Charakai attack and the Bikashi soldier in the antechamber. Hickory felt disoriented. *Where am I?*

The memory of her capture returned with a rush, and she clutched at her neck, seeking her pendant before remembering it was safely hidden. *Lucky I was wearing the helmet,* she thought, then realized her helmet cloak, sword, and knife had been taken from her. A familiar scent caused her to lift her head.

"Ah, the Earth woman—delivered into our hands by Balor, the just." Sequana laughed mockingly at her through the bars.

"This is indeed most fortuitous. Guards! Make sure her cell is secure. I don't want her leaving prematurely like our previous guests. If this one escapes, I'll have your heads on pikes and those of your wives and children, too." His voice faded as Hickory lapsed into unconsciousness once more.

Alone

Morning and night, they dragged her in front of the Pharlaxian leaders. Invariably, they asked the same questions. "Who are you working for? Why are you here?" And every day that Hickory remained silent, they made her suffer.

Sequana's lieutenants queried why she was allowed to live. He prodded the charts outlining Ezekan's defenses and armament displacement, saying, "This is our goal. Conquer the city, and all Avanaux will bow to us. We must not allow ourselves to be distracted from this task. Should we kill the Earth-girl? Possibly, but if we do, and her masters discover this, there will be reprisals. We do not know their strength, but I surmise it to be substantial—perhaps enough to delay us, perhaps enough to stop us altogether. No, I will not provide them with an excuse to interfere. We shall keep this one alive. There is no threat to us while she remains captive."

That did not deter them from trying to extract what information they could, short of killing her. Once a day, they provided Hickory with a bowl of porridge, a piece of cornbread, and a pint of water. If she was lucky, she would find a small slab of honeycomb or a few nuts hidden in her porridge. Hickory wondered which of her guards was prepared to risk Sequana's wrath to do her this small kindness.

Each evening, after stubbornly refusing to answer the Pharlaxian's questions, she was bundled off to her dark-eyed torturer. Tèkan sèra Sorbanne possessed a fiendish obsession with terror and took a mad pride in her professional skills.

At their first meeting, she'd circled Hickory slowly and explained, "Torture is an art form." She drew the tails of her whip across the palm of her hand. "Excruciating pain can be inflicted immediately, of course, if time is short. But unfortunately, there have been instances where the prisoner has died before the knowledge can be extracted."

Tèkan smiled and caressed Hickory's shoulder with the lash. "Much better, when time permits, that the information we seek is drawn out one piece at a time, using an instrument perfectly matched to the subject's persona."

She walked behind Hickory and whispered in her ear. "Sometimes, the anticipation alone can cause a prisoner to tell much of what they know, but I always discover more.

"This is one of my favorite pieces," she said, trailing her fingers along a row of implements laid out neatly on a bench and picking up a metal face mask. The mask was eyeless with a gauze-covered grill for the mouth and leather straps that fastened behind the head. A slow, devilish smile spread over the torturer's features, and she forced the mask against Hickory's face.

Hickory struggled, but the two guards held her firm. It was black as pitch inside the mask. Hickory's breath came quickly, hot against her face.

Tèkan said, "Yes, I think this is for you. It is a little slower, but it has never failed me." She removed the mask, laid it to one side, and walked to a cage on the bench. She put her hand inside and gently lifted out a tiny creature. "This is my pet, Sasha. Isn't she pretty?" She stroked the animal's head and held it close for Hickory to see.

Hickory's mind filled with dread. The creature was small, about the size of a field mouse, but its teeth and claws were like needles. It rubbed its ear affectionately against Tèkan's finger. "Sasha is pregnant. This will be her seventh litter. She will give birth sometime in the next ten days." She blew gently on the creature, then dropped it into the upturned mask and rammed it against Hickory's face.

Desperately, Hickory held back the scream that would mean her opening her mouth, and she squeezed her eyes and lips tightly together. Her pulse pounded in her temple, and her breath snorted in quick bursts through her nose. The tiny creature scuttled between the mask and her face, scampering over her eyes, poking its snout into Hickory's nose and into an ear, mewling and seeking a way to escape.

Tèkan held the mask in place for a few seconds before removing it and putting the frightened animal back in its cage. "Sasha's kind are compelled to give birth in the light of day. She will do anything and go to whatever lengths are necessary to make sure this takes place. She cannot eat through the mask, but she will burrow through your cheeks or neck to escape when her time is near." She smiled at Hickory. "Sasha is a caring mother."

Back in her cell, Hickory couldn't free her mind from the smile or the glint of madness in Tèkan's black eyes. When the horror subsided enough to let her nod off into a nightmare-filled sleep, the guards woke her every hour until it was time to see Sequana again.

Each day, the mask was strapped to her face only for a few minutes. Each day, the creature became more agitated, and by the end of the first week, Hickory's face was bloodied by small slashes and punctures.

In the middle of the second week, her face became infected, and one eye remained closed, crusted with pus. Tèkan doubled her agony by breaking a finger or removing a fingernail—one each day. When they returned Hickory to her cell, the pain and anticipation of what would inevitably happen caused her to

The Alien Corps

hallucinate.

She imagined Sasha and her family were in the cell, staring at her. In her demented state, she tried to convince the creatures to leave as she'd done with the Charakai, but they refused to go. Starved, mentally and physically exhausted, she realized she could hold out no longer. Tomorrow or the next day, the animal would start her birthing sequence, and in her panic to reach the light, she would rip through a cheek or an eye socket and gnaw her way to freedom.

Hickory awoke the following day to find her daily meal had been delivered while she'd slept. Alongside her porridge lay a damp cloth and a small jar of ointment. Crying softly, she thanked her benefactor, wiped the blood and grime from her face, and smeared on the balm as best she could with her broken fingers. The healing properties of the salve relieved the incessant itching she had borne, and she was able to think more clearly about her situation.

She wondered whether the torture would stop, even if she told Sequana the truth, but she knew Tèkan loved her work and Sasha too much for her to stop now. She decided that the next time they took her to Sasha, she would crush the little creature with her teeth until it was dead. She would see how much Tèkan liked that.

The guards did not come for her in the evening as they usually did, so she fell asleep on the cell floor. She woke with a thin shaft of light playing on her from the window high on a wall. From this, she judged it must be past morning. Her body shook from a fever, and her hands and feet were bound. *They must have done this while I slept. But why?*

She struggled to release the ropes, but the knots were too tight. Something wasn't right. It felt too quiet. Soldiers should have been on the parade ground, but the usual sounds of clashing swords and lances were absent. Usually, the chieftains would be shouting encouragement to their charges by now. Perhaps they'd all been called to the cavern for some reason. She crawled across the floor on her elbows to protect her broken fingers until her back reached the wall and then forced herself to her feet.

She hopped to the cell door and pressed an ear against the wood. Nothing. Were the guards asleep, or were they at a meeting, too? She shouted as loudly as she could, but there was no response. Hickory searched the cell but found neither food nor water. She was starving and thirsty. Sliding to the floor, she closed her eyes and waited for her jailers to return.

When she woke again, it was dark, and there was still no sign of the Pharlaxians. Thanks to the ointment, her face seemed a little less painful. She thought about that. Did the one who left the medication know everyone would be called away? It seemed likely, given that the jar and cloth were left in

The Alien Corps

plain sight.

She felt hot tears roll down her cheeks. Surely, they must have left someone to guard the prisoners? She called until she was hoarse, becoming more desperate as the minutes passed. She realized no one would come. The fighters were gone, the guards were gone, and the other prisoners had disappeared, too. Hickory had been abandoned, left here to die.

"Help me, help me!" she croaked, hoping her amulet was still transmitting. She knew it was unlikely to work in this stone complex, but her father wouldn't come for her even if it did.

He can't interfere. He won't interfere. His precious duty won't let him.

The Admiral had never come when she needed him. He'd always left her to her own resources, pretending it was for her own good. It would make her strong, he'd promised, able to handle whatever life threw at her and be independent.

Bullshit!

He was just plain selfish. He is only interested in his career. He kept enough room in his busy schedule for only one child. His precious, sycophantic son—sucking up to him to extract a morsel of consideration, panting after him like a puppy, dependent on his approval, always seeking some sign of love. Not she! She had no problem admitting the Admiral didn't love her. That's how she thought of him these days.

The Admiral, with a capital A. It was more fitting than "father." The only act of fatherhood he'd ever performed was to plant the seed of life in her mother's belly.

She lay back against the cold wall of her prison, drained by the bitterness of her feelings. Her thoughts strayed to the baby that had begun to develop in her womb, the son who'd never had any chance at life, and she wept. He would have been three years old today.

She'd waited so long since the disaster of Aquarius IV to have a second chance to prove herself, only to fail again. She shivered. Her father's image came to her once more. She would never see him again. She wouldn't be able to tell him about her baby. There was an ache in her heart and a piece missing from her soul. *My life story. I'm going to die here. I'm going to freeze or starve to death or, more likely, die of thirst.*

The face of the Teacher swam into her vision. *Is he truly the Son of God, the Messiah come to save us all?* Now, she would never know. She giggled crazily. *Unless I meet him when I die, and he's sitting across from me at the right hand of the Father.* Would he appear to her like Jesus or like Kar? She laughed out loud, then forced herself to concentrate.

He was unusual. The strangest and, at the same time, the most giving, gentlest person she'd ever met. Hickory recalled how she'd felt when Kar touched her shoulder. Peace. Beautiful, all-encompassing peace. And forgiveness, and love, unfettered love for all … for her.

She struggled to release her sword belt, praying the pendant was still where she'd placed it. Relieved, she clasped it close to her breast. *What would Talya do in my position? She wouldn't waste her time blaming others or wallow in self-pity over missed chances.* She had the feeling Talya would never, ever, give up.

Hickory had hoped for years that her father would return, walk into her life again, and fill it with light, and she would have welcomed him—she knew that. Even now. His lack of affection for her hurt, yes, terribly, searingly, no matter how hard she tried to push it away. The Teacher had shown her she could still love her father—did always love him, she realized with shock. *I wish I'd done something more. Too late now.*

She could feel the cold seep into her bones and the lethargy overcoming her will. Her head drooped.

I forgive you, Dad. I love you, Dad.

❖❖❖

She woke to the tickle of a spider crawling up her arm. She shook it away, shivering and yelling in terror as it scurried into some hidden cranny. Ever since her mission in Aquarius, she'd held an irrational fear of spiders.

A sound in the corridor outside broke through her

fear, causing her heart to surge with hope. Someone or something was nearby. She heard a murmur of voices.

"Help me!" It came out as a croak. "Help!" she repeated, louder this time. She heard an excited shout and saw the door at the end of the corridor burst open.

"Hickory! Thank God!" Jess ran to her cell with Mack at her side. They unlocked and pushed the bars aside. Jess knelt and held a water bag to her cracked lips, then loosened her bonds.

Hickory stared wide-eyed. I*s this another illusion?* Her voice broke as she saw her friend leaning over her. "Jess? Good old Jess. Good old, reliable Jess. Have you come to rescue me?" Her swollen lips formed a faint smile.

Jess looked into her eyes and felt her forehead. "She's burning up," she said anxiously.

"I'll get the meds from the saddlebag," said Mack as he hurried from the cell.

Hickory gulped greedily and grasped Jess's arm, afraid she would disappear.

Jess gently extracted the pendant from her bloody hands and placed it over Hickory's head.

"How did you find me? Did my father—"

"Kar-sèr-Sephiryth," Jess said. "We were passing Torane about halfway to Ezekan when we saw a crowd gathered. It was the Teacher and his followers.

The Alien Corps

Kar was shocked to see us there without you. When we sorted out our stories and realized you must still be in the Pax's camp, we rushed here as quickly as we could."

"It would have been pretty funny if you'd arrived, and I'd already gone." *Or maybe not so funny if I was dead.* Hickory shivered. "Did you tell the admiral what was happening here?"

"I haven't spoken with your father since we left the city four weeks ago. But Kar said he would go on to Ezekan and pass on the information to the high priest and your father."

Mack returned with a blanket and wrapped it around her. He took a pouch from his saddlebag, measured some of the contents into a bowl, and pounded them with the handle of his knife to release a thick, milky liquid. He combined the extract with some water and forced her to swallow it. "Drink up, Hickory. This brew doesn't smell too great, but the Teacher said if you have any injuries, this will help you heal more quickly. He thought it might come in handy."

Hickory swallowed the potion. It tasted vile, but Mack insisted she finish it.

Mack continued, "Before we caught up with Kar in Torane, we ran into the Pharlaxian army camped between the Ctarak and Trasel rivers. We stayed there long enough to get a count and then gave them a wide berth. The next day, we bumped into the Teacher. If we'd known you were in such a bad way, we would have moved more quickly. I'm sorry."

She wasn't sure whether he was sorry for arriving late or for forcing her to drink the disgusting medicine.

Jess wore a guilty look on her face. She flushed and couldn't meet Hickory's eyes.

Hickory glanced at Mack, then back to Jess. The rebel army wasn't the only thing that delayed them. "It's all right, Jess. I don't blame you for anything. You deserve whatever happiness you can find in your life. I'm happy for you both—honestly, I am. And the Intel you have on Sequana will be vital. Help me up. I need food and drink—lots of drink."

Jess and Mack filled her in while she ate. Perhaps it was the concoction Mack prepared, but the dry bread and rations tasted like a sumptuous feast, and she had to force herself to concentrate on what they were saying.

"We estimated two thousand Avanauri soldiers were at the camp, but more were arriving all the time. Most were armed with swords and knives, but about fifty carried assault rifles—Bikashi assault rifles. We saw about thirty Bikashi in the vanguard, armed to the teeth but wearing only light body armor. They're not expecting too much opposition."

Hickory was dismayed. *A platoon of fully armed*

The Alien Corps

Bikashi soldiers? If they fought the Ezekan army in the field, it would be a massacre. Then again, if he had any sense, the High Reeve wouldn't send many, if any, of his troops into direct combat. Much better to defend the city from behind its walls.

Mack filled in some of the missing pieces. "Our intel places the number of government forces at around two thousand regular troops inside the city walls and probably another six thousand or so volunteers. But they all carry traditional weapons, including fixed crossbows on the walls—easy pickings for the Bikashi. But that's not the worst part." He paused, looking at Jess to continue.

"Go on, Jess," said Hickory. "Give me the whole story, and then we can get out of here."

"Look at your face and hands. My God, what did they do to you? We're not going anywhere until you get some sleep and feel a bit stronger. I'm not having you dying on me."

Hickory swore. She was sore and weary, but things were moving fast, and she needed to get to Ezekan if she was going to be able to change anything. The Alliance and the Avanauri administration needed the complete picture of the enemy's strength. "Tell me now, Jess. I can sleep on the road."

Jess's face colored. "Sorry—I'm worried about you, but of course, you're right. We need to get to Ezekan quickly." She drew breath. "The rebels are bringing siege engines with them. That's why they're moving so slowly. There has to be at least twenty of those monsters. I counted battering rams on slings, catapults, towers, ballistae, trebuchets, and some I've never seen in our history books. All were being pulled along by teams of yarraks. I reckon the city is in trouble. If they can't match the Pax in the field, Ezekan will be reduced to rubble."

It was a disaster in the making. If it weren't for the Bikashi, the Alliance would be forced to abide by the non-interference policy, but her father wouldn't stand by and watch the non-aligned strip the planet of its crynidium. The problem was that the Bikashi might well have prevailed before the admiral realized what was happening. She needed to get this information to him.

Return to Ezekan

Tess did what she could to make Hickory comfortable in the back of the cart, but every rock and rut along the way felt like she was in the hands of her torturer once more. Outside Tontine, they killed and roasted wild lupus, thinking the meat would give Hickory strength. She ate ravenously, apologizing to the others for her appetite, then promptly threw up.

She drank more of the Teacher's mixture and was amazed by its medicinal properties. Hickory's health improved quickly; the cuts and welts on her face developed thick scabs, and the swelling of her fingers subsided. Each day, she insisted on exercising and testing her body to the limit.

Six days passed, and a pillar of dense smoke appeared on the horizon. They pushed on past nightfall and arrived at the small village of Hartlepool as the aurora faded. It lay in ruins, its houses, hotel, and temple reduced to rubble. Corpses littered the streets. They searched amongst the wreckage, looking for survivors. They found only one, barely alive.

"So many…" Oridanke-sèr-Frenchin was the holy man of Hartlepool. He'd fallen into a ditch after being shot through the lungs with an arrow during the initial attack. "So many," he repeated, red froth bubbling at his mouth. "They are a plague of insects darkening the sun. And he … he is evil incarnate." Jess covered his shivering body with a blanket. "There was no reason," he said. The priest raised his head a few inches, desperate to explain. "He needed an example to show the world—and he chose our community." His eyes strayed from Jess to the heavens, and he sank back to the ground.

Reluctantly, they left the dead to enrich the earth and journeyed throughout the night. Just before the sun came up, they saw, on the horizon, trails of smoke from the revolutionaries' campfires. At the crest of a hill, they looked down into the valley. A large military encampment spread out before them: hundreds of tents, dozens of flags and war machines, thousands of soldiers and followers, and almost as many yarraks.

The camp was already awake. Some soldiers wore the skins of Violators and other beasts with heads still attached. Many busied themselves in the paddock, preparing their charges for battle. Others stoked up smoking night fires to cook the morning meal.

"Look," said Hickory, pointing to the pavilion at the center of the camp.

"Sequana. He looks mightily pleased with

The Alien Corps

himself," said Mack, focusing his spyglass on the Pharlaxian leader. Sequana wore a battle vest etched with the infinity symbol and a black silken, calf-length robe trimmed with chrome. The rebel leader stood with his hands on his hips while two servants laced up his knee-length boots. He was talking to the Bikashi commander, Vogel, who was apparently agitated, waving his hands to encompass the camp.

"What's his problem?" said Jess.

"Hard to tell from here, but he's angry. I think it's because the army should be ready to march on the city," Mack said, looking grim. "Sequana may be the leader, but he doesn't have much idea how to conduct a war. Have a look at Vogel's men. They're ready to go."

Thank God for small mercies. "We're going to have to skirt the army to reach the city," said Hickory. "The admiral probably knows the worst by now, but we still need to brief him, and I have an idea that might help even the odds a little."

"What's going on over there?" said Jess, pointing. "On the far side. That's the Teacher, isn't it?"

"How the hell did he get caught again?" said Mack, passing his spyglass to Hickory.

Hickory looked through the glass. "It's him, all right. He's standing in an open wagon, tied to a post." *I can't figure him out. He doesn't seem to make any effort to avoid his enemies. It's almost as though he wants to be captured.*

"I don't like the look of it," said Jess. "I think they're going to burn him alive."

A squad of soldiers marched to the cart where the Teacher was imprisoned and pushed it to the army's front line. Shouts of derision and abuse and coarse jokes and laughter followed them. The Teacher's gaze never strayed from the path ahead.

"We've got to do something," said Jess. "We can't just stand by and watch him die."

"Watch him die?" echoed Hickory. Her eyes flicked here and there, looking for inspiration. "We must get to the city. They have to be warned. There's got to be five thousand soldiers here." Her shoulders slumped. *Maybe he'll be all right. He's escaped from them before.* She recalled her conversation with the Teacher the last time they'd met and made her decision. "Okay, this is what we're going to do. We can't leave him here alone, so one of us will need to stay. The other two will hightail it to the city, raise the alarm, and return as quickly as possible. If they want to make an example of him, they'll keep him alive to show off in front of the city gates."

Mack pulled Jess close and said to Hickory. "You and Jess head for the admiral. I'm going to get as close as I can to Kar-sèr-Sephiryth. Maybe I can do something. At the least, I won't let these guys burn him."

The Alien Corps

Hickory nodded. An arrow to the heart would be a better fate.

Mack smiled into Jess's upturned face. "Don't worry, I'll be careful. You be careful, too." He kissed her, then started down the hill towards the camp.

Hickory and Jess boarded the wagon and turned Brutus's head away from the rebel army. When they looked back, Mack had already disappeared. They rode on, taking a wide berth to avoid any outriders scouting along the flanks.

◆◆◆

Ezekan was in turmoil when they arrived. Refugees from outlying towns and villages had poured into the city throughout the day after the government decreed the gates would be locked at dusk. The guards had already closed the side gates, and families were being turned away. Those at the back of the queue were becoming ugly. Hartlepool was common knowledge. No one wanted to be left to the mercy of Sequana.

Hickory and Jess tried to drive the cart through the tightly packed crowd, but the mob closed around them, and they found themselves stuck. Desperate, they climbed onto the yarrak's back and unhitched him from the cart. They urged him forward, forcing the angry crowd aside. A squad of reinforcements arrived from the city to bolster the guards just as Brutus squeezed his way between the closing doors.

They left Brutus at the embassy and ran to the administration building, climbing the stairs two at a time. When they reached the government chambers, they were met by two armed guards standing outside the High Reeve's offices. "Where do you think you're going?" said one.

"We must see the High Reeve immediately. We have vital information for him," Hickory replied.

The guard looked Hickory up and down and smirked. "He's busy. Unless you have an appointment, you cannot enter."

"We've just come from the Pharlaxian camp. We must see the High Reeve now," argued Hickory.

The second soldier raised his spear threateningly. "Not unless you have an appointment. Those are our orders."

Frustrated, Jess tried to force her way through, and the soldier pushed her roughly away. "Another move like that, and I'll skewer you, Castilie." He pointed the spear at Jess's chest.

Hickory lost patience. She seized the spear by the shaft and wrested it from his hands, then forced the naur against the wall with the point at his neck.

Jess drew her sword and pointed it at the other guard.

The furor drew Josipe-sèr-Amagon from his office further down the hall. "What is happening here?" he said brusquely. "We all fight on the same side. Save your anger for the Pharlaxian enemy."

Hickory released the soldier and handed him back his spear.

He muttered in a surly tone, "We had orders."

"And I'm giving you another one." Josipe glared at the naur, who stiffened to attention.

Both soldiers looked at Hickory and Jess sheepishly, mumbled an apology, and then stood back to let them into the central offices.

The Chief bid them wait outside Yonni-sèr-Abelen's suite and knocked on the door for admission. A few minutes later, he returned and ushered them inside. "You're lucky. The High Reeve is keen to speak with you. Go straight in. I must leave now. Until we meet again." He smiled grimly at Hickory and Jess. "I wish you luck in these evil times."

Sèr-Abelen turned from the window as they approached. "Hickory Lace and Jess Parker, I've been waiting for you. Your father will be relieved to hear you are safe, Commander Lace."

Hickory and Jess stopped two yards from the High Reeve and bowed low in greeting. "It is good to see you, Yonni-sèr-Abelen. You have spoken with my father recently?" said Hickory. She searched for some emotional response from the High Reeve but could sense nothing. *Total absence. Very unusual. He must have a solid natural shield.*

"Quite recently. We maintain what I believe you refer to as a video link between us, which, although strange, has proven to be valuable. We will talk with the admiral presently. First, though, I would like you to tell me what has happened to you these last few weeks."

The smile he gave them did not reach his eyes, and Hickory glanced at Jess before replying. *Mine,* she signaled.

"The story of my capture and torture by the Pharlaxians is of little worth, High Reeve."

"I agree. I am more interested in what you can tell me about the naur, Kar-sèr-Sephiryth."

Hickory nodded. "The Teacher has been captured by the Pharlaxians. As we speak, he's being transported in a cage to Ezekan. They intend to publicly humiliate and execute him before the gates of the city. But all this, I am sure you already know."

The High Reeve shook his head, and his eyes flashed with annoyance. "We don't have time to play games, Miss Lace. I want you to tell me your findings regarding Kar-sèr-Sephiryth's claims of divinity."

"That would be an enormous waste of your time, Yonni-sèr-Abelen. I've yet to reach any conclusions, but the head of my order will be the first to hear them when I do.

The Alien Corps

"It would be more productive to discuss the information we obtained about the rebel forces. It will also save time if we include Admiral Lace in these discussions." She raised her eyebrows and stared into his eyes.

A sardonic smile twisted the lips of the High Reeve. "You may call me Yonni, commander. Let us talk to the admiral."

◆◆◆

Neither the admiral nor the High Reeve gave much away as Hickory presented her account. Still, the information on the Bikashi numbers was clearly new to the admiral, and the High Reeve moistened his lips at her assessment of the Pharlaxian forces and the siege engines.

"The Pax has been building these things under the direction of Vogel and his people. Jess saw them at work and has prepared a detailed report on logistics for you." She nodded to Jess to continue.

"They've quite a factory going," said Jess. "They've been using natural materials, so they're not detectable by scanners, even if you could use them, Admiral Lace." Her face colored as she glanced at the High Reeve. "My guess is they will be able to breach the city walls in a matter of days if Sequana manages to bring up all his heavy equipment."

Hickory's father nodded his approval. "Thank you, both. Please pass on your report to Lieutenant Brandt as soon as possible, Jess.

"Commander, I'm glad to see you pulled through." He pursed his lips. "A pity about the damage to the comms equipment. I'd like to have had this information before they started to move. What about Alex Mackie? Where is he?"

Hickory and Jess looked at each other. Jess told the admiral about Kar-sèr-Sephiryth's role in Hickory's rescue.

"We think this is a special individual, a truly generous and gentle being, and we would like to do what we can to help him, regardless of our professional assessment." She took a deep breath. "The last we saw of Mack, he was hiding outside the lines of the Pharlaxian camp. He hoped to reach the Teacher and free him. We don't know whether he succeeded." She didn't continue, but all in the meeting knew if Mack had been discovered, there was a good chance he was now dead.

The High Reeve's eyes narrowed as Jess finished her report.

Hickory coughed. "The main thing is, sir, what are we going to do about the Bikashi? If the government forces have to take on the Pharlaxian army head to head, the Bikashi will wipe them out." She glanced apologetically toward the High Reeve.

The admiral grimaced. "I'd like to tell you we will come riding in like the cavalry to your relief, Yonni,

The Alien Corps

but I'm unable to give you that assurance. At least, not yet. However, I will take this to my superiors and argue the point as strongly as I can—assuming you will request our assistance?"

Yonni-sèr-Abelen shrugged. "I hardly have any choice, do I? Either you humans descend on my planet armed with your devilish weapons or I let the Pharlaxians take the city. Either way, I feel we are headed for a time of unparalleled conflict. Things will change dramatically on this planet, and not for the better, I fear. However, I will have the request drawn up and signed by the Senate leaders this afternoon."

Hickory felt some sympathy for the High Reeve. He was in an impossible position. She wasn't sure the Alliance's mission would survive either. She came to a decision and cleared her throat.

"There is one possibility we could pursue that may allow the Prosperine people to sort out their problems with only a little help from the Alliance." She hesitated. "It's a high risk, but doable. The first step is for Jess and I to get out of the city without being seen."

Rescue

The admiral and the High Reeve agreed to her plan. Yonni said he would arrange for their secret departure from the city. Now it was up to her and Jess and Mack—if Mack was still free and if they could find him quickly enough.

Kyntai and Mirda were delighted to see Hickory and Jess when they arrived at the embassy. Kyntai looked behind Jess, expecting to see Mack, and both naurs were upset to hear their new master wasn't with them.

Half an hour later, Hickory and Jess donned the hooded Avanauri cloaks with the square shoulders favored by the rebel soldiers. They didn't have time to change the dark coloring of Jess's skin, so she wore the extra protection of a face scarf. They waited a few minutes until the aurora disappeared from the sky, and then the boy drove them to the temple.

The high priest had been forewarned and led them down the steps to a secret exit hidden behind the Sacred Sword grotto. He explained that the passage

The Alien Corps

was built by priests in times past to escape persecution. The door led to a tunnel that rose steadily upwards and emerged on a mountain track a few hundred yards from the city walls.

The night sky was clear and glittered with stars, and an orchard stretched for miles below them. There was no sign of the enemy. Hickory now considered the Pharlaxians the enemy, which, given her plans, seemed appropriate.

She sent Kyntai back to look after Brutus. He appeared glad to go. The youngster had never experienced war, but Hickory didn't doubt his youthful imagination would fill in the horrors omitted by the storytellers.

They followed the track down into the trees. Jess crouched and signaled Hickory to stop. A band of archers carrying longbows trotted past, not more than a hundred yards from them. They waited until the party was out of earshot and then moved on. "Forward scouts," whispered Jess. "The main body can't be far away."

"Half a day at most," agreed Hickory.

Several hours before dawn, they emerged from the trees onto the eastern edge of the goldengrass plains that swept away to the sea. The terrain rapidly deteriorated, becoming crisscrossed with gullies and ravines that made it difficult to negotiate in the dark.

By the time they climbed the crest of a hill and

spied the rebel camp sprawled out below, a pink flush on the horizon was invading the indigo of the night sky.

"What do you think?" Jess said, afraid to express her fears that Mack might have been killed in a failed attempt to rescue Kar-sèr-Sephiryth.

"If Mack's alive, he'll be down there." She didn't say she was unable to reach his SIM because Jess already knew.

"How are we going to find him?" whispered Jess, peering through her spyglass at the myriad of tents in the valley.

"If their previous practice is anything to go by, the Teacher will be on public display. We should be able to spot him unless Mack managed to find a way to set him loose." Hickory could feel the anxiety emanating from her friend.

Jess nodded her agreement.

Hickory searched the area with her spyglass, but all was quiet. She thought there should be more movement about the camp if the Teacher had escaped. A moment later, she found him. "He's still in the cart at the front of the army. There's no sign of Mack."

Prosperine's sun was still below the horizon, and they decided to make use of the semi-darkness to reach the camp. They edged down the hillside using the rocks and scrub for cover, stopping at every hiding

The Alien Corps

place to listen for the sound of sentries.

Fifty yards from the first tents, they spotted a night patrol. Two guards met up with their compatriots, then turned and walked a hundred yards to a third duo. Hickory realized the pattern would be repeated around the perimeter of the camp. Sequana was taking no chances.

Hickory and Jess waited until the guards passed them, then slipped through the lines. They reached the tents without being discovered, then tugged the hoods over their eyes and strode into the camp towards the carriage holding Kar-sèr-Sephiryth.

It was quiet. The only sounds were the snoring of soldiers in their tents and the whoop-whoop of a nocturnal predator. A group of half a dozen grizzled warriors sat around an open fire, talking in subdued tones about tomorrow's action. Others slept where they lay, their heads resting on their armor and their weapons nearby. One stalwart drained the last few drops of his wine before he threw the flask away and stumbled into his tent.

Two bored-looking guards carrying spears stood beside the prison wagon. Hickory motioned for Jess to wait in the shadow of a tent until she'd gained the guards' attention, then strolled over.

"Salutations, friends. So this is the so-called Son of Balor, eh? Not much to look at, is he?"

One guard laughed. "There never was much to

look at, but since the Bikashi talked to him, there is even less."

Hickory could see the welts and bruises on the prisoner. Despite the pain he must have been feeling, his eyes lit softly on her. Hickory's heart caught in her mouth. "They've done a good job on him," she responded.

The second guard looked more closely at her and weighed his spear in two hands. "I do not recognize you, soldier. Pull back your hood so I can see your face."

"Won't do you any good," said Hickory.

Jess crept up behind the guard and cracked him over the head. Before he hit the ground, Jess leaped at the second soldier and put her knife to his throat, stifling his cries with her other hand. "If you want to live, keep still," she whispered into his ear.

They tied both guards securely to a wheel and stuffed gags into their mouths. Hickory climbed onto the wagon, cut the Teacher's bonds, and whispered in his ear. "Be quiet now. We don't want to alarm the camp. There—you're free. Can you walk?"

Hickory and Jess helped The Teacher down from the wagon. He rubbed his wrists and stretched his legs, then went to the unconscious guard and checked his breathing. Satisfied, he rose. "He will recover. Thank you, Jess and Hickory. I've been tied to that stake for a long time, but if we walk slowly, I will

The Alien Corps

regain my strength."

"We were hoping to find our friend here. Have you seen him?" said Jess as they supported the injured naur by the arms and led him towards the edge of the camp.

"I have some good news, Jess. Mack is courageous, and he is alive. He made a valiant attempt to free me but was unfortunately caught. The Pharlaxians put him in the cage with me, and we talked briefly. He told me that you were on your way here, but Vogel took him away before I could tell him of my suspicions about Gareth's death."

Hickory and Jess looked at each other dumbfounded and came to a standstill. "What about Gareth's death? Do you know who was responsible? If so, you must tell us," said Hickory.

"Hickory, Jess. Knowing you would come, I chose to stay to share my thoughts with you. I believe Gareth is alive."

A warm flush rose up Hickory's neck. She looked at Jess, who stared open-mouthed at the Teacher. Hickory's mind filled with a multitude of emotions. She was shocked by the Teacher's pronouncement but couldn't prevent her heart from soaring with a sudden burst of hope.

Just as quickly, the crushing certainty of Gareth's death brought her back to earth. She felt pity for Jess and sadness for the Teacher who wanted to help, to make things better. His treatment at the hands of Sequana must have affected him more than she'd comprehended.

"He is here, being kept under guard by the Bikashi. I can show you."

Hickory shook her head. "Kar...I'm sorry, but that's not possible. Gareth is dead." Her voice broke. "His body lies in the morgue on the Jabberwocky."

His large eyes rested softly on the two friends. "Please trust me; I can unravel this mystery. As I promised Jess, I took the message about the Pharlaxian army to the High Reeve in Ezekan. I would instead have spoken to the admiral, but I could not find him anywhere in the city.

"Yonni-sèr-Abelen refused to meet with me until he was told I had information about the strength of the aggressors. I was shown into his office, and as we discussed the details, my eyes were drawn to a document on his desk. He whisked it away before I could read much of what was written. However, I saw enough to realize it was an ultimatum from Sequana. The paragraph before his signature was a threat to hoist the head of a demon spy on a pike at the gates of Ezekan."

Hickory frowned. "And you think this was a reference to Gareth? Why not Jess, or me, or Mack?"

"Yes, I think it must have been. Jess and Mack had escaped from Sequana's war camp before he sent the letter, and you did not arrive there until after. Unless there is another human in your team that I am not aware of, the only possible solution is that he holds Gareth prisoner."

"No, that can't be. I saw his body…" Hickory trailed off.

"Hick…" Jess pleaded. "It's worth a look, isn't it?"

Hickory understood her anxiety, but Jess knew as well as she did what was at stake. The mission was more important than any individual. She felt sadness sweep through her. It was hard for Jess to lose Gareth, but there was nothing either of them could have done to prevent it from happening. *And now, to be presented with this glimmer of hope. How will Jess cope if the Teacher turns out to be wrong? Is it possible that what he says could be right? Oh, God, I wish I'd demanded the autopsy results when it became apparent Nolanski was working with Vogel and the Pax.*

Hickory handed her water flask to the Teacher. She remained torn between carrying out her mission and accepting Jess's plea.

Kar had shown himself to be a remarkable individual. There was an aura about him, something that attracted others and made them feel safe and special. And what about the miracles he performed, curing insanity and healing open wounds at a touch? And he looked much stronger now compared to just a few minutes ago.

Hickory remembered how fresh The Teacher had appeared in the desert after he'd broken out of the Pax jail. He must have walked over a hundred miles in only a few days. And there was the matter of that escape through a locked door, although he denied that. *It's all too strange. I don't understand how he can do these things. His abilities seem uncanny, and his resemblance to the biblical Jesus is astonishing.*

It was almost like he could read her thoughts. He smiled and returned the bottle. "I am not a magician, Hickory. Meditation, prayer, and belief in Balor help keep my head clear and diminish the pain. Come, I will take you to where they are holding your friends."

Hickory nodded. She would reserve judgment for later. She had come here to rescue Mack. The least she should do is try to get him away from this place. Keeping close together, they followed Kar-sèr-Sephiryth through the gray mist. He held up his hand, and they froze. A few yards before them, an Avanauri soldier hitched up his trousers and staggered back into his tent.

The fog parted momentarily, allowing them a glimpse of the Bikashi camp. Vogel's soldiers were billeted separately from the Pharlaxians. It seemed the two groups hadn't bonded well together. The Pax were clearly still nervous about having off-worlders around.

"Bikashi guards patrol their own camping area,"

The Alien Corps

whispered Kar-sèr-Sephiryth, "but if we move silently, they will not see us."

Hickory's eyes narrowed in the gloom. She counted twenty-six tents in the clearing and spotted a sentry standing at the entry to the biggest one. *That could be Vogel's sleeping quarters.* A light breeze sprang up, and curling wisps of mist revealed the shape of a steel cage and two armed Bikashi. She caught her breath. *They're using a negative energy device to conceal this place! Vogel is taking a huge risk.* She nudged Jess and nodded at the phenomenon.

Jess put her mouth close to Hickory's ear. "That's why we couldn't reach Mack. Nothing can penetrate that field. They must be mad or desperate. If the Alliance picks up that they're using this sort of advanced technology, the admiral will be sorely tempted to launch a strike force, regardless of the consequences."

"My guess is the field is just big enough to cover the area where Mack is being held, not the whole camp. A mini power source wouldn't be picked up by the admiral's scanners," said Hickory.

She noticed a console sitting to one side of the force field. It looked incongruous in the camp setting. *That must be it.* Hickory pointed. "Do you see it?"

Jess nodded and touched her shoulder. "Those two guards inside the force field," she whispered. "We need to deal with them before we try to cut the power."

"Any ideas?" asked Hickory.

Jess pointed to where some Bikashi mounts were corralled at the rear of the clearing. A large tree with overhanging branches stood just outside the roped-off area. Several yarraks were resting beneath the tree's canopy. "Maybe a distraction would work for one of them. But that still leaves the other guard wondering where his buddy has disappeared to."

"It'll be okay if he sees his pal returning to his post. Then, all we need to do is get him to come outside the field perimeter," said Hickory. She turned to face the Teacher.

"If this works, we'll need to get out of here quickly. We won't be able to return through the main camp. But I'd rather not leave our equipment and rides behind."

"I understand. What would you have me do?" the Teacher said.

"Titus and Brutus are tethered in an orchard just the other side of the ridge. Will you fetch them and wait for us on the back road to Ezekan."

He nodded. "I'll meet you there."

"Teacher—" she hesitated, uncertain of what to say. "Take this with you." She thrust the emerald-encrusted pendant into his hands. "Look after it until we reach Ezekan, and please be careful. If you're captured, they won't risk you escaping again. And… there's a lot we need to talk about."

Kar-sèr-Sephiryth extended his long, skinny arms and folded her to his chest. He stroked her hair and whispered. "Do not fear, Hickory. Part of this story remains unfinished for both of us. I have no intention of departing this world yet, and I look forward to our discussion." He let her go and smiled. "Extend my greetings to your friends."

Hickory brushed a tear from her eye as she watched him depart. They waited fifteen minutes to give Kar-sèr-Sephiryth time to slip unnoticed through the encampment, and then Hickory loped off.

She circled the Bikashi camp until she reached the other side of the yarrak enclosure. The old tree offered plenty of toeholds and places her hands could grip. She climbed steadily until she reached a stout branch extending over the compound.

Hickory snaked along the tree limb until she was as close to the sleeping yarraks as possible. She shook a branch, and the leaves rustled loudly. The yarraks lumbered to their feet, yipping in fright.

Moments later, a guard approached to investigate. He moved cautiously, peering over the rope fence and murmuring to the beasts. "Hey, now. What's all the noise, Enixtra? Something disturbs you, eh? One of those Pharlaxians try to take you away?" He looked around suspiciously.

Hickory waited until the Bikashi drew near to the tree and then jumped. The guard looked up, startled. Hickory fell heavily on the guard's head, and both landed awkwardly on the ground. Hickory rolled away and leaped to her feet, but the guard didn't move. Blank eyes stared at her. She checked for a pulse but found none.

Grimly, she pulled his clothing over her own, donned his helmet, and picked up the spear. She took a few deep breaths and trotted back to the compound, waving her arms at the second Bikashi. "Hey, there's a problem with Enixtra. I need some help!"

The second guard took a few steps outside the forcefield's perimeter and shouted back, "*Frackist!* You know it's against orders to leave our post. Get back here, or—"

His threat was cut off by Jess, who approached from behind and knocked him on the head with the pommel of her sword. Catching the guard as he fell, she laid him gently on the ground.

Blowing hard, Hickory discarded her headgear and joined Jess at the control panel. "The other soldier's dead. I landed on top of him and accidentally broke his neck, poor sod."

"Tough luck for him," said Jess, grimly. "Let's get this shield down before the other one wakes up."

"Have you figured out how it works?

The Alien Corps

"I think so. There's an alarm system, though. I just need to—ah! That's it."

Jess and Hickory looked up as the barrier flared, and they saw the previously invisible area clearly. Several posts with chains attached were anchored into the ground, and a rough log table sat in the middle of the virtual cell. They could see a figure hunched over it.

"Forcefield is down. We're in. Let's get Mack and get out of here pronto," Said Jess.

They sprinted to the table. Mack was asleep and handcuffed to one of the post-chains. His clothes were dirty, and one eye was swollen like a boiled egg.

Jess caressed his head, pushing his hair back from his forehead. "Mack," she whispered urgently. "Mack, wake up. You're being rescued, you daft thing."

Mack rubbed his eyes and stared in disbelief from his one good eye. "Jess? What are you doing here? Don't you know you're in the middle of a rebel army?"

He saw Hickory smiling at him and pushed himself from the table to his feet. Staggering, he grasped Jess to him. "Oh, God, it's so good to see you. I felt for sure we were goners."

Hickory looked around slowly, unable to speak. She felt a heavy weight land in her stomach. Jess was more forthright. "What are you talking about? We need to get you out of here straight away. Your story can wait." She tried to drag him with her, but Mack shrugged himself free.

"No, you don't understand. It's Gareth. He's here."

Hickory felt rooted to the spot, her mind laboring to accept the truth. *The teacher was right, after all?*

Mack looked from one to the other. "Oh, for heaven's sake. He's here. Gareth's right here! Look." He shuffled across to the opposite side of the confinement area. "He's in a bad way. He's been tortured—I think mentally as well as physically. He's just about given up.

Gareth… Gareth, come on, mate! Wake up. Look who's here." He leaned down and shook the sleeper. The bundle of rags on the ground stirred, and a hand emerged to draw back the hood. Hickory and Jess gasped.

"It *is* you!" said Hickory, her eyes wide and her heart hammering.

"But, but, you're… you're dead," said Jess, tears coming to her eyes.

She looked at Mack, who grinned and nodded to her. "It is, Jess. It's Gareth," he said.

"Mother?" The croak was quiet and hopeful, and then the tone hardened, and his voice rose. "No. Just another trick you're playing on me, you bastards, but

I know what your game is, and I won't play. You hear me? I won't play!"

"Shhh!" said Hickory. She came to his side and placed an arm around him. "We won't hurt you. We're your friends."

"We're here to help you," said Jess. "Come on, Gareth. Get up. We have to get you both away from here, pronto." She dragged Gareth to his feet and looked at Mack. "Can you manage?"

He nodded. "I'm okay."

Gareth mumbled incoherently as they made their way to the yarraks. Hickory tried to keep him calm, but he struggled when they reached the pen. "No, no, no! Let me go. Wherever you're taking me, I'm not going. I don't know anything—I'm just an engineer."

Hickory realized Gareth was raving, his mind still locked in whatever prison Vogel had created for him. She hoped his condition was temporary, but he would surely give them away if he kept this up. "I'm sorry, Gareth, but this is for your good as much as mine." She hit him firmly on the jaw, and Gareth collapsed into Jess's arms.

"He can share a yarrak with me. You two should ride together," she said. Ignoring the shocked looks on Jess and Mack's faces, she heaved Gareth onto one yarrak and then led the animals away from the Bikashi camp.

When Hickory judged they were out of earshot, they mounted and urged their steeds to full speed.

Full speed for the yarraks was little more than a jogging pace, but the beasts could keep that up for several hours without a rest.

Gareth came around not long after they'd set off and expressed surprise to be galloping along beneath the stars. He was lucid and listened with interest as Hickory told him about the body on Silver Hill she'd been sure was his.

"Some poor, unfortunate lookalike Vogel used to throw you off the scent," he said. "I saw him being put in a cell. He bore a passable resemblance to me, to begin with, and they would have made sure he was pretty much unrecognizable before they dumped him."

Now they were on their way, Hickory could think about what had happened. "The poor sod. He *was* you, Gareth. I was so convinced. I'm so sorry."

"Don't be. It's not your fault." He shuddered and fell silent.

"Why was Vogel so interested in you?"

"He wasn't to start with. He left me for Sequana to deal with. After my first session with the interrogator, he dropped in for another chat." The muscles in his neck twitched. "I told him exactly who I was—everything about me, everything! I couldn't stand the

The Alien Corps

pain anymore.

"He wanted to know about my expertise in faster-than-light technology. He told me the Bikashi system wasn't nearly as advanced as the one developed on Earth." Gareth giggled quietly to himself, his eyes wild. "He decided I was just the person to help design a better FTL, one they could use when they got their hands on the planet's crynidium. He said he would help me…"

Gareth's eyes closed, and his voice faded to silence. Hickory thought he'd fallen asleep. "Gareth?"

"Yes, yes. I'm here. Vogel said he would help me, and I thought anything would be better than being left in that dungeon. Hickory, the boy… he was an ensign who should have left for Earth on leave. He…" Gareth's eyes wandered wildly, and he sobbed.

Hickory sensed he was being haunted by the screams of his dead twin.

"I…I can't remember much of what happened after that. They took me somewhere. I know they used drugs on me, and there were a lot of people asking questions, Bikashi scientists, but I didn't know where I was. Most of the time, I was being questioned or put to sleep." His shoulders slumped, and then he giggled. "They did things to me, and I can't remember what. I can't remember!"

Hickory was silent for a moment, holding him tightly to her. "It's all right, Gareth. Everything will be all right. You're safe now. Try to sleep. I'll wake you when we get to Ezekan." She thought about Vogel. *I hope I get the chance to meet you again.*

As arranged, they rendezvoused with the Teacher along the old road, a half-day journey to Ezekan. Mack backtracked a few miles to check whether they were being followed while the others ate some rations and made hot tea from some leaves stored in Kar-sèr-Sephiryth's pouch.

Hickory worried about Gareth. Physically, he looked drawn, and he'd lost weight, but it was his mental well-being that concerned her most. He seemed to blink in and out of reality without warning, and when he was in that other place, there was a slyness about him that was utterly foreign.

She spoke with the Teacher. "Is there anything you can do to relieve his pain?"

Kar-sèr-Sephiryth glanced to where Gareth sat on the grass, disconsolate, his head hanging down, and his back bowed. "I will do what I can."

Fifteen minutes later, he returned to Hickory's side. "Gareth is very sick. He cannot bring forth what has happened to him. I have tried to ease his mind, and in time, he will recover, but it would be dangerous to pressure him into remembering. When we reach the city, I will prepare something to help heal his body."

Hickory had hoped for more, a miracle perhaps. A snap of the fingers and hey presto! Gareth would be

The Alien Corps

cured, and the old Gareth would be fully restored. She realized how futile this was. *Past events can't be altered, nor can their consequences. Even when Jesus was on the cross, and he begged, his Father would not take away his suffering.*

Mack hurried into camp. "Bikashi—about a dozen of them, less than an hour behind us."

They mounted their steeds and set off at the yarraks' top pace and did not rest again until they'd climbed the mountain and passed through the hidden gate to the city.

War

Hickory hadn't slept since she'd arrived, but adrenaline kept her going. *Time enough to rest when this is over.* Her father had sanctioned the plan, and now she stood on the outer wall watching the rebel horde assemble on the plain less than a mile away. She worried about Gareth, but he'd told her he felt better and was helping Jess and the city's smiths fit out the balloons for warfare—Prosperine style.

The rebels' approach to the city was hampered by the orchards along their route, and they'd been forced to wait for the massive war engines to catch up with the main force.

Josipe-sèr-Amagon was tasked with further delaying the rebels. Working through the night, he and the city guard strung chains between trees and planted clusters of sharpened stakes in deep trenches. They dug rows of parallel ditches two thousand yards from the walls, spiked them with upward-pointing spears, and covered them with branches.

The Alien Corps

Grim-faced Avanauri guards, soldiers, and ordinary citizens crowded the walls alongside Hickory. The High Reeve had armed the latter with spears, swords, and bows. Those who missed out carried their own weapons—slings, scythes, and sabers with elaborate handles, passed down from parent to eldest child ever since the war with the North. Children, not yet old enough to wield arms, held long poles sporting triangular house flags to indicate the strength and direction of the breeze.

Hickory looked back to the airships and hoped the wind wouldn't get any stronger. The courtyard below her buzzed with Avanauri citizens running back and forth. Naurs and nauris dragged catapults into place between the outside and inside walls. Yarraks towed carts piled with rocks to be stacked beside them. Others hurried to store food and water beneath the parapet to be distributed by aging naurs and children as the need arose.

Although satisfied they'd done their best with the available resources, Hickory wished they had a score of assault rifles to even up the odds a little. Her father was adamant on that score. He didn't want to escalate this into a war between the Bikashi and the Alliance. "If this is to be a holy war," he said, "our side will be aligned with the forces of light."

The slaughter caused by modern Bikashi weapons would terrify the city's defenders. The off-worlders were branded demons even by their own side because of their unholy appearance and use of "devilish" weapons.

The clerics nurtured a belief in the righteousness of the defenders' cause by providing blessings and absolution and distributing amulets to the troops. They hoisted sacred statues of Balor, Connat-sèra-Haagar, and other war heroes on top of the fortifications and positioned them to face the enemy.

A horn sounded from far away, echoing eerily against the walls. Everyone stopped what they were doing and turned to face the sound. On top of a hill five miles distant, a lone figure appeared. Sequana stood in his stirrups and raised his staff. A mighty roar surrounded him as his army, led by his generals, crested the rise. In the center of the horde, the artillerists hauled their war machines.

Sequana pointed right, left, and then center. The enemy artillery trundled to the front of the ground troops. Hickory searched for the Bikashi and found them astride their mounts at the rear of Sequana's main force. It looked like they would be held in reserve until needed.

The Pharlaxian army continued to advance. The city defenders jeered when the leading trebuchet toppled into one of Josipe's pits.

Immediately, a platoon left the enemy's ranks and combed the area for further traps. Although coming under heavy fire from the defenders, they succeeded in planting crossed flags in several places to indicate the location of the traps.

The main force advanced until it was within two thousand yards of the walls. Rebel artillerists ratcheted the counterweight into the firing position and levered the first projectile into the sling. They released the trigger, and the massive counterweight fell; the long arm revolved, gathering speed until it reached the optimum height, and the sling whipped its load toward the walls. The rock fell harmlessly short, causing the defending forces to jeer.

Cavaliers urged their yarraks to drag the engines forward a further fifty paces. The second rock smashed into the wall midway up, breaking into debris and dust. The next shot sailed over the wall and shattered in the courtyard, injuring several of the auxiliary support.

Sequana ordered all his war engines to advance and commence bombardment. Rocks and fiery projectiles rained down on the city.

Defenders took shelter beneath their shields but couldn't escape the barrage. All around, the injured screamed in agony from ruptured limbs and burning skin. Some lay sprawled on the ground, missing arms or legs. Others were dead from no apparent cause.

Hickory heard a thump next to her. She turned, and the body of a nauri fell into her arms. Where its head had been, there remained only ragged bone, torn flesh, and gurgling blood. She pushed the corpse away and bent over, gagging.

At ground level, beneath the parapet, a captain held a bloody hand to her side and shouted orders, urging her troops to greater effort.

"Fire!" The long arm of the catapult swept forward, releasing its cargo.

"Reload," she roared. "Move yourself, warrior! Bring those rocks over here."

Projectiles flew overhead in both directions. Pots containing combustible liquids smashed on the ground inside the walls. Naurs and nauris screamed in panic as rancid clouds of smoke and flames erupted, consuming tents, war machines, and defenders.

The wounded were rushed to makeshift field hospitals, their limbs dangling from stretchers. Hickory spotted Kar-sèr-Sephiryth working among them. He glanced up from attending to an injured soldier, her pendant dangling on his chest, and she could see his lips move in prayer.

A salvo of rocks and flame exploded against a tower, and parts of the wall collapsed, landing in a cloud of dust and stone. Hickory activated her SIM. *Jess, what's your status? We need you now.* She ducked as a shower of broken rock fell towards her.

The Alien Corps

On our way. I hope you can give us cover. We won't last long once the Bikashi realize what we're up to. Hickory watched the fleet of airships approach from the city center, trailing puffs of vapor as their pilots cranked up the thrust to full speed. They crossed the wall, and the defenders gazed open-mouthed at the sight. Jess had organized for the aircraft to be fitted with sirens, and the resultant cacophony was alarming.

Hickory shifted her gaze to the Bikashi. They hadn't moved yet. It was time for her to do her thing. She took a deep breath and searched within her mind until she located the empathic receptors. She could sense the power build in response to her intense concentration. Electrical impulses began to swirl around, speeding into her SIM and back to her nerve centers faster and faster. Her head ached, but she delved deeper, and the electricity crackled in her nostrils and behind her eyes. Flashes of white-hot bursts of energy increased in strength and frequency until she felt as though her head might explode. She reached out above the advancing army, over the ridges and hills, over the rivers and mountains, and when she thought she could no longer hold the command, she felt the contact.

We are Charakai. We come.

◆◆◆

The aircraft advanced ever so slowly towards the Pharlaxian forces. In the lead balloon, Jess signaled to

Gareth, who waved back. She hoped the boy was ready for this. He'd assured her he was fine, but the state of his mental health was still problematic. The Teacher promised Gareth's memory would return piece by piece, but Jess didn't like the hunted look often present in his eyes.

When they got home, she would organize a holiday for him with the girls and Mack and herself. He'd like that. St Moritz, perhaps. Somewhere nice and cold, where they could go skiing and throw snowballs at each other. Have some fun. When they got home. *If they got home.*

She ducked instinctively as a projectile flew past, missing her by only a few feet. *I hope that was accidental, and they're not firing at us.* More rocks were in the air on their way to the wall, passing harmlessly by the flying ships. *Another few minutes, and we'll be inside their minimum range, and then…*

◆◆◆

The walls of the city were severely damaged. They still stood, but for how much longer could they take this pounding? Hickory watched anxiously as the dirigibles approached the rebel war machines. She saw the first bomb being bundled over the side of the leading ship and watched it tumble through the air and strike the ground beside a ballista.

This was Gareth's unique contribution to the city's defense. Each gondola was loaded with canisters

The Alien Corps

containing gunpowder surrounded by close-packed stone pebbles.

The bomb burst in a flash of noise, smoke, and fire. Earth and rock soared in a deadly salvo, smashing into the wooden structure and transforming it into lethal shards that felled many of its operators. The rest panicked and ran.

Suddenly, the air was filled with the noise and smoke of simultaneous explosions as the remaining flying machines unleashed their deadly cargo. The acrid smell of gunpowder and burning flesh drifted to the defenders on the wall, who cheered wildly. The airship squadron demolished three of the war weapons, killing dozens of their crew before the Bikashi arrived within striking distance.

Vogel issued a command, and his troops knelt and opened fire on the balloons. Deadly missiles exploded from the muzzles of the guns and flashed towards their targets. The aircraft and their crews were an easy mark for the experienced shooters. The ballons disintegrated with a roar and a blinding flash, leaving only a cloud of vapor to say where they'd been. Within minutes, more than half were obliterated.

The cheering from the defenders turned into cries of terror at this display of demonic power. Some fled their posts in despair but weren't the only ones. Some among the Pharlaxian forces threw themselves to the ground and hid their faces. Hickory watched grimly.

This was what her father had been afraid of. The use of high-tech weapons against the superstitious Avanauri was unconscionable.

The temple priests, led by the High Reeve and the Chief, urged the deserters to return to their posts. For the moment, the naurs seemed to comply, but for how long? The dirigibles scattered to avoid the snipers, and two of the balloons crashed in mid-air and collapsed. Two others managed to discharge their bombs before hitting the ground.

Watching through her spyglass, Hickory was shocked to see one of the downed craft was Gareth's. "Gareth!" she cried. "For crying out loud." She searched the smoke anxiously and saw bodies lying unmoving on the ground. As she scanned the area, another balloon touched down amongst the smoke and then immediately took off. Hickory picked out Jess, scuttling across the field towards the crashed vehicles. Her heart leaped. "Go, Jess. Find him and get the hell away from there," she muttered.

And then her attention was drawn to the Pharlaxian main force. Sequana had seen the impact the Bikashi riflemen were having on the defenders and urged his supporters forward. "To the city, to the city!" he roared.

◆◆◆

A dark shadow spread across the battlefield as the sun was eclipsed by thousands of leather wings. Vogel was the first to hear the Charakai approach. He turned around, puzzled, and saw the first wave swoop. A hundred screeching raptors extended their necks and talons and plunged towards him. Desperately, Vogel shouted a warning to his men. "Watch out. The enemy is behind you. Kill the reptiles, kill the birds!"

The Charakai's leathery wings folded, and they fell amongst the troops. Razor-sharp talons clawed at faces and hands in a bloody frenzy. Cruel teeth savaged necks and tore strips of flesh from unprotected areas of the body. Vogel's troops panicked and fired into the air and onto the ground, killing and injuring their own people as well as their attackers.

Hickory watched from the walls. The Bikashi had no hope. There were already fifty Charakai to each soldier. Though the soldiers fought like demons, they were no match for the slashing talons and stabbing beaks.

The enemy retreated, and the remaining air yachts resumed their barrage of the war machines. Sequana desperately tried to rally his troops to no avail. The ground was swarming with Charakai feeding on the dead. Hickory decided she would allow them to have their fill, and then she'd send them home.

She spied movement at the edge of the Bikashi battalion. Vogel! He and two of his men were scrambling away from the massacre. They'd abandoned their guns and were running backward, swinging their sabers at a dozen or so pursuing Charakai. She swung her glass back to where she'd seen Jess and spotted her pursuing Gareth. He was making a beeline for Vogel.

◆◆◆

Gareth stared at the ceiling but saw nothing. The cerebral inhibitors they'd inserted in his brain had robbed him of his sight, and he wept with the pain and sheer terror of it.

The Bikashi surgeons had little experience dealing with the complexities of the human nervous system. Finding the right connections was a matter of trial and error for them. If their transference protocols were to work effectively on him, he should be in a theta wave, non-REM sleep, but the pain kept him conscious most of the time.

In his lucid moments, Gareth was aware they were using a cocktail of psychotropic drugs and amphetamines to lower his resistance. The fact that they kept trying was the only indication they hadn't yet extracted the information they wanted.

The drugs gave rise to vivid dreams. People and objects floated in and out of his awareness. The Teacher, wearing a crown of thorns, morphed into Jenny crying tears of blood. Sequana and Vogel transmuted into Hickory and Jess. They were angry, shouting something at him he couldn't quite understand.

The most frightening visions were of him and Carole on

The Alien Corps

the deck of the Pride of America. They were arguing. She'd drank too much and was clinging with one hand to the steering wheel, swaying back and forth with the roll of the sea. He was furious because he'd found Carole embracing Jack in the main cabin.

"Slut! You betrayed me," he shouted.

Her laughter was carried away by the breeze. "You're such an innocent, Gareth. Jack and I have been an item for months."

"But...but why are you—"

"Why am I still hanging around you? You're rich, you silly boy, and I like to be around money."

"You said you loved me."

"Love you? You are the last person in the world I'd fall for—a complete nerd. You're supposed to be brainy, but you are so stupid! At least Jack is a man, not a boy."

The yacht pitched violently, and Carole lost her grip on the helm. She staggered to the stern, her eyes wide with surprise. She seemed to regain her balance until the boat shifted again, and she plummeted backward over the rail.

Gareth lunged. His fingers brushed one foot as she fell, but she eluded him. He watched her head collide with the anchor chain and blood gush from her scalp as she disappeared below the surface.

"No," he cried, "it wasn't like that. We were friends, just friends."

At times, the scientists would stop feeding him the

hallucinogens and try to talk him into cooperating with them, but he was obstinate, and they always put him back into this state of half-truth, half-lie.

He refused to reveal the critical information they needed. Still, he knew he'd given them some, and it was only a matter of time before they got everything. The one constant in his nightmares was Vogel. Vogel's questions, Vogel's threats, Vogel's pain, Vogel's love, Vogel's promises, Vogel's torments. He hated him.

◆◆◆

Gareth dragged himself into the present. His enemy was climbing the slope just ahead. He forced himself to move more quickly. The Teacher had done an excellent job healing his body and had eased the turmoil in his mind. But Gareth knew there was only one cure for his emotional and mental suffering, and the proximity to Vogel drove him on.

Jess was close. He'd told her to go away, back to the city where it was safe, but she was stubborn, too. She was still a few yards behind him, keeping up a stream of pleadings, begging him to stop. But he'd seen the devil escape Hickory's crows, and he would not stop until they came face to face. He smiled thinly, thinking about his revenge. He would kill him slowly, painfully, with his own hands. He'd have to get rid of Jess. She would interfere and try to stop him, but this was what he had to do. He wouldn't rest until it was done.

The Alien Corps

The fiend was up ahead. Two of his minions ran alongside him, one with an arm hanging limply by his side.

The flying reptiles had evidently given up the chase and returned to easier pickings on the battleground.

Gareth howled like a wolf on the hunt.

Vogel looked back and hissed. He snapped at his two companions, and they started back towards Gareth.

Gareth paused, and Jess reached his side, panting.

"What the hell are you doing?" she said. "Are you trying to get yourself killed?" Her face was screwed up in pain, and Gareth saw her leg was bleeding.

"Looks like you're the one in trouble," he said, nodding at her leg.

"It's only a scratch, and I think we both have a bigger problem to worry about."

The two Bikashi blocked their path, feet apart, swords pointed in their direction.

"No," said Gareth, "this is just a temporary inconvenience." He moved swiftly forward and lunged at the unscathed Bikashi.

"Jezus!" swore Jess. She crossed swords with the other before he could engage Gareth. The alien's injury slowed him down, but he was still a powerful adversary. Jess felt herself being forced backward by sheer brute strength. She lost her footing and fell, rolling to one side as he swung his sword down, narrowly missing her. From the ground, she swiped at his leg. Her sword caught fast in the plastisteel armor protecting his knee. She tugged to release it, her sword pulled free, and blood gushed from the wound.

The Bikashi roared and staggered back. Jess leaped nimbly to her feet, stepped to his lame side, and brought her sword across his neck. His severed head rolled downhill as his body collapsed. She turned swiftly to aid Gareth but saw his opponent lying face-up, eyes staring sightlessly, and a bloody gash across his throat. Jess searched around and saw Gareth fifty yards ahead, on the heels of Vogel. She cursed again and began to run.

◆◆◆

The battle was in full swing. With the Bikashi removed from the equation and most of the war weapons destroyed, the High Reeve gave the order to meet the rebels in the field. Soldiers poured from the gate, positioning themselves in a phalanx in front of the walls. A horn blew, and they marched forward to engage their enemy.

Hickory ran down a flight of stairs and jumped to the ground. This war was now reduced to a skirmish between two domestic foes. She'd done what she could to even up the score. The rest was up to the Prosperine people. Her father would be happy if the

Pharlaxian menace was eliminated, but even if they won the day, he would find a way to come to terms with them. The main danger had been the Bikashi presence, and they'd been dealt with, except for Vogel. While he was free, he was still a threat. She'd last seen him running from Gareth with Jess in hot pursuit, and that worried her. Both could end up dead. She went to the stables, saddled Titus, and coaxed the animal into a fast trot.

The opposing armies faced each other. The Ezekani forces split into three and launched a pincer movement to attack the flanks of the rebels who were advancing in a solid block. The Pharlaxian lieutenants responded by sending their cavalry to harass the arms of the pincer. Fifty mounts rode out to engage each arm, sweeping wide to attack.

Hickory found herself caught between the pincer arm and the rebel riders. She urged her mount to greater efforts and narrowly avoided being caught in the melee.

A long arrow followed her out and lodged in Titus's hind leg. The yarrak stumbled beneath her, and Hickory was thrown head over heels to the ground. She tucked herself into a ball and rolled forward, then gained her feet. Titus struggled to rise, nickering in fear and pain. Hickory ran and seized the reins, rubbing the yarrak's nose in reassurance. She looked around anxiously, but there didn't seem to be any immediate danger. "It's all right, boy, you'll be okay. Let me take a look."

The arrow had gone through the yarrak's lower leg. As far as Hickory could tell, it had missed the tendon and the bone. She gripped the arrow shaft. Titus trembled, but Hickory snapped it off at the head and withdrew it quickly from the flesh. The beast trumpeted, and Hickory hugged his head, whispering into his ear. "It's all done, Titus. You're a brave boy, aren't you?" Her mount nuzzled her hand. Hickory placed her forehead against the beast and centered her thoughts on one command. *Home.*

She watched the beast limp away in the direction of Ezekan before she continued her journey. The battle had moved on, with government troops and rebel sympathizers engaged in hand-to-hand fighting. Her best chance of finding Gareth was by avoiding the hostilities. That meant heading north and then west once she was beyond the rival armies.

It took longer than she expected to bypass the more intense battles. She veered into a fruit farm, thinking it would be a shortcut and provide her with good cover.

She didn't count on others having the same thought and was startled when three rebel soldiers stepped from behind some trees and blocked her path.

Where do you think you're going, nauri?" said one. "You won't escape retribution so easily." He drew his

The Alien Corps

sword and advanced towards Hickory. His companions formed a semi-circle around her.

"I won't be so simple to kill," said Hickory, adopting a defensive posture. Her feet and body were well balanced, and she pointed her sword towards the leader.

He licked his lips and glanced at his companions. "Give us your purse and that fine sword, and we'll let you go."

"Before or after you kill me?" said Hickory.

He laughed, yelled fiercely, and rushed forward, his sword raised above his head. Hickory sprang towards him, and her sword sliced through his leather vest into his chest. He screamed and collapsed. Hickory regained her defensive stance, and the two remaining adversaries circled her warily. Hickory's sword swished in front of one, then the other. Her first opponent sought to attack while her back was turned, but Hickory swirled and slashed his neck, then turned to plunge her sword deep into the heart of her final opponent.

"Very impressive, Earth woman, but futile."

A chill went through Hickory. *Sequana*.

The Pharlaxian leader looked down at her from the back of his yarrak. A dozen mounted guards flanked him. "I admit to making a mistake. I should have killed you when I had the chance." He shook his head.

"I believe we would not have quite so much trouble now if I had. You are responsible for the destruction of my war machines, are you not?" His voice was bitter. "I thought so."

He pursed his lips and sighed. "It seems Yonni-sèr-Abelen will win the day. Our people fight valiantly, but without the Bikashi, they are no match for the Ezekani forces. It is, I fear, only a matter of time."

Hickory looked around. The area behind her was clear of trees. She wouldn't get very far trying to outrun them.

Sequana's face was like flint. "I will flee to the North, humiliated, like a violator with its tail between its legs, yes. But only temporarily. I will be back—Balor will not be denied his victory. For you, Earth woman, this time, there is no escape. Your stay on Prosperine is at an end." He motioned to his guardsmen. "Kill her."

The riders nudged their yarraks forward, and Hickory resumed her fighting stance. There were too many. It was a pity it had to end like this. She felt no fear, just disappointment. She hoped Jess and Gareth would survive and raised her sword.

"Hickory!" The cry came from the treetops. "Grab the rope!"

An airship materialized between the branches. Mack gripped the gunnel of the gondola and hollered at her, "Come on, we've got you. Grab hold."

The Alien Corps

Hickory dropped her sword and gripped the rope with both hands. The balloon moved slowly, dragging her along the ground.

The Pharlaxians recovered quickly from their surprise, and Sequana urged them to attack.

Mack leaned out from the carriage and tossed a bomb at the cavalry. It exploded in front of the leading yarraks, sending the Pharlaxian riders into disarray.

The pilot gunned the engines, and the balloon gained height. The branches of the trees buffeted Hickory as they flew. Her grip on the rope loosened, and she could feel her hands slip. She shouted. "Mack, I'm going to fall—pull me up or put me down, but do it now!"

Mack and his co-pilot hauled her up, grasped her jacket, and heaved her into the gondola. Mack knelt beside her and looked at her anxiously. "Are you okay?"

His voice sounded far away, and she could hardly hear her own when she answered, "Thanks to you, although I think my hearing's gone. How did you know where to find me?"

"Titus. We saw him approach in the distance, and when he came through the gates alone and hurt, I feared the worst. I set off straight away. I reckoned the yarrak made a beeline for Ezekan after he was shot. All I did was follow the direction he came from. Luckily, I was in time."

"Lucky for me," Hickory said, looking over the edge. The Pharlaxian leader and what was left of his guards were riding swiftly northwards. "Not so much for them. I wonder if we've seen the last of him."

"The High Reeve won't rest until he's caught, or dead. We can forget about Sequana," said Mack.

"I hope you're right. But we've urgent business to deal with. Do you think we might fly this craft of yours to the West? We need to find Gareth and Jess."

"Jess?"

"Yes, she's gone after Gareth. They're both chasing the Bikashi commander."

Retribution

The blacksmith had done quality work honing the short leaf-blade sword to the sharpness of a razor. Ideal for thrust and cut, it glittered in the light. Sabin had told him it was tempered with crynidium hardened in fire and would slice through chain armor. It rested comfortably in a scabbard on his back.

Gareth knelt and searched the ground for signs of the Bikashi. The sandy soil made it easy to track him. Vogel must have climbed over the top of the ridge up ahead. *He can't be far.*

He'd never been far away from him, watching over the shoulders of the scientists, sharing his meals, and taking him for daily walks around the deck. They would discuss trivial nonsense, and Vogel would tell humorous stories of his dealings with the Bikashi High Command.

And then there were the lies—hundreds of lies. Myths about the Galactic Alliance and the reasons why the Bikashi were thrown out. Vogel insisted his people were a peaceful race, and the Alliance considered them a threat only because of their superior trading skills.

He swore the Alien Corps was a willing partner in the Alliance's strategy. He claimed Hickory was under her father's spell and knew the Bikashi were being maligned. He said Jess had been duped by Hickory and the G.A..

Vogel told him so many half-truths and lies and pumped him so full of drugs that he no longer knew what to believe. Gareth flinched. The torture they'd inflicted on him was in his head. The alien always apologized for the pain. He didn't want to hurt him. If only Gareth would realize the Alliance was responsible. Because of their greed, they consigned every non-aligned planet to use FTL drives that were slower than those of the Alliance planets. He was sure Gareth would want to help if he only realized the truth—and he would make the pain stop.

Gareth's knowledge would only put the Bikashi on a level footing with Earth's allies. Wasn't that the fair and reasonable thing? Otherwise, their race was doomed to always take second place, to be servants to the Alliance. Earth and the others didn't want any competitors spoiling their monopoly. They were morally corrupt and determined to keep their foot on the throat of the Bikashi people.

Lies and half-truths all designed to weaken his

The Alien Corps

resistance. Some things were true. The Bikashi FTL *was* primitive, Cortherien and the Space Corps probably *were* in bed with the Alliance, and Jess would believe anything Hickory said. But could Hickory be working hand in hand with the admiral? Anything was possible.

Gareth clambered to the top of the slope. On the other side, a steep descent of loose rocks and boulders ended abruptly at a cliff face that plunged a half mile to the rocky coast. Vogel was halfway to the cliff, following a winding path towards the edge. *Where does he think he's going to?* There's no way the Bikashi could escape unless he could fly. Gareth decided to take the short route. Ignoring the path, he headed straight down, slipping and sliding on the loose scree.

The Bikashi almost reached the cliff edge. He looked around and spotted Gareth bearing down on him. He turned to face him, knife at the ready.

Gareth leaped the last few feet. He barreled into Vogel, and they tumbled over and down in the dust, grasping at each other until they collided with a boulder and rolled apart. Vogel recovered more quickly from the jarring impact and struck out at Gareth with his boot. Gareth deflected the kick and grabbed his leg as it went by, sending the Bikashi to the ground and jolting his knife free. Both jumped to their feet and crouched, facing each other.

"Earthman! Why fight me? What's the point? The

Alliance has won, and your kind will keep the crynidium. The Bikashi will suffer for the Galactic Alliance's treachery for decades. Let me go on my way." He glanced at the ground where his weapon lay.

Gareth watched him warily. His voice was scathing. "You know what the point is, Bikashi." He advanced a step and kicked Vogel's knife away. *You tortured me. Physically and emotionally experimented on me to the point where I thought I'd lost my sanity.* "You think I will let you just walk away?" He laughed mockingly.

"I did what I did to help my people. It was necessary. I took no pleasure in it."

Gareth took a step to one side and began to circle Vogel. Tears tickled the corners of his eyes, but he held them back. "You tried to destroy my beliefs, my friendships, and my freedom, and for what?"

"For the greater good, Gareth."

"Your greater good—not mine," said Gareth. He heard the rattle of falling stones and glanced over his enemy's shoulder. Jess had almost caught up with him. Dust rose, and boulders dislodged, rolling down the slope in front of her. He saw her lose her footing and skid along on her back over the sharp rocks.

She came to an abrupt halt forty meters from the antagonists. "Gareth, no!" she shouted as he reached behind and drew his sword.

The Alien Corps

Vogel launched himself at the lighter and younger human. He grabbed Gareth's neck with one hand and smashed his other fist into the boy's face. The sword fell from Gareth's hand. His legs gave way, and he staggered backward. Vogel unbuttoned his jacket and took out a handgun. He glanced quickly at Gareth's unmoving body, then spinning around, he turned the weapon on Jess. "Stay where you are. One more step, and I'll kill the boy."

Gareth stirred. He felt light-headed from Vogel's attack but lunged at the Bikashi's arm and wrestled it away from Jess. The gun discharged, and a burst of energy blasted the ground near her feet.

Vogel swung his free arm, and his elbow connected Gareth's temple with a sickening blow. The young man fell to the ground. He didn't move.

"You foul pig," said Jess. She advanced towards him, her fists clenched.

Vogel sneered. "You arrogant humans. You think you're superior to every race in the galaxy." He squeezed the trigger. Nothing happened. He squeezed again with the same result.

Jess snorted through clenched teeth. "Despite everything, you couldn't break him. He was too strong for you." Her voice shook. "I thank God Earth has no death penalty. You're going to rot in an Alliance prison for the rest of your pathetic life."

The Bikashi twisted his head to look over the cliff

face. He turned back and laughed bitterly. "I'd rather die—but I doubt it will come to that."

The Bikashi fighter plane rose silently over the bluff. It hovered there, canons trained on the clifftop. The pilot beneath the canopy gesticulated urgently.

Vogel whispered briefly into his comms, then spoke. "It seems your admiral is no longer taking a passive role. I must leave you now." He cast a final look at Gareth, then spun around and moved quickly towards the waiting plane.

Gareth rose like a shade from the ground. He scooped up his blade and hurled it after Vogel. The weapon spun through the air and sliced through the Bikashi's armor, impaling him in the back.

Vogel jerked forward, then turned stiffly to face his nemesis. He reached behind him, sucked in a quick breath, and drew out the sword. Staring disbelievingly at Gareth, he shook his head, then tossed the blade over the cliff edge. The Bikashi staggered into the plane, the door shut, the engines whined, and it blasted off.

◆◆◆

Hickory and Mack watched Vogel's plane soar into the stratosphere. They released some air from the balloon and landed gently at the edge of the cliff. Mack jumped out. He rushed to Jess and hugged and kissed her.

"Gareth, Jess. Thank God you're alive," said Hickory, tethering the balloon to a large rock. She grasped Gareth by the shoulders and pulled him against her.

"Whoa," said Gareth. "Does this mean we're engaged?"

Hickory pushed him away. "Idiot boy. You'll be lucky if I don't court-martial you. What happened with Vogel?"

"He got away, but I winged him pretty good, I reckon. Lost my sword, though." He looked disconsolate, then raised his eyebrows, and a smile lit up his face. "I'm sure Sabin can make me another."

"You won't need it. The war is over. Sequana's gone, Vogel's gone. The rebels have laid down their arms. There are only some stragglers left to mop up."

Jess disengaged herself from Mack's embrace. "And the Teacher? Is he all right?" she asked.

"Last time I saw him, he was attending to the wounded," said Mack. "Funny thing, he had a crucifix around his neck."

"Maybe it's time for us to have a talk with him," said Jess.

"Not before I have a bath and a good night's sleep," said Hickory. "Come on. All aboard. We've got a long flight back to the city."

Return to Earth

The Jabberwocky carried a full complement of passengers and crew. Mackie took leave from the Alliance and traveled with Hickory's team. Admiral Lace was also on his way to Earth, and James Brandt accompanied him.

Gareth renewed his acquaintance with Jenny, and Hickory saw a difference in how the two were relating. They tended to keep to themselves most of the time. Gareth was gradually recovering his full health, thanks to Kar-sèr-Sephiryth's ministrations. However, some of the mental scars remained, and he was less playful and more reflective than when the two had previously met. Jenny seemed to appreciate the new, more mature Gareth.

Hickory, Jess, and Mackie were sitting around the table in the conference room, being debriefed by Admiral Lace.

"It's a pity you let the Bikashi get away," the admiral told Jess.

"We're lucky to be alive, sir," she said. "He only

The Alien Corps

left because he feared the Alliance were on their way."

George Lace massaged his temples with his fingers. "A little bit of subterfuge there. I thought it might help if the Bikashi believed we were entering the arena. We put some chatter over the air to that effect. It seems to have worked."

"He might be dead anyway, sir—" began Mack.

The admiral shook his head. "I don't expect the parting pinprick he received from Gareth will have done him any permanent damage. No, he's probably being interrogated by the Bikashi high command as we speak. Can't say I feel sorry for him."

Hickory frowned. She took a sip of coffee before asking her question. "Surely, it doesn't matter any longer? The Bikashi threat has been nullified, hasn't it?"

"For the moment, yes. But if Vogel survived, he could prove to be a dangerous adversary in the future. We've put a security net in place around the planet. That will warn us of any future alien infiltration. It will be safer when all the Bikashi are on the space side of the net. Our people are rounding up the stragglers now."

"The Prosperine government has agreed to this?" said Hickory. She expressed mild surprise but, knowing her father, realized there was likely more to it.

"The government has made some very sensible decisions in their people's best interests," said the admiral.

"You've negotiated an agreement with the government to trade for crynidium." It was a statement, not a question. Hickory sensed the truth of it. She shook her head. "What else have you agreed to?"

"We will provide the Avanauri people with schools and universities specializing in the sciences and engineering. We'll start off slowly, but we think they'll learn quickly. Improving their education should have a positive effect on their society and culture."

"Plus their religion?" said Jess.

"Perhaps," said the admiral, "but the Teacher is the wildcard there. What's your assessment of him, commander?"

Hickory lowered her eyes. Should she tell him what she really thought? In truth, she wasn't sure, and she really wanted to discuss her findings with the prefect before finalizing her report. "You mean, do I believe he's some supernatural being, another Jesus, a Son of God? I can't decide what he is, not yet, at any rate. But he's a unique individual with skills and talents I haven't seen in anyone before. The Teacher's ability to heal is amazing, and he often knows what will happen before it does. He also seems to possess inexhaustible supplies of energy and comes across as incredibly wise and sensitive." She paused, looking into her father's eyes.

She and Jess had talked with the Teacher about his beliefs and his unique abilities. He'd been forthright, answering all their questions. He'd told them everything they wanted to know and a bit more. When it was time for them to go, they'd been reluctant to leave the peaceful healing power his presence brought them. "Remember my words," he'd said as he returned the pendant to Hickory. "You are knight commanders of Balor. Your work here is finished for the present, but we may meet again." He smiled enigmatically.

How would her father react if she said Kar-sèr-Sephiryth was the Son of God? She decided to spare him. "Do I believe all that adds up to him being the Messiah? It adds up to him being a very advanced Avanauri—far ahead of his contemporaries. And I think that's what the blood tests and the results of the brain scans will show us. We know the Avanauri race is close to a flashpoint where they will undergo massive growth in their brain cells. I would guess Kar-sèr-Sephiryth is the first of the new society. I hope that's true because it means the future of this race is bright indeed."

◆◆◆

Hickory reported to Cortherien first, then met the admiral for lunch at the reconstructed Fortunato al

Pantheon. They ordered tagliatelle with white truffles, fresh fungi porcini, and a flask of the house white. The admiral waited until they'd eaten, then told her the secret he'd kept from her for almost twenty years. "We should have told you when you were young, but your mother wanted to wait until you were a bit older." He paused, twisting the wedding band on the finger. "Did you never guess? Never wonder why you were the first in the family to have your astounding empathic ability?" His eyes searched hers.

Hickory shook her head slowly, and he sighed. "Jack Manson was my best friend ever since high school. We went to university together, we drank together, we did everything together. And then, I joined the Agency, met your mother, and fell in love.

"We were happy, I truly believe we were, and if it hadn't been for Jack, she would have been content to be with me. We spent six incredible months traversing the Galaxy. I wanted it to go on forever. My world was perfect, you see. I had Angela, a great job, and a bright future. When I asked her to marry me, she said yes. We went home to meet our respective families, and I introduced her to Jack." He shook his head slowly.

The truth set Hickory's heart in a whirl. She felt dizzy as his meaning sank in. She recalled the Teacher's last words. "When the time comes, remember this father, who is not your father, loves you. Forgive him for any wrong he may have done to you, and your heart will be healed." Only now did they make sense.

She tightened the grip on her father's hand while he told his tale. His revelations came as a shock, but she needed to know everything. He continued. "Nothing was the same after that. Jack was an empath, you see, and he and Angela—well, they fell hard for each other. While I offered her stability and a predictable, planned future, he promised excitement, adventure, and the thrill of the unknown.

"She was hopelessly in love with him. I tried to warn her Jack was no good for her—all right, I was jealous, but I also knew him. I told her it would be a brief, tempestuous affair, and then Jack would grow tired of her, and she would be sorry."

Hickory could sense the mixture of sadness and regret sweeping through him. She knew she should feel sorry, but she couldn't contain the rapture building in her heart or the bright tears in her eyes. She held her breath, willing him to continue.

"She didn't listen, and I couldn't have been more wrong. They were mad for each other and married six months later. I was devastated. I immersed myself in my work and tried to make myself forget them. I became a dedicated officer—fast-tracked as a future star, one of the whiz-kids."

Absentmindedly, he drew his fork along the tablecloth, creating a series of parallel lines on the white surface. He paused and then shook his head as though he still couldn't believe what he was about to tell her. "Two years afterward, I heard Jack had been killed in a car accident." He placed the fork beside his knife. "I went home immediately for the funeral and stayed. I still loved Angela, and she now had a one-year-old baby to care for. We saw a lot of each other. We shared our memories of Johnny, as she called him, and she talked to me about their life together. It was the most natural thing in the world when I returned to my post four months later, and she came with me."

He raised his head and smiled at Hickory. "You can guess the rest. We were married, and I like to think your mother came to love me—at least a little. I know we were happy. I even loved you, Hickory."

The sparkle in his eyes fled, and he pressed his lips together. "After she died, you became a constant reminder of how much I'd lost. Your memories of her on her deathbed didn't leave you for years. You relived them every night. I couldn't bear it."

He leaned over the table and grasped her hand. "But you and Mike are all that's left of her. I don't want to lose either of you. I always thought I would when you realized I wasn't your father."

It was too much for Hickory to take in. Who was this "Johnny," apparently her biological father? And how was it possible he could die in a traffic accident? That part of the admiral's story struck her as odd.

The Alien Corps

Did Johnny have the same power to call animals as she? Hickory hoped, in time, she would find out. She left the admiral, still unsure about her feelings for him. Hickory thought he'd told her as much truth as he was capable of at this time, but certainly not all of it. His confession was worth something. At least it was a start.

◆◆◆

She strolled across the sand towards the group of adults playing volleyball. Jess saw her first and let out a cry. "Hick—you're here!" The other players turned and ran to meet her. Jess's twins outsprinted everyone and embraced her enthusiastically. Hickory staggered under their combined weight.

"Hey, it's okay. I've arrived. Nice to see you, too." She laughed, then greeted Jess and Mack. Gareth came up, hand in hand with Jenny Morrison. Jess took Hickory's arm and led her to a table laid with tropical fruits and bottles of cold wine.

Jess poured champagne for all and raised her glass for a toast. "Here's to the completion of a successful mission." They clinked glasses and drank, and then Jess filled them up again. "And here's to the engagement of Gareth and Jenny. We all wish you great happiness."

Jenny blushed, and Gareth looked sheepishly at Hickory and shrugged. "What can I say? She's the first girl I've met who's really interested in intra dimensional fifth-tier catalytics."

Jenny put her finger to his lips, and Hickory noticed the diamond ring she wore. It was great to see everyone having a good time, she thought. It looked like the holiday and his love life were helping Gareth recover from his ordeal. Jess and Mack enjoyed each other's company, too. She felt a small stab of jealousy but pushed it aside.

"What happened with the prefect? How did he take your report?" said Jess.

"Pretty well. A little disappointed I wasn't able to be more definite about Kar-sèr-Sephiryth. But he's decided to travel to Prosperine and meet him for himself. I don't think he's quite given up on him yet."

"That I can understand. The Teacher is a remarkable person and as close to divinity as I will ever see," said Gareth.

"Don't be so sure," said Hickory. "Cortherien has confirmed my return to permanent active duty. He's given me another assignment. Apparently, there's an amphibian race on a planet called Atlantis, a few hundred light-years from Earth. He wants me to take a look. I'll need to put together a team. We leave in three weeks."

Gareth and Jess grinned at each other. "We'd better get in some practice then," said Gareth. "Time for a swim, Mother. Race you to the water!"

The End of the Alien Corps

Dear Reader, thank you for reading the first part of the Prosperine Series. I sincerely hope you enjoyed it, and I would be delighted if you were to spread the word by leaving a review at your local online store. Part 2 of the series, Rise of the Erlachi, is available in paperback and eBook formats.

P J McDermott

Main Characters

(Born of Fire, prelude to the Prosperine Series)

Father Alberto Battista: Vatican Archaeologist, joint finder of Philip's ossuary.

Talya: a young female apprentice archaeologist and joint finder of Philip's ossuary.

Bishop Verroni: Head of the Vatican Christian archaeological division.

Pope Innocent XIV: 2086 – 2105. Former Dean of the Pontifical Academy of Roman Archaeology.

Cardinal Jean Rousseau: Head of the International Theological Commission at the Vatican.

Professor George Hussain: Jacob M. Alkow Professor of Archaeology at Tel Aviv University.

(Book 1: The Alien Corps)

Commander Hickory Lace: lecturer at the Saint Philip Research Academy (SPRA) and special operative of the Alien Corps.

Prefect Pierre Cortherien: cardinal and CEO of the Saint Philip Research Academy (SPRA).

Admiral George Lace: Hickory's father, admiral of the Intragalactic Agency (IA), whose role is to protect the interests of the federated planets.

James Brandt: IA lieutenant, reports to Admiral Lace.

Jess Parker: Pilot, an expert in computer-human interface, Hickory's friend.

The Alien Corps

Gareth Blanquette: Former SPRA student, genius, and expert in faster-than-light (FTL) theory, as well as technology.

Jenny Morrison: Junior lieutenant of the Jabberwocky, an FTL interstellar transport.

Jebediah Nolanski: I.A. Cultural Exchange Attaché in Ezekan, the capital city of Avanaux.

Alex Mackie: IA lieutenant, reports to Admiral Lace.

The Avanauri

(Avanauri names comprise a personal name and a surname. The surname is inherited from the mother. The two names are linked by sèr if male and sèra if female. Hence, Yonni-sèr-Abelen is Yonni, son of Abelen; Connat-sèra-Haagar is Connat, daughter of Haagar.)

Balor: The supreme being of Avanaux (the southern continent of the planet Prosperine)

Connat-sèra-Haagar, legendary heroine and victor of the ancient wars against the Erlachi.

Kar-sèr-Sephiryth: Prosperine religious leader, teacher, and prophet.

Yonni-sèr-Abelen: High-Reeve of Avanaux.

Josipe-sèr-Amagon: Chief of Peacekeepers.

Sequana-sèr-Kira: the Pharlaxian leader – also known by his code-name, *Ecknit*.

P J McDermott

Lieutenant Thurle-sèr-Gammons: peacekeeper, nephew to Josipe-sèr-Amagon.

Sabin-sèr-Adham: a weapons maker in Ezekan.

Kyntai: Young naur, stable boy.

Mirda-sèr-Sidhartha: Ambassador Nolanski's assistant.

Yamu-sèra-Jahini: a mad woman.

Other Alien Characters

Vogel: A Bikashi infiltrator on Prosperine.

Saurab and Jakah: Members of the Dark Suns, smugglers.

Organisations

The Galactic Confederation of Aligned Planets (also known as The Galactic Alliance, the Alliance, The Aligned Planets, the Federated Planets, and the GA). The Alliance is the political body comprised of representatives from member planets. This body presides over numerous Divisions and Agencies dealing with interplanetary concerns, the most important of which are:

➢ *Intragalactic Security Agency*, also known as the Intragalactic Agency or IA, (responsible for the protection of and neutralizing potential threats to the efficient operations of the GA)

➢ Administration Division (responsible for ensuring member planets' compliance with the

Confederation Charter.) They also have a role in policing Confederation law.

> *Legal Division* (handling disputes, contracts, trade agreements)
> *Commercial Division* (including management of trade operations)

The Alien Corps: the operational arm of the Saint Philip Research Academy (SPRA), set up by Pope Innocent IV to investigate and assess Christian–like religions on distant planets. The Charter for the SPRA and the Corp is 'to explore possible instances supporting the universal nature of the Son of God.'

The Dark Suns: a loose association of smugglers from around the galaxy with no home planet.

Non-aligned planets (NAP): A cooperative of planets existing outside the IA and in competition with them.

The Bikashi: natives of the Non-aligned planet, Auriga – the sworn enemy of the GA.

Saturnine Raiders: An alien race that migrated to Prosperine three hundred years ago after their home world entered a nuclear winter.

The invisible: a gang of vicious thugs, muscle for hire.

The Pharlaxian Party (Pax) Hard-line opposition to the government, especially its policies on religious doctrine. They are armed and organized fundamental radicals.

P J McDermott

By the Same Author

Book 2 in the Prosperine Series

Hickory Lace and her cohorts in the Alien Corps have defeated the coalition of Bikashi invaders and Pharlaxian rebels. As a result, the strategic agreement between Earth and the province is alive and well.

But the Alliance has received word that the Pharlaxian leader, Sequana, who disappeared after the final battle, is mobilizing the northern clans of Erlach.

Sequana has his hands on a symbiotic high-tech weapon that could threaten not only Earth's interests on Prosperine but Planet Earth itself.

The Alien Corps

Book 3 in the Prosperine Series

When Hickory Lace placed the Sword of Connat into the claws of the telepathic Riv-Amok, she trusted the beast would bury the weapon in a desolate region of Prosperine known as the Scarf. She'd hoped it would never be seen again.

Only a few months pass before a call from the Admiral sends shivers down her spine. A Bikashi jet has been spotted scouting the area.

In the third book of the Prosperine series, Hickory faces her greatest fear, discovers the secrets to Prosperine's past, and unravels the mystery of the Teacher.

P J McDermott

Book 4 in the Prosperine Series

The alien known as *the Teacher* is missing and presumed dead after his spacecraft plunged into the fiery inferno of Prosperine's sun.

Hickory is devastated by the tragic loss and has isolated herself in a small town in a remote part of North Queensland.

A tiny flicker of hope he might still be alive takes her back to the Corps for one last mission on the homeworld of Earth's greatest foe, the Bikashi.

The truth she uncovers on the enemy planet ignites a fierce new purpose in her heart.

Coming-of-Age Fiction

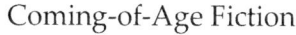

Small Fish Big Fish

When Jamie McCarthy sees some money lying on the floor of the corner store, he thinks his luck is in. But sometimes, what seems like Fortune's kindly smile can be a mask hiding a twisted and cruel face.

The seemingly harmless act of keeping the money triggers a series of events that drags Jamie into a quagmire of deception and criminality, pursued by an adversary who appears determined to destroy his life.

P J McDermott

About the Author

PJ McDermott was born in a one-bedroom tenement flat above the local cinema in Paisley, Scotland.

As a schoolboy, he spent most of his time in the library reading science fiction books day and night and reveling in the genius of Asimov, Herbert, and Le Guin. These days, he's more into the fantasy novels of Robin Hobb and Alex Weir.

He lives by the beach in Australia with his wife, two wonderful daughters, and grandchildren, Mia, Ryder, Patrick, and Ethan. Please visit him at his website: https://www.awesomescifi.com

Printed in Great Britain
by Amazon